The House Guest
A J WILLS

Cherry Tree Publishing

The House Guest

Copyright ©   A J Wills 2023

This book is a work of fiction. Any resemblance to actual persons,
living or dead is purely coincidental.

Prologue

The car crept up and slowed to a stop, showering the pavement with a fine spray of rainwater that had puddled on the road.

She didn't notice the make nor the model. Only its colour. A deep burgundy that reminded her of those boiled sweets she ate when she was a little girl.

A window buzzed down a few inches.

'Do you need a lift?'

She shivered as a trickle of water ran down her forehead and into her eyes. Her clothes were soaked through. The skirt that barely covered the top of her thighs and the tiny crop top that was perfect for the club, but not so great for walking home in the rain, drenched and sticking to her goose-pimpled skin.

She knew better than to accept lifts from strangers. She wasn't stupid. But as she glanced down at the broken heel of her shoe, the numbing chill of the November rain penetrating her bones, the offer was tempting. And anyway, she had her phone. If anything funny happened, she'd call the police.

'That would be amazing,' she gasped, her teeth chattering. 'Thanks.'

She hurried around the back of the car, pulled open the passenger door and sighed with relief when she was hit by a fug of warm air and the scent of expensive perfume.

'You look frozen. Let me turn the heating up.'

'You're a lifesaver. Thank you so much.'

She cupped her hands around a vent, the soft leather of the seat sticky on the backs of her legs.

'Where do you live?'

'Up past the old prison,' she said. 'Pilgrim's Avenue.'

A light above the dashboard dimmed and went out. The inside of the car fell dark. As they pulled away, the doors locked with an ominous clunk.

Was that normal?

Of course it was. She was being paranoid. She shouldn't be so judgemental. They could have driven past and left her. Instead, they saw she was in trouble and stopped to help. She shouldn't think so badly of people.

'Do you normally walk home in the rain without a coat?'

She laughed, running a hand over her hair, squeezing the rain down the back of her neck.

'I was at a club with my boyfriend. We had an argument and I left without him,' she said.

He was probably already home. Maybe she had overreacted, but when she saw him chatting up that woman with the blonde dreadlocks at the bar, something inside her flipped. He told her she was being possessive. That she was being a drama queen, so she stormed out, forgetting she didn't have her purse or any money for a taxi.

It was only when her heel snapped and she was taking shelter under a tree that she realised how stupidly impetuous she'd been. Thank god someone had taken pity on her.

'I really appreciate this,' she said.

'No problem. Relax and I'll have you home in no time.'

She took a deep breath and settled into the seat, her head falling back as she allowed her eyes to close.

'What brings you out so late?' she asked.

The driver didn't reply. Eyes fixed on the road ahead. Hands lightly gripping the wheel. Lips turned upwards in an enigmatic smile.

She had no idea there was someone else in the car. Someone hiding on the back seat. Not until she heard the rustle of clothing.

She jolted upright, tried to turn. But it was too late.

They were trying to put a hood over her head. No, not a hood. Something else. A plastic bag. Strong hands around her neck, drawing it tight.

When she took a breath to scream, she sucked the bag deep into her mouth. There was no air. No oxygen. Nothing to breathe.

Panic ballooned in her chest, her eyes wide with terror.

3

Her phone slid from her grasp, slipping into a crevice down the side of her seat, out of reach.

Her head throbbed with its own heartbeat. Her mind a white flare of alarm and fear.

And the more she fought, the tighter they pulled the bag around her neck and face.

Her arms and legs became heavy, her mind a chaotic battleground trying to make sense of what was happening. A tendril of terror coiled around her spine and, as the cloying thin plastic hit the back of her throat, the darkness closed in and the fight in her evaporated.

Chapter 1

'Do you have the bag for me?'

The dark saloon is parked in the shadow of a tree at the rear of the car park, away from prying eyes. A fine mist of rain is falling, soaking into my uniform and threatening to wreak havoc with my hair.

'Are you sure you want to do this?' the woman in the car asks as I peer in through the window. 'I mean, won't you get into trouble?'

Strictly speaking, what I'm doing *is* wrong. There are clear rules about this sort of thing, but sometimes you have to follow your gut and say to hell with the consequences.

'It's fine,' I assure her. 'What's the worst that could happen?'

'You could lose your job.'

'Do you have the bag or not?' I'm getting soaked out here.

She clambers out, pulling the hood of her coat over her head. She scoots around the back, lifts the tailgate, and reappears a moment later with a canvas bag. The sort of bag you might take for a weekend away in a fancy hotel. Not that I can remember the last time Frazer and I took a weekend away anywhere, let alone to a fancy hotel. We don't go anywhere these days.

'Take it with two hands,' the woman advises.

She dumps it into my outstretched arms. It's surprisingly heavy. The first pang of doubt creeps in. I'm hardly going to be inconspicuous walking into the building like this.

Oh, well. Too late now. A promise is a promise.

I've timed it to coincide with the changeover when the night shift should be too occupied with their handover from the day team to notice me with a suspicious-looking bag. And anyway, I doubt anyone's going to question me. They're all far too busy.

As I stride towards the brightly lit entrance, sliding doors swish open. I waltz past the reception desk without a second look, hugging the bag close to my chest. Into the lift, which thankfully I have to myself, and up onto the second floor.

I have to put the bag down momentarily to swipe through a security door and struggle to pick it up again before it swings closed.

'Almost there,' I whisper to my precious cargo.

There's a gaggle of nurses gathered around the central desk, listening intently as they swap notes about patient conditions, medications and routines.

I was right. No one pays me the slightest attention as I lumber past, sweat and rain mixing on my forehead in an unsightly sheen of moisture. My arms are killing me and I'm glad to make it onto the ward without mishap.

Freddie's eyes are closed and his twiggy arms are resting at his sides over the top of his blanket. His face is partially covered by an oxygen mask and his wispy white hair sticks out at all angles on his pillow.

I lower the bag to the floor and draw the curtains around his bay. It's not unusual. We often draw the curtains to give patients some privacy, especially when they're being treated or we need to bathe them.

'Freddie,' I whisper. 'It's Marcella.'

His eyelids flutter, and he groans. He doesn't have long left. He'll be lucky to make it through the night now the cancer's finally caught up with him. It's one fight he's not going to win.

I glance at the monitor at his side, quietly bleeping and flashing with his vitals. His heart rate is slowing. He's slipping away. I'm just glad I've been able to do this one last thing for him.

As I lift the bag onto the bed, it comes to life, squirming and wriggling unnaturally.

I pull open the zip and a dog's head pops out like a canine jack-in-the-box.

Freddie's eyes spring open and the dog barks.

'Shhh!' I whisper as the dog squeezes out, his little tail wagging with excitement at being reunited with his owner. He rushes up to Freddie's face and plasters it in sloppy wet kisses with his pink tongue, while whining with pure excitement.

Freddie's face lights up. He peels the oxygen mask from his nose and mouth. 'Knuckles,' he grins, his voice gravelly and weak.

'Maggie thought you'd like to see him one last time,' I say, unexpected tears moistening my eyes.

Freddie's sister put the idea of a last visit into my head when she told me how much Knuckles was missing Freddie.

'Thank you,' he croaks as the dog, a short-legged Jack Russell with cute brown patches and huge black eyes, sniffs around the bed.

Freddie raises a weak arm, his skin papery thin and bruised, to stroke the animal, his rheumy eyes wet with tears.

'It's my pleasure. Maggie had to sedate him to get him into the bag, but I think he's pleased to see you.'

Unfortunately, Knuckles' pleasure at seeing his owner is short-lived and his attention is quickly distracted by all the strange smells. The overpowering stench of disinfectant. The lingering odour of over-cooked cabbage. Stale sweat and plastic sheets.

Before I can stop him, he's jumped off the bed and is sniffing around the floor.

'Knuckles, come back here,' I hiss, but he's moved around to the other side, out of my reach.

I hurry after him, but I'm too late to stop him cocking his leg and urinating down the side of the bedside cabinet.

'Bad dog,' I chide as a golden pool forms on the floor.

Knuckles looks at me defiantly and barks three times. An annoying yap like a miniature siren. At this rate, the whole hospital's going to know he's here.

'And stop that. You'll get us both into trouble.'

He barks again, pawing the floor with his back legs, as if he's trying to tell me who's the boss.

'Right, you'll have to go back in your bag if you're going to be like that.'

Behind me, Freddie chuckles. I'm glad one of us is finding this amusing. Then he coughs. A chesty, hacking cough that wracks his body.

'It's okay, Freddie. Sit up and have a drink of water.'

I raise his mattress and place a plastic beaker of water to his lips. His body relaxes, and he sinks back into the bed.

Now where the hell has that bloody dog gone?

'Nurse,' Freddie gasps.

I don't remind him I'm not an actual nurse. I'm an assistant. Or what management prefers to call a "healthcare support worker". It just means I'm the one who helps with all the patients' needs, offering a friendly face or helping them wash, move around or get dressed.

'Yes, Freddie?'

'Thank you,' he says. His eyes fold closed as he sags into sleep.

'That's my pleasure. I'm glad I could reunite you both.'

The curtain rips open with an angry fizz.

I spin around.

The matron's standing there with a face like a raging tempest and Knuckles tucked under one arm, his legs dangling free and his tail wagging furiously.

Shit.

'Don't be angry. I can explain everything,' I say.

Chapter 2

'You can't fire me,' I shriek.

'This isn't the first time we've had to have words,' the matron reminds me, crossing her legs as perches on the edge of her chair. 'You were already on a warning for your timekeeping...'

'But —'

'And now this. You know animals aren't allowed on the wards. There are strict rules about it. It's unhygienic. They carry a serious risk of spreading infection.'

'It was only for a minute. I just wanted to let Freddie... I mean, Mr McLean, see his dog one last time. He misses him.' At least he saw the funny side of it, although Maggie was mortified when I handed the dog back and told her what had happened.

'That might be the case, and if you'd spoken to me about it in advance, we might have been able to make some arrangements, but to smuggle an animal onto my ward behind my back is unforgivable.'

I lower my head and stare at my knees. I can't believe she's sacking me.

'I was only trying to do the right thing,' I mumble. 'Use my initiative, like you said I should.'

'That's not what I meant, and you know it. I can't have staff working on this ward who I can't trust.' She glances at a sheet of paper on her desk. 'Problems have been building for a while, haven't they? You're regularly late for work and when you are here, your head's always in the clouds. You make mistakes and you're forgetful.'

'The patients like me.'

'Be that as it may, I don't think you're cut out for the job, Marcella.' The matron's face softens and she sighs. 'Look, you're a lovely girl, but I need someone reliable on my ward. How old are you now?'

'Twenty-eight.'

She shakes her head sadly. 'Old enough to know better. I'm disappointed. I expected more from you.'

'I'll try harder,' I protest.

'I'm sorry, my decision's final. You'll hear in writing from HR in the next few days, but I don't want you back. Sorry, Marcella, but I'd like you to clear out your locker and I don't expect to see you again.'

So that's it? Fired. Sacked. Thrown out on my ear. What am I supposed to do now?

Frazer's going to go mad. We've not long moved into the flat and I'm not sure how we'll afford the rent on his wages alone.

I'll have to tell him. I'm sure he'll understand. Although maybe not so much when he realises we might have to let the flat go.

I can't face calling him right away, though. It'll be better if I speak to him face to face. But first I need a drink. I think I deserve one after the day I've had. And so, rather than heading home after I've changed out of my uniform and cleared my meagre belongings out of my locker, I head for my favourite pub in the centre of town.

I was only planning on having one. A quick drink to console myself and for some Dutch courage before I speak to Frazer. But one drink quickly turns into two. And when a guy at the bar offers to buy me one more, it seems rude to refuse. Time passes in a blur. I make new friends, convinced I'm the life and soul of the impromptu party, laughing and joking with anyone who'll talk to me, until my jaw aches and the memory that I've just lost my job forgotten in a drunken haze.

It's gone eleven when I finally stumble out of the pub to make my way home. I've no idea how much I've spent on drinks, but it's money I can't afford now I don't have a job. But who cares? Something will turn up. Something better. It's not as if I'm leaving a highly paid career.

It hits me how drunk I am when I step out onto the street. It's as if someone's softened all the bones in my legs and made it impossible to walk in a straight line. I giggle to myself as I zigzag along the pavement, my world spinning.

I probably should have rung Frazer to let him know I was going to be late. He'll be worried about me, although checking my phone, I'm surprised he hasn't tried calling, especially with all those women who've gone missing in the city recently. Maybe he's gone out too.

My stomach rumbles, turning in on itself, hollow and tight. I've not eaten since lunchtime, so it's no wonder the alcohol's gone straight to my head. I'm sure I'll pay for it in the morning, but so what? I don't have to get up and go to work. I can stay in bed all day if I like. Screw the hospital. Screw the job. And screw the matron.

I creep down the ramp that leads to the under-pass under the ring road, my toes pressing into the ends of my shoes and my fingers brushing along the handrail, careful not to fall. I'd hate to end up back at the hospital as an emergency in-patient. That would be mortifying.

As I reach the bottom of the ramp, the entrance to the underpass looms. A gaping hole into the unknown. My pulse quickens. I must have walked through here a million times, but now a slither of fear snakes down my spine. For the last few weeks, the police have been warning women in the city not to walk home alone at night.

Seven women have vanished now. Or maybe it's eight. I've lost count. It's been all over the news. All of them have vanished as if they never existed. And the police don't seem to have the first clue what's happened to them.

I shudder. But I'm sure I'll be fine. There's a police station on the other side of the road. You'd have to be crazy to try to snatch someone here.

It doesn't quell my racing heart, though, especially when I hear footsteps behind me. Someone matching my pace, or maybe travelling quicker than me.

I speed up, occasionally bumping my shoulder against the wall as I struggle with my balance.

The footsteps draw closer.

I imagine a hand clamping over my mouth from behind. Pulling me down. Overpowering me. Dragging me to a waiting van.

The light at the end of the tunnel draws nearer.

A dark shadow appears ahead. The indistinct outline of someone approaching in the opposite direction. I dive into my bag and scrabble around for my keys to use as a weapon.

The shadow grows bigger and darker.

Two figures appear.

A young couple, hand in hand. She's staring into his eyes, hanging on his every word. They don't even acknowledge me as they breeze past.

As a tsunami of relief washes over my body, I ease up to almost a dead stop.

Someone grazes past me from behind. A man on his phone. He walks past wordlessly and disappears out of view as I put my keys back in my bag, feeling foolish. I let out a breath of relief.

Ten minutes later, I'm back at our flat. I lock and bolt the door behind me and slip off my jacket.

The place is in silence. No sound coming from the TV. Or music playing. Which is odd.

'Frazer?' I call, hanging my jacket and bag on a hook at the bottom of the stairs.

Nothing.

I can't believe he's gone to bed already. Frazer's a nighthawk, rarely asleep before midnight or later.

I creep up the stairs, conscious not to stomp in my semi-drunken state. I don't want to annoy our neighbours below.

The curtains have been left wide open, but strangely, the place is in darkness.

I flick on a light. It's blindingly bright. Too bright for my tired eyes.

Frazer's not asleep on the sofa in the lounge, nor in bed. Odd that he didn't mention going out tonight. But then again, neither did I. Maybe it was a last minute, spur-of-the-moment thing with some people from work.

At least it spares me having to tell him I've lost my job tonight and that until I can find something else, we'll have to rely on his wages.

I should take myself off to bed, but the rush of adrenaline from the walk home has left me feeling wide awake. Plus, with my earlier alcoholic euphoria burning off, I'm heading rapidly towards a darker place. It's not somewhere I want to go tonight. I need another drink.

There's some white wine in the fridge left over from the weekend. I pour a large glass, emptying the bottle and tossing it into the recycling bin. One more drink and then I'll turn in. Hopefully, I'll be asleep when Frazer gets back and I won't have to talk to him.

An envelope on the kitchen table catches my eye.

It's a plain white envelope with my name written on the front. I recognise Frazer's looping handwriting.

In all the months I've known him, he's never once written me a letter. Text messages and voice notes are our usual channels of communication.

A dark stone sits heavily in the pit of my stomach.

I put my glass on the table and tear the letter open, ripping out a sheet of folded lined paper inside.

I read it quickly, my eyes scanning the words, struggling to make sense of it.

Is this for real? Or some kind of joke?

My legs give way beneath me, and I crumple to the floor, my throat thick with emotion.

This can't be happening. Not today of all days.

It's as though my entire universe is falling apart.

Chapter 3

Dear Marcella,

I'm so sorry, but by the time you read this, I'll be gone.

I know this is the coward's way, and I should have found the balls to talk to you to your face, but it's easier like this. For me, at least.

I've tried to talk to you about how I've been feeling lately, about us, but you won't listen.

I can't go on as we are. And so I think it's best for us both if we start afresh.

I hope you understand. I know you'll be angry with me, and hurt, but hopefully, in time, you'll find someone new. Someone who truly loves you in the way you deserve.

Please don't try to contact me. I've cleared out my belongings and the rent's paid until the end of next week.

I'm so sorry.

Frazer x

He's leaving me? What the hell?
Or more accurately, he's already left.

I flip the letter over, hoping it's one of Frazer's stupid pranks. All one big joke at my expense. But the back of the letter is blank. No 'Gotcha'. No laughing face emoji. No nothing.

Seven measly lines of apology. That's all I get?

He was fine this morning. Maybe a little quiet, a tad sombre, but he's often like that first thing. Mornings don't suit him.

And when exactly did he try to talk to me about how he was feeling? That's just his way of making out this is my fault. To lay the blame on me and to make me feel guilty.

He's met someone else. That must be it.

He's been going on about that girl in the office. What's her name? Sally or Sadie or something? I bet it's her. I bet that's where he is right now, cosying up to her and telling her how I don't understand him. Well, she's welcome to him.

I scrunch the letter into a ball and hurl it across the kitchen. It bounces off a wall and when it lands on the floor by my feet, I angrily kick it into the corner. How dare he.

Well, fine. I'm better off without him. He had a dreadful taste in music, anyway. And he always left toast crumbs in the butter. And he was incapable of putting his dirty plates and mugs in the dishwasher, always leaving them on the side as if we shared the flat with a magical cleaning fairy whose job it was to tidy up after him.

I grab my wine, head into the lounge and flop onto the sofa. Could the day get any worse?

Without a job or Frazer's wages, I'll never be able to afford the rent on this place. I have until the end of next week and I'm going to be homeless. And it's not as if I have much in savings. Everything I earn goes on food and bills. The odd takeaway. The occasional night out.

Oh, god. I shouldn't have spent all that money in the pub tonight. I've no idea how much I blew through, but I had no inkling this bombshell was about to land.

I swipe away the tears in my eyes with the back of my hand, ashamed he's made me cry. I can't believe he's done this to me.

The thick silence of the flat weighs heavily on my shoulders. It's too quiet. I snatch up the remote and switch on the TV. Anything to fill the void. I need the sound of voices to chase away the crushing loneliness. The hollowness of despair.

I watch and listen with my mind numb as a bald weatherman in a dark suit explains how low pressure is driving in from the west, bringing with it rain and strong winds.

'Yeah, that's about right,' I mutter under my breath.

I turn the sound down to a low murmur in the background and grab my phone.

My first instinct is to call Frazer, to beg him to come home. But even though I'm drunk, I can see that wouldn't be a good idea. And besides, I'm not going to beg. Let him stew on it. I bet he's expecting me to call and when he doesn't hear from me, he'll come crawling back.

I absentmindedly flick through my apps. I open YouTube. The first recommended video is a travel vlog all about Ibiza, hosted by an impossibly good-looking couple who start every sentence screaming, 'Check it out!' into the camera while parading around in their swimwear. Still, they've filmed it beautifully. The sea is a cobalt blue and shimmers under a cloudless, azure sky. And the coast looks divine. Crisp, sandy beaches below dramatic rocky inlets. What a great job, travelling around the world and making videos about how amazing their lives are.

When the video ends, I'm served up another from a dour German influencer comparing the merits of the three Balearic Islands. I have a sudden yearning to pack my bags, jet off and leave my troubles behind. But of course, I can't. I don't have the money, apart from anything else.

On the TV, a late-night regional news bulletin comes on. My eyes flick between my phone and the screen, dividing my attention between them both. The top story is about a police appeal for witnesses after the disappearance of yet another woman in Canterbury. They flash up her picture. She has peroxide blonde hair, plump lips and long, thick, black eyelashes.

It's a reminder of how foolish I was to walk home on my own tonight. Anything could have happened.

The presenter moves on, giving updates about the opening of a new cancer centre and a protest against sewage being discharged into the sea, before revealing how one family has been forced to use a food bank because they can no longer afford supermarket prices. It's all a bit depressing and does nothing to lift my mood.

Finally, the bulletin wraps up with a story about an old farmhouse on the North Downs, which is in line for an architectural award. They briefly show footage of the building, which has a striking glass and steel extension bolted obtrusively onto an original brick dwelling. The two parts of the building are so boldly juxtaposed, I'm surprised it was granted permission at all, let alone shortlisted for an award.

I can only imagine living in a house like that, surrounded by the countryside and the sound of birds singing. It's not fair. Some people can't even afford to buy food.

The footage cuts to an older couple standing side by side with the house in the background, sunlight glinting off the expanse of glass that dominates the frontage of the new extension.

A pang of jealously twists my gut. How can they afford a house like that? They must have so much money. The man explains how he designed the rebuild himself and how he'd battled with the council for months to let him build something so contemporary and out of keeping with the rest of the property.

His wife gazes at him adoringly as he speaks, with a smug, self-satisfied smile. No wonder. I bet they don't have to queue up at the food bank for tins of beans and bags of pasta. They're obviously loaded. It makes me sick.

I bet it's equally amazing inside. Imagine what it would be like waking up in a place like that every morning. Drinking coffee on the terrace. Watching the world go by through that vast pane of glass. Everything new and gleaming.

I sigh as my finger hovers over the off button on the remote.

But then the couple's names flash up on the screen.

There's something about them that triggers a niggle of recognition at the back of my brain. Something that makes me continue to watch, fascinated.

I hit the pause button on the satellite box, freezing him with his mouth open and her with her eyes half-closed like she's in a drunken stupor. It's *her* name that rings a bell, but I can't for the life of me think why.

Maybe a patient at the hospital? Someone I knew at school or college? Someone I've met at the pub?

No, it's nothing like that. I don't recognize her face at all. It's just the name.

Carmel Van Der Proust.

And then it hits me. It's such an unusual name, it has to be her. I know the name from the court papers. The signature on the report that condemned my sister to a life hardly worth living. She'd be about the right age and I'm sure they said in the piece she was a psychiatrist.

She should have been struck off. But look at her now with her fancy house and her handsome husband and that smug smile.

And what makes it worse is that I doubt she has any idea of the damage she's done. How she's destroyed my family. And probably countless others like mine.

And yet here she is, gloating about her wonderful life on TV, while everything I hold precious has slipped through my fingers like fine sand.

It really isn't fair, especially when I've lost everything.

It stokes a fire of fury in the pit of my stomach.

It's infuriating as hell, but what can I do about it? Absolutely nothing.

Chapter 4

My hangover the next morning is every bit as bad as I deserve. My head throbs, my stomach is tender, and there's an unpleasant sticky film in my mouth. But what's worse is rolling over, discovering Frazer's side of the bed is empty and remembering he's gone.

Not only that, but I have no job and, by the end of next week, nowhere to live. In my sleep, I'd been able to forget how my life is crumbling to dust. Now it hits me again with the force of a piledriver.

I sink back into the pillow with a groan of despondency. What's the point of getting up when I have nothing to get up for?

Maybe Frazer's tried calling or sent a message while I was sleeping. I snatch up my phone, but there are no messages or missed calls. I could try calling, I suppose. If I talked to him, maybe I could change his mind and make him realise he's made a terrible mistake.

He said not to contact him, but what do I have to lose?

I make the call and press the phone to my ear.

A scratchy silence is followed by a click and Frazer's voicemail kicks in.

'This is Frazer's phone...'

I hang up.

The sound of his voice threatens to make me cry, but I'm not leaving a message for him to ignore. I'll try again later.

I need something to take my mind off my misery. Social media probably isn't the solution, but I casually open Facebook and flick through a dozen pointless updates, boring memes and cat videos.

I might post something suitably enigmatic myself later, to reflect my current dark mood. The kind of thing that normally winds me up when other people do it.

Even a bed of roses has its thorns (wilting rose emoji)

Ha, that will get people talking.

I open my Instagram account, expecting my feed to serve me my usual diet of glamorous celebrity shots and updates from strangers I follow, sharing images of their amazing travels abroad to far-flung and fabulous places.

But my feed is full of pictures of amazing houses and incredible grand designs. Architectural masterpieces in stunning mountain-top locations. Quirky new builds and modern cabins in the woods.

Strange. I must have been flicking through them last night before I went to bed, for some unknown reason. It's not like me.

And then I remember the news story on TV. Carmel Van Der Proust and the house her husband designed, which has been shortlisted for an award. I guess I was trying to find out more about them and became sidetracked.

My stomach tightens. My sense of injustice hasn't lessened overnight. In fact, I feel even more aggrieved that the woman who stole everything from me and my sister is living the life of wealth and luxury, and worse, is gloating about it on TV.

I can't help myself. I need to know more about her. Even a quick internet search on her name throws up thousands more images of the house, showing off beautifully lit interiors, stunning exteriors set against dramatic sunsets, aerial shots, pictures of the couple inside and outside the house, and even a magazine feature that paints such an idyllic image of their life, it makes me want to hurl.

As I scroll through pages and pages of hits, it's almost as if Carmel is taunting me.

It drives me crazy with anger.

She has everything she could ever want, that anyone could ever want, and I'm not even going to have anywhere to rent in a few days.

And then a crazy thought occurs to me.

It's stupid, but I can't shake it.

She doesn't deserve that life. She's done nothing to merit it other than bring misery and suffering. I'm more deserving than she is.

I don't know how I'm going to do it yet, but I'm going to steal that life from right under her nose. Call it compensation for how she mistreated my sister.

That's the problem when you have so much. You have everything to lose.

Me? I have nothing to lose.

Two hours later, with a stomach awash with painkillers and coffee, I jump on a bus to Wychwood, a village just outside Canterbury, close to where I've established Carmel and her husband have renovated that old farmhouse I'm now so familiar with.

I sit on the back seat with my knees pulled up to my chest and my ears buried into my shoulders. Nobody pays me the slightest attention or, god forbid, tries to talk to me as we rumble out of the city and into the countryside where the first flush of spring leaves is tingeing the trees green.

Until last night, I knew nothing about Carmel Van Der Proust. Her name was just a scrawled signature on a report. The faceless psychiatrist who condemned Hannah to that awful hospital where all the doors have locks and bolts, there are bars on all the windows and haunting screams punctuate the night. It was a total hellhole, liable to drive the sanest person mad.

Eventually, the bus grinds to a halt in the middle of Wychwood, a village with a pretty stone church and a row of red-brick cottages with neat gardens and crooked roofs. I hop off and take a moment to find my bearings.

The house is less than a mile away, according to the map on my phone. The quickest route appears to be along a footpath that cuts through the churchyard and across some fields to the south. I don't mind the walk. Anyway, I could use the fresh air to clear my head.

I sling my rucksack over my shoulder and head off. The church is in a beautiful spot, surrounded by a graveyard dotted with lichen-covered grey headstones, mostly from the nineteenth century. I slow to look at some of the more prominent ones marking the deaths of some strange characters with names like Septimus, Peregrine, and Octavia. One headstone in particular catches my eye. It lists six names, all of them children from the age of eight to three, all with the same surname, all of whom died on the same day in the summer of 1925.

I kneel at the grave and use my thumb to wipe away a patch of moss. Brothers and sisters? I wonder how they perished. A fire, perhaps. It's terribly sad.

I'm procrastinating. I didn't come all this way to get distracted by gravestones.

The path through the churchyard leads to a muddy trail through a field budding with the green shoots of a new crop. Eventually, I emerge onto a narrow lane and I catch my first glimpse of Shadowbrook Farm.

A glint of sunlight on glass through the trees. A snatch of a towering old brick chimney. A pockmarked tiled roof. But that's all. The property is well-hidden in a secluded spot. I'll need to get closer if I want to see it in all its glory.

At the top of the lane, I find a pair of decorative wrought-iron gates hung on a pair of flint pillars leading to a drive that descends towards the old farmhouse. A slate plaque with the name of the property confirms I'm in the right place.

Although the gates are open, I still can't see much of the house. So, with a quick glance around, I march confidently down the drive with my pulse threading rapidly through my veins.

At the bottom of the drive, the house I've been studying all morning on the internet is instantly recognisable. It's nestled on the side of a hill and surrounded by woodland. Instead of a garden, a wild meadow of long grasses and cow parsley grows unfettered, stretching beyond a paved terrace, complete with a long wooden table and a dozen chairs.

The house is a crazy blend of the old and the new. The original farmhouse has been masterfully renovated and restored, but attached to it now is an enormous, ultra-modern, single-storey metal and glass extension. It's a jarring contrast between two styles, but I can immediately see why they've done it. You don't need to be an architect to understand it's a beautiful location and that by creating a bank of floor-to-ceiling glazing, they've made the best of the stunning views, as well as presumably flooding the house with light.

My legs grow heavy as I approach. Everything about the house and its location is perfect. If I lived here, I'd never moan about anything ever again. In fact, I don't think I'd ever leave. It's simply stunning. I picture myself on the terrace sipping a gin cocktail in my bikini, soaking up the sun. I bet it's an amazing party pad, too. You could fit hundreds of people in a house like this. Maybe have a DJ on the patio with a bar and circus acts wandering through the garden to entertain people...

'Hello? Can I help you?'

I almost jump out of my skin.

Chapter 5

There's a man cradling a steaming mug, with one hand casually in his pocket, his eyes narrowed.

I recognise him instantly. Rufus Van Der Proust. Carmel's husband. The architect who designed the renovated farmhouse.

I stare at him, conscious my jaw is opening and closing, but no words are coming out.

'Did you have a delivery?' he says.

'What?'

'A parcel? The front door's around the side.'

'Oh, no,' I say.

Do I look like a courier?

He raises his eyebrows, encouraging me to explain what the hell I am doing at the house if not delivering a package.

'I, um, sorry, I was just...'

I've been planning what to say on the journey over, but suddenly words fail me.

Get a grip, Marcella. You only have one shot at this.

'I saw you on the TV,' I blurt out. 'Talking about the house and the award.'

'Oh, right,' he says, but he looks perplexed.

'My name's Marcella Middleton. People call me Mars.' I stride towards him and offer him my hand. He's far more handsome in the flesh than on the TV. Although he's much older than me, he's tall and exudes a self-assured confidence. He has wiry, sandy hair coiled into tight ringlets, and a hooded brow which shades intense, chocolate-coloured eyes.

'And what can I do for you, Mars?'

'I run a YouTube channel,' I lie.

'A YouTuber?' he says the word, elongating the vowels, like it's an unfamiliar expression from another century he's trying out for size. 'An influencer?'

'That's right.' Oh god, this is crazy. I can't believe I'm actually doing this. 'I was interested in shooting some films about the house, for my channel.'

Obviously, I don't have a channel or even the first clue about making a film, other than what I've seen other people doing. But then again, how hard can it be?

'Oh, what's your channel?'

A hot flush sweeps my body, and I feel damp patches spreading under my arms. 'Well, to tell you the truth, I've not actually started it yet. I've been looking for the right project to launch it.'

Rufus nods as if that all makes perfect sense. 'But it's going to be about architecture, is it?'

'That's right. It's something I've always been interested in and nobody is really doing much on it at the moment,' I say, the lies continuing to spill easily from my lips.

'That sounds really interesting.' He nods his appreciation. Maybe it's not such a bad idea after all.

'Obviously, I'd like to talk to you about the house and how you came up with the design. I mean, it's so striking,' I say, getting into my stride.

Rufus strokes his chin. 'Yeah, it's all about treating these historic buildings with sympathy while dragging them kicking and screaming into the twenty-first century.'

What a load of pretentious waffle. I nod enthusiastically, as if I couldn't agree more.

'Lots of people hate it,' he continues. 'Fortunately, the planners saw the value of bringing the building back to life. Eventually.'

'That's fascinating,' I say, suppressing the desire to yawn.

'So what would it entail?'

'Sorry?'

'The filming? What would you need?'

'Well, I'd really like to understand what the building means to you and how you make use of the space,' I say, regurgitating the phrases I've heard a million times on some of the house renovation programmes I've watched on TV over the years.

'That was a really important consideration for me when I first sat down and thought about the kinds of designs we could incorporate. First and foremost, it had to be a house that worked for us, you know?' Rufus says.

'That's so important,' I agree, although I don't know what he's talking about.

'And what about your wife? She must love what you've done with the place?'

'Carmel? Oh, yeah, totally. In fact, she's had an enormous influence on the interior design. She has quite an eye for it, actually.'

Yeah, I bet she does.

'So to really understand the building, I need to understand you,' I say.

'Yup, makes sense. I get that.' Rufus nods again, like he's really buying into my vision.

'So how would you feel if I moved in with you for a bit? I mean, to really embed myself in the experience of the house and make the film as strong as it can be?'

My skin tingles.

'Move in?' Rufus blinks rapidly and clears his throat.

'Only for a few days,' I add quickly. 'It would give me the chance to get lots of filming done, inside and out, plus talk to you both about the project. I was hoping I could make a whole series of films about it.'

I hold my breath, waiting for his answer, as he stares into his mug and swirls its contents around. I'm hoping I've not misjudged the situation, and that Rufus is as vain about the project as I think he is. Vain enough to let a complete stranger into his house, if it means even more publicity for his wacky renovation.

'And your boyfriend wouldn't mind you moving in here with us?' he asks.

My cheeks flush. Is he fishing? 'I don't have a boyfriend,' I mumble. 'I live on my own and do as I please.'

At least that's true since last night when Frazer walked out on me. Not that Rufus has to know that.

A light sparks in his eye. 'Oh, right,' he says.

'Is that a yes?'

'Sure, why not? Although I'll have to check with my wife.'

'Oh, do you think she'll mind?'

He looks me up and down. His tongue darts out of his mouth and wets his lips. 'I wouldn't have thought so, but I'd better make certain. It's her house as much as it's mine. She's not in right now, but I'll talk to her tonight. Do you have a number I can call?'

My heart sinks. Just when I thought I had it all worked out. If he talks to Carmel, she's bound to say no.

'I could phone her if you like and run her through what I'm proposing,' I suggest. If she's not as vain about the house as Rufus, she could blow my entire plan out of the water with one word. I have to get her on side too.

'No, no, I'll do it. It's fine.'

'But you'll tell her you think it's a good idea?'

'Absolutely.'

He pulls out his phone from the back pocket of his trousers and I give him my number.

'You'll definitely speak to her tonight?'

He smiles sympathetically. 'Yes.'

'Great, thanks.'

'I suppose you'll be wanting to do something on the history of the house, too?' Rufus says as I'm about to walk away. 'The old stories and rumours?'

'Absolutely.' I'll agree to anything if it gets me a bed in the house for a few days.

'Because it wasn't called the House of Horrors for nothing.'

'The House of Horrors?'

'You didn't know? I thought it was local folklore.'

I shake my head. 'I've never heard of it.'

'Six young children murdered by their father back in the nineteen twenties? Ring any bells?'

My mind's transported back to the graveyard I walked through earlier and the headstone with the names of six young children etched into it. All died on the same day. Buried in a family plot.

'I think I may have seen their grave on my way over.'

'Their bodies were buried at St Mary's in Wychwood, so yes, probably.'

I feel my eyes widen. 'Why'd he kill his own children?'

'Who knows? But rumour has it he had some kind of breakdown.'

'Is the house... haunted?' I ask with a shiver, glancing up at the building and eyeing it in a new light. Maybe I don't want to stay here after all.

Rufus throws his head back and laughs. 'No,' he says. 'Not as far as I know. I've certainly not seen or heard anything.'

'That's pretty creepy, though.'

'Only if you believe in that kind of thing. Anyway, when you come back—'

'*If* I come back.'

'Then I'll tell you all about it.'

'Okay, that's a deal,' I say.

It sounds curious, but I'm not entirely convinced I want to know, especially if I'm going to be staying here overnight.

Chapter 6

I'm so excited by what lies ahead and the prospect of actually moving in with Rufus and Carmel that I almost forget Frazer's gone. It hits me as I let myself into the flat. It's like being caught under an emotional rockfall that forces the air from my lungs.

'Frazer?' I call out. Maybe he's changed his mind and come back after a night apart to think things over.

But the flat's deserted and I'm greeted by a deafening silence punctuated only by the distant rumble of traffic and the sound of children playing in the school across the road.

I've never felt more alone.

How could things have gone so badly off track between us without me realising?

I already miss his smelly trainers. The smear of shaving foam and snicks of black stubble in the bathroom basin. The way he'd drape the damp dishcloth over the kitchen tap to dry. All the little things that used to irritate me are now reminders of what I've lost.

I don't know where I'll go when I have to move out. Without a job, who in their right mind is going to offer me a tenancy? And it's not as if I have any family to turn to for help, either. I've not spoken to my mother in years and I don't know where my father's living. We lost touch a long time ago.

A hollow pang of hunger gnaws at my core as I remember I've not eaten anything all day.

I wander into the kitchen to make myself a sandwich. I find half a loaf in the bread bin, but it's covered in mould. With a sigh, I dump it in the bin and grab a packet of instant noodles in the cupboard over the microwave instead.

'Hey, what are you doing home? Shouldn't you be at work?'

My heart almost bursts out of my chest in shock. 'Hannah! You scared the life out of me.'

My sister's curled up on the sofa in the lounge, plaiting her hair.

'Sorry, I thought you saw me.'

'What are you doing here?'

'I was bored,' she says. 'Where's Frazer? Not left you, has he?'

I've never been able to hide secrets from Hannah. She can read me like a book. But that's twins for you. It's as if there's been an invisible thread between us since the day we were born, Hannah exactly three minutes before me.

After all these years, I still find it weird how near identical we appear. Looking at her is like staring into a mirror, although I can spot subtle differences. Her front teeth are slightly crooked and her left eye slants fractionally upwards, although most people wouldn't notice. She still thinks she's prettier than me, though.

These days, we make more of an effort to be distinct. I choose to keep my hair shorter and dye it a darker shade of brown. And we've never been into wearing the same clothes, even when we were little. That would be freaky. We're sisters, not clones.

'Oh, my god. He has, hasn't he?' Hannah screeches when I don't answer.

I glance at the floor, unable to hold her judgemental gaze. I never seem to have any issue attracting men. It's holding on to them that's more of a problem.

'I don't want to talk about it,' I say.

'I knew it! I thought there was something going on when I saw all his clothes had gone.'

'You've been snooping around the flat while I've been out?' I plant my hands on my hips and stare at Hannah with incredulity.

'I was looking for one of your jumpers and saw the wardrobe was half empty. Anyway, that's not important. Tell me what happened.'

'Nothing happened. He walked out and left me. That's it.'

'That's it? I warned you if you didn't treat him right, he'd go, didn't I? But you never listen to me, do you?'

'Shut up, Hannah.'

'Is that why you're not at work?'

'No,' I say. I take a deep breath. 'I quit.'

Hannah stops playing with her hair and stares at me, open-mouthed. 'What? Why?'

I shrug. 'Dunno. I guess it wasn't the right job for me.'

'Marcella,' she says in that tone of voice she likes to take with me, like she's our mother. 'What happened?'

'Nothing.'

'Nothing?' She raises an eyebrow.

'I'm going to get a new job. A better job. One that pays more money.'

'Right,' she says. She flicks her hair over her shoulder, focusing her full attention on me. 'What job?'

'Actually, I'm waiting for a call about a new venture.' I draw my shoulders back and meet her gaze with a challenge.

'What venture?'

'I'm going to be working for myself from now on. I'm launching a YouTube channel, if you must know.'

'YouTube?' She laughs. 'You?'

'What's so funny about that?'

I might as well have told her I've applied to become a NASA astronaut the way she's gawping at me in disbelief. She's never had any faith in my abilities.

'What do you know about running a YouTube channel?'

'It's not rocket science.'

'And what's this YouTube channel,' she makes inverted comma signs with her fingers in the air, 'going to be about?'

I suppose she's going to find out, eventually.

'I've found the psychiatrist they assigned to evaluate your mental health after the fire. Her name's Carmel Van Der Proust. I remembered her from the court papers,' I explain.

'So?'

My lips turn up into an involuntary smile. 'She's married to an architect and they've recently renovated an old farmhouse up on the Downs. I've asked if I can make some films about the project.'

Hannah frowns and cocks her head to one side. 'Why?'

'I had to find a way of persuading them to let me stay. Honestly, Hannah, you wouldn't believe it if you saw it. This house is massive. They're obviously loaded. It's not right. She's all over those lifestyle magazines, showing off how amazing her life is, boasting about how rich she is, and we've got nothing.'

'Why would you want to stay with them? What are you planning?' Hannah asks sternly. 'I don't want you getting into any trouble.'

'I just thought if I could get a little closer to her, and find out more about her, I could...'

'You could what?'

I shrug. 'She should pay for what she did.'

'How?'

I tap my foot impatiently on the carpet. 'You should see the place. It must be worth millions. It's not fair.'

'Life's not fair.'

'Well, you might have forgiven her, but I can't.'

'Who says I've forgiven her? I don't even know her.'

'You don't sound very enthusiastic.' That's typical of Hannah, just because it was my idea and not hers.

Hannah shakes her head sadly. 'You've got more important things to worry about. You've lost your job. Your boyfriend's walked out. And what are you going to do when you can't pay the rent?'

'Why do you always have to be so negative?' I snap, my anger rising. She's supposed to be my sister. A little emotional support now and again wouldn't go amiss. 'I'll work something out.'

'You're a mess, Mars. You want to worry less about what other people are doing and sort yourself out.'

'Yeah? Well, that's great coming from you, isn't it?'

'What's that supposed to mean?' Hannah asks, folding her arms over her chest.

It's a low blow. I shouldn't use her mental health problems as a weapon. But I've said it now. 'Nothing.'

'No, come on. Spit it out if you've got something to say.'

'Just forget it, alright.'

She has such a way of getting under my skin. I love her to bits, obviously. She's my sister. But she really knows how to push my buttons.

'You're a selfish cow,' she cries. 'And self-centred. Always putting yourself first.'

I spin around, about to give her a piece of my mind. It's about time she heard a few home truths.

But the words jam in my throat as my phone rings in my pocket. I don't recognise the number, but there's only one call I'm waiting for.

'I need to get this,' I mutter.

I don't want Hannah listening in, so I head into the bedroom and pull the door closed.

'Marcella? It's Rufus Van Der Proust. We spoke earlier.'

'Did you talk with your wife?' I ask, clutching my T-shirt anxiously.

'Yes, I spoke with Carmel,' he says, his tone even and measured. 'We'd be delighted to have you stay with us for your filming.'

'You would?'

I can't believe it.

'As I said earlier, it sounds interesting.'

'Right. Yes. Thank you.'

They've actually agreed to it. This is insane.

'When do you want to start?' Rufus asks. 'We can be fairly flexible and work around you.'

My mind's all over the place. I can't think straight, so I say the first thing that comes into my head. 'What about tomorrow?'

'Tomorrow?' He hesitates. 'Sure, why not? Can you make it over here after we've finished work for the day? We could talk through your ideas over dinner.'

Chapter 7

With butterflies fluttering in my stomach and my mind churning, I retrace my footsteps through the church in Wychwood, across the field and up the lane to Shadowbrook Farm with a heavy rucksack filled with as many clothes as I can carry slung on my back.

When I reach the house, I head for a door under an oak-beamed porch that's flanked by a pair of perfectly pruned bay trees in terracotta pots. It's almost too perfect to be real.

I knock and wait, excited and fearful in equal measure.

When Carmel answers the door, I'm momentarily thrown.

Finally, I'm face to face with the woman who ruined everything. The woman I'm here to destroy. On the bus journey over, I'd tried to prepare myself for this moment, but it still comes as a shock.

She greets me with a smile. It curdles my insides. 'You must be Marcella. How lovely to meet you,' she says, but there's no warmth to her tone.

'Mrs Van Der Proust —'

'Call me Carmel.'

She was probably an attractive woman when she was younger. She still has a good figure and is wearing a full face of make-up. Bright red lipstick, which has smudged on her front teeth, a hint of blusher and dusky eyes. I'm not sure about the short-cropped haircut though, especially as she's let it go completely grey. Almost white. She probably thinks it looks sophisticated, but it ages her. It's not a great look.

She's dressed casually in a plain top matched with dark, slim-fitting jeans, but all the fabrics look expensive and even though she's probably older than my mum, she manages to make me feel dowdy.

My jeans are ripped at the knees, and my T-shirt is crumpled and threadbare. It's what I thought a YouTuber might wear, and it's important, until I win their trust, that I keep up appearances.

'Your house is amazing,' I say, stepping inside and admiring the decor.

It's all elegantly minimalist and tastefully done. They've painted the walls in muted pastel shades, left gnarled, twisted old wooden beams exposed, and tiled the floor with expensive-looking polished flagstones.

I kick off my muddy shoes in the hall and follow Carmel into a stunning kitchen, which although is in the older, original part of the house, is surprisingly modern. The cupboards are all pristine white and the worktops uncluttered by anything as unseemly as an electrical appliance. I can't even see any taps by the sink. A bowl piled high with lemons and limes is the only sign that it's a working kitchen and not a showroom in a home improvement store. What kind of people live like this?

Rufus rushes into the kitchen, looking flustered. For a moment, I think he's going to wrap me up in a hug and kiss me on both cheeks, which would be inappropriate given we've only met once. Instead, he offers me his hand, which I shake stiffly. It's all a bit awkward.

'Would you like me to show you to your room?' he asks.

'Thank you.'

Carmel glances at her watch. 'I have a call to make, so I'll leave you with Rufus to settle in. You'll join us for dinner, though? I'm interested to know about the film you want to shoot.'

'That would be lovely. Thank you.'

'Good,' Carmel says. 'I'm looking forward to hearing all about it.'

I have to jog to keep up with Rufus as he takes my rucksack from me and trots out of the kitchen into a spacious hall. I catch fleeting glimpses into some incredible rooms, all styled in the same minimalist, sophisticated fashion.

Upstairs, he guides me along a galleried landing. Some doors to the bedrooms have been left open, giving me a further peek into the sort of opulence and luxury I could only dream of. It must be an incredible place to live.

'Most of this floor is finished now,' Rufus says as we sweep past a stunning bathroom decked in white marble and gold. 'But we've put you upstairs.'

My imagination runs away with itself, wondering what kind of room I'll be staying in. Whether I'll have my own en suite. A huge double bed. A window with a view across the valley.

But my excitement is short-lived as Rufus continues on up a rickety, dark staircase that disappears into the gloom above, at the back of the house.

'We thought you'd be happier staying in one of the attic rooms,' he says.

The stairs creak and groan under our combined weight and there's a definite drop in the temperature as we climb. The skin on my forearms puckers and I shiver.

At the top, Rufus reaches for a light switch. A naked, overhead bulb hanging from the ceiling comes on, lighting up a grim landing with exposed floorboards. There are three doors, all pulled shut. It couldn't look any more different than the splendour of the rooms below.

'Unfortunately, it's the one part of the house we still have left to finish,' Rufus explains, 'but we thought up here you'd at least have your own space, which you'd appreciate.'

He pushes open a door to reveal a basic bathroom. No white marble or gold in here. Just a stained enamel bath, a cracked basin and a toilet angled into the corner.

'I'm sure it'll be fine,' I say through gritted teeth.

'And this is your room,' he says, throwing open the door opposite.

I peer inside, my spirits sinking. There are two ancient-looking metal beds on either side of the room, plus a chest of drawers and two bedside cabinets. There isn't even any carpet and the beds haven't been made up. A duvet has been heaped on the end of one of the lumpy-looking mattresses, a set of bedclothes folded neatly next to it. I guess I'm supposed to do it myself.

What makes it worse is that there are no proper windows. No views of the outside world. Only a tiny skylight with a limited view of the darkening sky. It's no better than a prison.

'Carmel thought you'd be happiest up here,' Rufus says.

'Thank you. It's very... cosy.'

'I'm glad you like it.' Rufus stands in the doorway, watching as I take my rucksack from him and dump it on the spare bed.

'I suppose I ought to set out the ground rules,' he says.

'Ground rules?'

'Just a bit of housekeeping while you're under our roof, so we all rub along together nicely.'

I'm supposed to be a guest. Is this how they treat all their visitors?

'You can have the run of the house during the day,' he explains. 'Help yourself to food. Anything you like. The cupboards and fridge are usually pretty well stocked, and I'll find you the wifi code later. Carmel and I often work from home, so you'll see us around if you need anything. The only real stipulation is that we would ask you to be in your room by nine. We retire early and Carmel's a light sleeper. So please keep the noise to a minimum.'

'Oh, okay.'

'Because you don't want to get on the wrong side of Carmel.' Rufus laughs nervously. 'Is there anything else you'd like to know?'

I glance around the room, hoping he's joking and that really he's going to offer me a comfortable bedroom with a super king size bed, thick pile carpet and my own en suite in the main part of the house.

'No, I don't think so,' I mumble.

'Great,' he grins. 'We'll see you for dinner then.' He checks his watch. 'We eat at seven, so that gives you time to freshen up and get changed. Then we can have a good chat about what you hope to achieve with your filming.'

Freshen up and change? Does he expect me to dress up for dinner? It's a good thing I brought some dresses.

'I think this is going to be a really fun adventure for all of us,' he adds. 'We can't wait to get started.'

He withdraws from the room and pulls the door shut.

As I listen to his footsteps thud down the stairs and fade away, I slump on the bed with a sigh. The room isn't cosy. It's oppressive and cold. And now I'm stuck here. This isn't what I imagined it was going to be like at all. But there's nothing I can do about it. I'll have to make the most of it.

At least I'm being cooked for tonight, and hopefully, over dinner, Rufus will fill me in on the details of the children who were supposedly murdered in the house, like he promised.

In the meantime, I need to work on the next phase of my plan, because the more I see of the house, the more I'm convinced there's no one less deserving of it than Carmel Van Der Proust.

Chapter 8

St Mary's Church, Wychwood
September 12, 1925

The verger was running late. Damned bicycle. Three times he'd had to stop en route to re-inflate a punctured tyre, and now he was hot and irritable.

'A sluggard's appetite is never filled, but the desires of the diligent are fully satisfied,' Albert Bates muttered under his breath as he leant his bike up against the mighty oak that shaded the porch over the entrance to the church. He hated tardiness, in others and himself.

His agitation was further compounded when he discovered the door was unlocked and the church open for anyone to wander in.

Strange. The vicar, presumably. He must have popped in on some urgent ecclesiastical business. Although he hadn't mentioned it earlier.

Albert propped the outer door open with a brick and let himself into the nave.

'Hello?' he called out, his voice echoing. 'Anyone here?'

Perhaps the Reverend James Bennett had popped in and in his haste forgotten to lock up. Not that the village of Wychwood was a hotbed of criminality. It's just Albert didn't trust anyone. It was always better to be sure than sorry.

He poked his head around the door of the vestry and the sacristy, but there was no sign of anyone, nor thankfully that anything had been touched or taken. They'd had some trouble in recent months with some young lads from a neighbouring village who'd been set on causing trouble, throwing stones at the windows and such like, but they'd not been seen for a while. Hopefully, they'd moved on.

Albert shrugged to himself and swung his satchel off his shoulder. No harm done, but he'd have a word with the vicar later. Can't have the church left open and unattended like that. It was asking for trouble.

He pulled out a paper bag filled with bread-crumbs he'd collected from his morning loaf and headed back outside.

A haunting stillness enveloped the grounds as a hazy sun climbed above the bell tower, burning off a low hanging mist clinging to the gravestones, like angels' breath ascending to heaven.

Albert pulled out a fistful of crumbs as a pair of goldfinches darted out of a hedge and flew low over his head, chirruping a warning. Beautiful creatures with their flashes of gold and scarlet.

He shuffled over to the patch of lush grass by a bench along the flint wall that encircled the grounds and scattered the crumbs liberally for the birds.

From the corner of his eye, something caught his attention. Something in the tall grass growing around the rusty iron fence by Henry Randall's grave. Something out of place.

A brown leather notebook. He recognised it instantly. The Reverend Bennett's notebook that he carried with him at all times to jot down his poems and musings. But what was it doing out here?

A chill shiver ran down Albert's spine. He edged towards the notebook and picked it up. Dew had soaked into the leather, causing it to turn slimy like soap, its pages curling and distorted.

And then he saw the hand at the end of an outstretched arm.

Albert gasped, his heart leapfrogging in his chest.

The Reverend Bennett was lying face down on the ground, his cassock rucked up around his legs. Jewels of dew dappled his hair. His wire-framed glasses twisted and cracked on the ground at his side.

'Reverend?' Albert croaked, his voice snagging in his throat. 'Mr Bennett? Are you alright?'

Albert's knees creaked as he lowered himself. He shook the vicar's shoulders.

'Can you hear me, Vicar?'

When he rolled the body over, he discovered a gruesome open cut ran from the vicar's hairline to his eyebrow. It was bloody and swollen, his hair matted and sticky. His eyes were shut. He wasn't breathing.

Albert pressed his ear against the man's chest and listened for a heartbeat. Willing there to be one.

This couldn't be happening. The Reverend Bennett was the kindest, gentlest, most considerate, godly man he knew. But there was no heartbeat. No breath. And although Albert was no doctor, he knew a dead body when he saw one.

'Help!' he cried out. 'Somebody help me, please.'

No one came. He'd have to raise the alarm with the village constable himself.

He feared his own heart was going to give out as he ran to the police house, his knees aching and his hips protesting.

He hammered at the door until the red-faced constable answered.

'It's the vicar,' Albert wheezed. 'I think he's dead.'

Walter Cooper threw on his uniform and hurried with Albert back to the church.

Cooper shook his head sadly, then paced the scene, peering around graves and poking his truncheon into the grass.

'I found this,' Albert said, remembering the vicar's notebook he'd shoved into his pocket.

Cooper examined it carefully.

'It's his notebook. He always had it with him,' Albert explained. 'What do you think happened to him? Do you think he's been... murdered?' He whispered the word as if it was a profanity.

Cooper's head jerked up. 'Murdered? Why would you think that?'

'I don't know... it's just...'

'No, no,' Cooper said. 'A tragic accident, I'd say.'

He tapped the nearest headstone with his truncheon. Elizabeth Mary Fletcher's tombstone. Born May 3, 1786. Died December 15, 1808, aged twenty-three.

'See the blood here?' He pointed to the top of the headstone. 'I'd say the Reverend Bennett tripped. Must have hit his head hard. Nasty business.'

Albert frowned.

'Looking at the condition of the body, I suspect he's lain here all night, which means he probably died some time last evening,' Cooper continued.

'What was he doing out here last night?'

Cooper puffed out his cheeks. 'When did you last see him alive?'

'Yesterday afternoon. At the funeral for the Webb children.' Albert bowed his head. Poor Reverend Bennett. What a way to die.

He took a step back, and almost stumbled, his foot catching on a rock half-hidden in the weeds and brambles that had sprung up around Joseph Frederick Whyte's gravestone. Born March 19, 1833. Died February 2, 1867, aged 33.

If he'd have looked more closely, he'd have seen someone had recently dropped the rock in a hurry. And that it was stained crimson, sticky with blood.

'So what happens now?' Albert asked.

'I'll contact the funeral director and ask him to collect the body.'

'And that's it?'

'I'm afraid so. I know the village will be upset, but it's just one of those unfortunate things.'

Chapter 9

St Mary's Church, Wychwood
   June 7, 1925

The Reverend James Bennett pushed the door of the vestry closed, removed his stole, a lush, dark green, the colour of nature itself, and hung it on its hook on the wall.

He loved Sunday service when the entire village came together for worship and commune. Today had been no exception. There had only been a few absentees, the pews packed with the old and the young, who'd hung on his every word.

He'd risen to his theme this week and had them enthralled with his lesson on compassion, reminding them how, when they embraced their neighbours in their darkest moments, they manifested God's love on earth.

Many of them nodded along, fixed in an almost transcendental state, despite the cries of a baby at the back and the mutterings of the restless Webb children who'd crammed into a single pew along-side their mother.

Sadly, the only moment he'd had the children's full attention was when he reminded them of the parable of the Good Samaritan, who'd taken pity on a stranger beaten and left for dead on the road to Jericho. They liked that one. Probably because of the gruesome details he'd used to embellish the story. He ought to make a note and return to it at a later date.

He slipped out of his pristine white surplice, hung it on its wire hanger, and pulled out his notebook from the pocket of his cassock. He took a seat at the table, picked up his faithful fountain pen, and unscrewed the cap.

But that's as far as he got before the door crashed open and a child burst in, giggling breathlessly as he glanced over his shoulder with nervous excitement. When he spotted the vicar, his face fell in horror and his laughter dried up.

With wide eyes of shock, the boy whipped off his cloth cap and bowed his head.

'Young Master Webb,' the vicar said, swivelling in his chair to appraise the impudent young intruder.

'I'm sorry, Reverend Bennett. I didn't know you were in here,' he mumbled sheepishly.

'It's the vestry, Stanley. Where else would you expect to find me?'

The boy stood forlornly, gazing at the floor, his cheeks glowing and his hair damp with sweat.

'What were you doing?' the Reverend Bennett asked.

'Hiding.'

The vicar raised an eyebrow. 'From whom?'

'Alfred. We were playing hide and seek and it's our turn to hide.'

The Reverend Bennett smiled. Boys will be boys, even in the House of God.

'Well, why don't you run along and play outside instead of causing chaos in the church. There are plenty of places to hide in the churchyard.'

Hurried footsteps tapped along the tiled floor outside and Agatha Webb put her head around the door, looking flustered.

'What are you doing in here?' she snapped at the boy, snatching his wrist and dragging him out.

The Reverend Bennett stood and held up his hands. 'It's perfectly alright, Mrs Webb. No harm done, although I've advised your son he'd be better playing outside.'

'I'm so sorry, Reverend. I only turned my back for a minute, and the next thing they're causing havoc.' She adjusted her fashionable cloche hat. 'Go on, get out,' she yelled at the boy, striking him on his backside as he ran away.

'There's no need to apologise. It's good to see the children having fun.'

She looked tired, her eyes dark and her shoulders stooped as if she was carrying a Sisyphean rock on her back.

She carved out a tight smile.

'How is everything at home? We've not seen William at church for a while.'

Her smile tightened further. 'Billy's fine.'

The vicar raised a disbelieving eyebrow. 'We miss him at Sunday service.'

Agatha chewed her lip and fiddled with her fingers. 'He says he's rejected the church. That he's lost his faith.'

The vicar frowned. Of all the villagers, William Webb was probably the one man who needed Christ in his life above anyone.

'Does he ever talk about the war?' he asked.

'Not really. He still gets night terrors, waking screaming, his body soaked in sweat. I'm afraid he's not the man I married.'

The Reverend Bennett nodded sagely. William was one of the lucky ones, medically discharged from the army during the war, and returned to his family. Several men from the village had not been so fortunate, their lives lost on the battlefields of France. At least Agatha had her husband home, even if he was missing a leg and suffering some kind of mental affliction.

He thought of the sermon he'd delivered earlier that morning. Of the need for compassion and understanding. 'Remember the power of patience and compassion,' he said. 'The road ahead may be challenging, but together, with faith, love and determination, you and your husband *will* find a path to healing and restoration.'

But Agatha shook her head sadly. 'I don't think it's going to be that easy. He hates me. He's so withdrawn and angry all the time, with me and the children.'

'I'm sorry to hear that. Come, sit awhile.' The vicar pulled out a chair and encouraged her to sit. 'Talk to me.'

She glanced at the door, as if contemplating whether she should leave. 'You're most kind, but you must be busy.'

'I'm never too busy for a parishioner in need.'

She saw his notebook, still open on the table. His fountain pen uncapped. 'What were you writing?'

'I like to keep a journal of my thoughts, and sometimes I write poetry. Maybe it's a way you could find solace too? I find it helpful to write in it every day.'

Her brow knotted, a wave of furrows creasing her pretty forehead. 'I don't think so.'

'No matter how hard it seems, you must stick by your husband's side and he will heal, with God's will. Remember your vows? In sickness and in health?'

'I don't think he's sick,' she said.

'Not all illnesses are visible to the human eye. Just as we encounter physical afflictions that are apparent, there are also those that dwell within the recesses of the mind and heart.'

Agatha played nervously with her fingers. 'The problem is, I don't think he's capable of love anymore.'

'I'm sure he loves you very much,' the vicar assured her. 'Even if he struggles to show it outwardly.'

'He won't come near me, or let me near him. He won't touch me. Hold me. I'm locked in a loveless marriage.' She dabbed at a tear in the corner of her eye.

'You have six children,' he reminded her.

'Love is not the same as sex.'

The Reverend Bennett's cheeks flushed with heat. He coughed to clear his throat.

'Give him time.'

'It's been eight years.'

He reached out to touch her hand. He should have known better. But they were alone and instinct commandeered his senses.

She recoiled as if his touch had ignited an electrical spark between them. And then she looked at him in a way no woman had ever looked at him before. Something forbidden stirred in the pit of his stomach.

He pushed it away, standing in a dizzying haze. His chair toppled backwards, hitting the floor with a thud, while outside, the sound of children's laughter filtered through the cold stone walls.

'I couldn't help notice how grown up Stanley is looking these days,' the Reverend Bennett mumbled, snatching at the first thing that came to mind to steer their conversation in a new direction. 'He has his mother's nose and determined spirit.'

'And his father's eyes,' Agatha whispered, raising her eyebrows.

The Reverend Bennett winced. How thoughtless to mention the eldest child.

'How is he with the children?'

'Not at all like a father. They might as well not have one.'

'Would you like me to speak to him? Maybe he'll confide in me.'

'Do as you want. I don't care.'

A crash from inside the nave made them both jump. A child's cry echoed through the church. The plaintive howl of pain.

'I'd better go,' Agatha said.

'Of course. I'll try to visit soon. Probably best not to mention it to William, though,' the vicar said.

But Agatha had already disappeared to attend to her injured child.

The vicar, alone again, returned to his notebook. He picked up his pen and wrote in capital letters, 'WILLIAM WEBB'. Then circled it.

William may have forsaken God, but God would never turn his back on one of his own children.

The vicar vowed to be true to his word. He'd speak to William and try to encourage him back to church.

If nothing else, visiting the house would give him the opportunity to see Agatha again.

Chapter 10

**Shadowbrook Farm, near Wychwood
June 10, 1925**

Agatha was hanging washing on the line, a white apron tied around her waist. She gave a little start when the Reverend Bennett called her name over the wind rustling the leaves in the trees.

'Mrs Webb, forgive my intrusion,' he said, mopping his brow with his handkerchief. It was a warm spring day heralding the start of a hot summer, and a tidy walk to the farm from the vicarage. 'I was hoping to catch a word with your husband if he's around?'

She lowered the cotton shirt she was hanging and stared at him with suspicion. Her two youngest, Dorothy and Edith, were playing around her skirts, hand-in-hand, singing *Ring a Ring o' Roses*.

'Down at the barn with the cattle.' She nodded in the direction beyond the farmhouse. 'There's a problem with one of the cows.'

The Reverend Bennett tipped his hat and set off along a hard-baked dirt path into the valley. It had been a long time since he'd last seen William, let alone spoken to him. Not since he'd first returned from France, struggling to master his balance on a pair of crutches and his trouser leg pinned up below his knee. It was a miracle he'd been able to return to working on the farm at all. It was too big an operation for one man, disabled or not.

The low, distressed bellow of a troubled animal guided the vicar to the barn, where he found William leaning into a pen. A cow, hoof-deep in fresh straw, was struggling to stand.

'What's happened to her?' the vicar asked.

William turned his head slowly and looked the Reverend Bennett up and down as if he was at the market appraising the worth of a two-headed ram.

'She's sick,' he growled.

'Any idea what's wrong?'

'No. She's been like it for a few days.'

The cow stumbled to its knees and lowed again, flicking its head in distress.

'We haven't seen you at church in a while, William. Everything well with you?'

William grabbed his crutches and turned awkwardly, almost slipping on the stone floor, slick with mud.

'I'm fine,' he answered in a lazy drawl, his mouth barely opening, as if it was too much effort to speak.

He'd lost weight in the years since the Reverend Bennett had last seen him. His chest was hollowed out and his arms spindle-thin. His eyes were hooded and dark, his skin sallow and his cheeks sunken. A man haunted by his past. A shell of a human being.

'Are you sure? Agatha thought you might need someone to talk to.'

William snorted. 'And you thought you were the man for the job?'

'I'd like to help, if I can. For Agatha's sake. And the children.'

'So she put you up to this? Spreading gossip and rumours about me, was it?'

'No, it wasn't like that. She's worried you might not be coping spiritually, which isn't any wonder after—'

'What do you know about it?' William snapped, glowering at the vicar, his black eyes boring into him as if the devil possessed him.

'You have a family who needs you. Six beautiful children and a wonderful wife.'

'I don't need counselling from the church.'

'No man is an island, entire of itself.' The vicar removed his hat and smoothed down his hair.

'You've got no right coming down here and poking your nose into other people's business. We're fine as we are.'

'Agatha tells me you've not been sleeping well. Are you still suffering from troubling dreams?' the vicar asked, replacing his hat and swatting at a fly that buzzed around his face.

'Troubling dreams?' William scowled.

'Night terrors. Nightmares. Call it what you will. It's nothing to be ashamed of.'

'Who says I'm ashamed?'

'You are not alone in this struggle. Remember that God is always with you, guiding and supporting you through your pain. Let His light guide you towards healing.'

William snorted dismissively. 'God?'

'It might help if you came to Sunday service. Many soldiers have returned from the war and found great comfort in the Lord's word.'

William hobbled closer until their faces were inches apart.

'Comfort?' William sneered. 'There's no comfort in the nonsense you peddle. I've listened to men in the trenches praying fervently for deliverance, only to be met with suffering and death. I've seen good men who've been gassed, gasping for breath, blood foaming at their mouths. Men, no more than boys, with their faces blown away, their stomachs turned inside out by a hail of bullets. Entire villages reduced to rubble and families torn apart. More misery and suffering than you could ever know. How could there be any divine plan in such destruction? How could a merciful god allow any of that to happen?'

The vicar lowered his gaze. How could he ever understand what the poor man had endured? The horrors he'd witnessed?

'It's natural to question and doubt during times of great suffering,' he said. 'But remember, God's love and presence might not always be evident in the midst of tragedy. Sometimes we find comfort and meaning in unexpected ways. Your experiences on the battlefield are a reminder of the importance of compassion and peace. Even in the face of senseless violence, we can choose to work towards healing and reconciliation, becoming instruments of God's love in a broken world.'

As William stared at him with his soulless black eyes, the vicar shuddered.

'Keep away from my wife,' he growled.

The Reverend Bennett's cheeks burned. 'She came to me in desperation.'

'I bet she did.'

'In a spiritual capacity.'

'Oh, yeah?'

'She's worried you don't love her anymore. That you're incapable of love, but I think she's wrong. Take the time to nurture yourself and love will find its way back into your life.'

William grunted. 'She told you that, did she?'

'She was distressed. She thought I might be able to help.'

William pushed past the vicar. The Reverend Bennett stumbled backwards, his feet slipping, his shoes covered in muck and dirt.

'Would you at least think about returning to church? I know it would make Agatha happy.'

'I don't think so.' William reached for a shelf in the shadows at the back of the barn.

He picked up a revolver. Military issue. A wooden handle. Dull tarnished metal. He swung out the cylinder with a flick of his wrist, and, leaning on his crutch, loaded it with ammunition from a cardboard box.

The Reverend Bennett edged away, his gaze fixed warily on the weapon.

'Sometimes a man needs to be cruel to be kind,' William said, snapping the cylinder shut.

He hobbled back to the pen where the cow was trying again to stand, but her legs buckled and wouldn't support her weight. There was something terribly wrong with her.

'I can't afford the vet,' William said. He raised the revolver to the beast's head, placed the barrel between her eyes, and fired a single shot.

The crack reverberated around the shed, startling a murder of crows from the nearby wood, and momentarily deafening the vicar.

The cow collapsed into the straw.

'Best thing for her to put her out of her misery,' William said. 'She wasn't going to get any better.'

He lowered the gun and slipped it in his pocket as the Reverend Bennett dug his fingers into his ears, trying to clear the ringing noise. A flush of nausea rose from his stomach. He wiped his mouth with his handkerchief and concentrated on keeping his breakfast down.

'Now I'm busy, so unless there was anything else?' William said, swaying unsteadily on the spot.

'Think about what I said, William. Your family needs you.'

'I think you'd better go.'

The Reverend Bennett opened his mouth to speak, but snapped it closed again. There was no point talking to the man when he was in this kind of mood. Maybe he'd try later. He owed it to Agatha.

She didn't deserve to be living with a monster. She deserved so much better.

He tipped his hat. 'As you wish, but think about my words.'

William snorted with derision. 'Don't come back,' he said. 'And stay away from my wife. If I hear you've been dripping poison in her ear again, I'll break every bone in your body.'

Chapter 11

The Vicarage, Wychwood
June 27, 1925

The hammering at the door was an unwelcome intrusion into the Reverend Bennett's thoughts. He was working on the lesson for the morning service, and besides, it was late. Who on earth was knocking at his door at this time of the evening?

With a sigh, he screwed the cap back onto his fountain pen and trudged wearily into the hall, noting the time on the grandfather clock. Almost half-past eight.

He prayed it wasn't an emergency. One of the village elders at death's door or a parishioner suffering a spiritual crisis that was going to eat into the rest of his evening.

Another frantic volley of blows on the door urged the vicar to hurry.

'Yes, yes, yes, I'm coming,' he muttered, adjusting his glasses as he went.

He unlocked the door and heaved it open.

He was surprised to find Agatha on the doorstep, her head bowed and her shoulders hunched. If he wasn't mistaken, she was crying.

'Agatha? What's wrong?'

She peered up at him from under a wide-brimmed hat and he gasped. Her left eye was puffy and almost entirely closed up, an aubergine purple bruise following the contours of its socket.

Tears streamed down her cheek, and her face crumpled in distress.

'I'm sorry,' she wailed. 'I didn't know where else to go.'

The Reverend Bennett glanced over her shoulder and ushered her inside.

She sat on the edge of the divan in the lounge with her knees together and her fingers snaking around each other in her lap. As her skirts rose, the vicar couldn't help notice an unusual mark on her calf. A birthmark that looked for all the world like an angry dragon.

He snapped his gaze away, embarrassed that he'd been looking.

'Agatha, who did this to you?' he asked, fearing he already knew the answer.

'He didn't mean to,' she sobbed, dabbing her nose with a balled-up cotton handkerchief. 'But he was so angry.'

The vicar took a deep breath, suppressing a rising tide of fury. What kind of a man strikes a woman?

'It's been getting worse,' she continued. 'He's always so full of rage. And the night terrors aren't getting any better. When he wakes, as he does most nights, his eyes are focused on some kind of horror I cannot see, as if he's reliving all the terrible things he saw on the battlefield over and over again. As if his mind won't let him forget.'

The Reverend Bennett took a seat at her side and placed his hand in hers. Her fingers were rigid and cold. She stretched her back and winced with pain.

'What is it?'

'I think I may have a broken rib,' she said.

The vicar jumped up. 'I'll call the doctor.'

'No!' She grabbed his hand and pulled him back down. 'I don't want anyone else to know.'

'But you're hurt.'

'Please,' she begged.

The way she looked at him, with such desperation and sadness, made up his mind. He wouldn't do anything to cause her any further distress.

'Has he hit you before?'

She shook her head. 'He's threatened it. Raised his hand to me, but he's never hurt me before.'

'Where is he now?'

'At home with the children. I don't know how much more I can take. You don't know what it's like.'

'His mind has been wounded, just as war has scarred his body. I'm sure he never meant to cause you any harm,' the vicar soothed. 'I've been praying for you both, and in time, I'm sure things will improve, with God's will.'

'And how long is that going to take?'

'I know this is a difficult time for you, but you need to lean on your faith. Take comfort in prayer and remember God is present in your struggles and will never forsake you.'

'I don't know if that's enough anymore.' A fresh wave of tears and misery wracked Agatha's body.

The Reverend Bennett was seized by the sudden urge to throw his arms around her and hold her tight. But he knew he mustn't. Especially as he recognised he'd developed unnatural feelings towards her in recent weeks. For the love of God, she was a married woman. He shouldn't be thinking about her like that.

'You need to find patience with yourself and your husband. Healing takes time, but with love and understanding, you can navigate through this storm and find a path towards restoration and reconciliation,' he said.

'Yes,' she croaked. 'I know you're right, but it's so hard. I'm living with a stranger and I'm worried what he's capable of in the middle of the night, when he wakes staring blankly at the wall. I worry what he'll do when he's not quite himself. If he thinks I'm somebody else.'

'Patience and belief,' he reminded her. 'And you'll grow stronger together.'

She picked at the handkerchief in her hands, lost in her own torment. And then she stood suddenly, wiping her eyes. Collecting herself.

'I'm so sorry, turning up here like this. Whatever must you think of me?' She smoothed down her skirt, straightened her spine and pulled back her shoulders. 'I'm sure you were busy.'

The vicar waved a dismissive hand. 'Nothing important. I was only working on tomorrow's lesson. Will I be seeing you all?'

Agatha put a knuckle to her blackened eye. 'It might be best if we give it a miss tomorrow. I don't want to start tongues wagging,' she said.

He shot her a weak smile. 'I'll ask everyone to pray for you.'

She looked horrified. 'You won't tell anyone, will you?'

'I'll mention that you're sick and that's why you couldn't be there.'

'You really are kind.' She threw her arms around his neck.

Her body was firm, warm, and sweet. He allowed himself to return her hold and breathed in the smell of her hair.

'If there's anything else I can do, you must let me know,' he said, clearing his throat as she pulled away from him.

'I just needed a friendly ear. But thank you.'

He walked her to the door, pushing an inappropriate thought out of his mind. She was married, he reminded himself. There could never be anything between them. His life was dedicated to Christ. Not to the pleasures of the flesh.

'Goodnight, Agatha. Safe journey home.'

She adjusted her hat and lifted her skirt as she stepped outside.

'I hope you don't think I'm making a fuss about nothing,' she said.

'No, not at all. I'm glad you felt you could come to me.'

'It's just that... it sounds silly, I know... but I'm worried that one day he's going to...' She shook her head. 'No, it doesn't matter. I shouldn't say it.'

'You can tell me anything, Agatha. It won't go any further.'

'Well, it's just, I'm worried that one day he might actually kill me.'

Chapter 12

On the stroke of seven, I tiptoe nervously down the stairs as the smell of something delicious wafts up from below and makes my stomach rumble. Even though Rufus and Carmel have invited me to stay, I feel like an intruder. An unwanted guest. It's all a bit surreal.

They're in the kitchen sharing a bottle of wine. Rufus is at the stove, with his back to the door, stirring a large pot while Carmel sits at the breakfast bar, poring over her phone.

She looks me up and down over the top of a pair of reading glasses, her eyes widening in surprise.

'You've changed,' she says, noting I've dispensed with my scruffy jeans and baggy T-shirt.

'Oh, I thought Rufus said...' I clutch at the hem of my dress. The heat of embarrassment rises from my chest to my cheeks. As if I wasn't already feeling awkward.

Rufus's eyes almost pop out of his head when he sees me. He takes a large gulp of wine.

I thought it would be smart for dinner, but maybe the dress is too figure-hugging. A little too plunging at the front, showing off too much cleavage. I don't wear dresses as often as I should, and only put it on because it usually makes me feel good about myself. Not tonight.

I've also tied my hair back and applied a touch of make-up. Only some lip gloss and eyeliner. But I can see now it's too much. Way over the top for a casual supper. I guess I was just trying to make a good impression.

Neither Rufus nor Carmel has bothered changing, and I have the urge to run away, strip off and wash my face.

'That's an... *impressive* dress,' Carmel says, but her tone suggests it's not intended as a compliment.

'I'll take it off,' I mumble.

'Don't be silly.' Carmel peels off her glasses with an infuriating smirk. 'Dinner's almost ready.'

She pours me a glass of wine, which I gratefully accept. I have a feeling I'm going to need some Dutch courage to make it through the evening.

'Why don't you take our guest through to the dining room, love,' Rufus says, clattering a pile of plates he takes from the oven. 'I'll bring the food through.'

With my cheeks still flushed and my head bowed, I follow Carmel into the vast glass and steel extension that makes up the new half of the house. I've only glimpsed it from outside, but inside it's enormous. It forms one long room, about as big as an Olympic-sized swimming pool, and is zoned into different living areas by the clever placement of furniture and mood lighting.

A long dining table has been set for dinner with a dozen tall candles whose flames glint in the vast expanse of glazing overlooking the garden.

There are no curtains or blinds. Just a long wall of glass. It's almost impossible to see out with all the lights reflecting off the glazing, but it's obvious anyone standing outside would have a clear view of everything going on in the house. I shudder at the thought.

'You can sit there,' Carmel orders, pointing to a place that's been set halfway down the table.

I pull up a chair, drape a napkin over my lap, and try desperately to think of something to say to punctuate the awkward silence.

'You have a lovely house.'

'Yes,' Carmel agrees, fiddling with a bulbous red earring that matches the colour of her lipstick as she takes a seat at the end of the table. Her lips are pinched as if she's just licked a spoonful of salt.

She was fine with me when I first arrived at the house, but I get the distinct impression she doesn't like me much, which is odd, because she doesn't know me. Rufus said she was happy for me to come and stay for a few days, but maybe she's not as pleased as he made out. Or is it the dress? She must have seen how he looked at me, his eyes bulging like full moons.

Fine. If she doesn't want to talk, I'm happy sitting here in silence. The thought of making small talk with her makes me nauseous, anyway. Even sitting at the same table ignites a fire of fury in my gut, especially now I can see with my own eyes the life she's living here with Rufus.

All this money and luxury. The perfect house. Her handsome architect husband. It's all been built on other people's misery. I bet she doesn't even remember Hannah's name.

Being here, seeing it all for myself, is a torture I could do without. But I have to remember why I'm here.

Rufus rushes into the room with two serving dishes filled with lamb shanks and heaps of creamy mashed potato, which he places in the middle of the table.

'Oh my god, this is amazing,' I coo, serving myself and forking a chunk of lamb into my mouth. It virtually melts on my tongue.

'It's nothing, really,' Rufus says, beaming with pride. 'Just something I threw together. We're lucky. There's an amazing butcher's shop in Wychwood.'

Carmel takes the tiniest mouthful of potato. 'He's fine as long as he has a recipe to follow,' she says bitterly. 'Typical man.'

Rufus shrinks into himself. If it was supposed to be a joke, he clearly didn't find it funny.

'Well, I think it's delicious,' I say, rushing to his defence.

'So tell me more about this YouTube channel,' Carmel asks, wrinkling her nose as if it's something squalid and unsavoury.

I put my knife and fork down on my plate and dab my mouth with my napkin.

'It was just an idea I had to celebrate the area's best architecture,' I explain. 'I wanted to feature some of the best work but also find out about the people behind the projects and what it's like to live in such amazing places.' I force a smile. 'Places like Shadowbrook Farm.'

'That's great, isn't it?' Rufus says to his wife.

'And how many of these films have you made?' Carmel asks with an arched eyebrow.

I chew my bottom lip. 'This is the first, but hopefully it will be the first of many.'

'Right,' she says, clearly unimpressed.

'I mean, this house, how you've blended the old with the new, is out of this world. How did you come up with the idea, Rufus?'

He swallows and washes his food down with another mouthful of wine, then folds his hands over his plate, elbows on the table. 'I'd been looking for a project like this to sink my teeth into for a while,' he says, clearly pleased to be talking about himself and his work. I nod my encouragement. 'Something where I could bring back a historic building to life and fuse it with something extraordinarily contemporary. We were lucky to find this house, although it had been abandoned and left as a virtual wreck for years.'

'It was a joint vision,' Carmel adds. 'And all the interior design was mine. Rufus doesn't have a clue about colour schemes.'

She's done an incredible job. It's beautiful inside and out. But I refuse to inflate her ego by telling her so.

'So with your agreement, what I'd like to do is film a series of short intimate films about the house and the two of you,' I say. 'How you use the space? What drove you to create something so radical? What makes you tick? I'll film it all on my phone and hopefully you'll soon forget I'm even here.'

'And how long do you intend to stay?' Carmel asks. I think I was right. She's not keen on me being here at all. I'm surprised Rufus talked her into it.

'A week? Maybe two, if you'll let me.'

'You're welcome to stay as long as you like,' Rufus says. 'And I guess you'll also want to explore the history of the farmhouse?'

I'd almost forgotten. The murders that happened here between the wars. I'd tried looking up details of the case online before I arrived, but there was scant information about it, other than a few sparse lines on a local history website.

'I guess that would be something interesting to explore, of course. You were going to tell me more about it,' I prompt.

'Don't scare easily, do you?' Carmel says, pushing her half-eaten meal to one side with a cruel grin.

'Stop it, Carmel,' Rufus warns. 'Like I told you yesterday, there were six children. The eldest was eight, the youngest only three.'

I recall the gravestone I saw at the church. All the names. The dates of birth. The same date of death. It's shocking when you see it literally written in stone.

'Their father killed them one by one after sedating them with a fruit punch he'd laced with whisky.

He smothered them with a pillow as they slept, then laid them all out side by side,' Rufus explains, the glow of a candle casting an eerie light across his face.

'That's horrible.' I shudder. 'How could a father do that to his own children?'

He shrugs. 'They think he killed his wife first, but they never found her body. She's probably buried out in the woods somewhere.'

'Jesus,' I gasp.

Carmel rocks back in her chair, cradling her wine glass, her lips curled up into a smile of delight. She's obviously enjoying my discomfort.

'And wracked with guilt, he took his own life. They found his body next to his old service revolver and with a bullet in his head,' Rufus says.

'He'd been in the war.' Carmel leans on the table, fixing me with cold, grey eyes. 'But he'd been medically discharged after his leg was blown off below the knee during a battle at the Somme. Some people in the village said it affected his mind. When he returned home, his wife, Agatha, and the kids bore the brunt of his erratic behaviour. He was sullen, withdrawn and prone to losing his temper.'

'What a sad story.' I push potato around my plate, my appetite ruined. 'Doesn't it bother you, living in this house knowing that all happened here?'

Carmel stares at me blankly, as if the idea has never occurred to her. 'It all happened a long time ago.'

'Yes, I know, but it's kind of creepy, isn't it?'

'You think the house might be haunted?' Rufus laughs. He raises his hands above his head and waggles his fingers, making a silly 'woo hoo' noise, as if he's a child pretending to be a ghost.

'Is it?'

'It's just a house,' Carmel says. 'Bricks and mortar. You're probably wondering where they found the bodies.'

An icy shiver runs down my spine. Not really, but I have a feeling she's going to tell me, anyway.

'At the top of the house, in the attic.'

I gulp. 'In the room where I'm staying?'

Carmel's eyes light up with glee. 'That's right,' she says. 'All six of them, laid out side by side, looking so peaceful, like they were sleeping.'

Chapter 13

After we've eaten, and my offer to help clean up has been politely turned down, I make my way wearily to bed with the story of the father who killed his wife and children playing on my mind.

I try to think of something else. But all I can think about are those six little bodies laid out in the attic, murdered by the man who was supposed to love and protect them.

I've never believed in ghosts, or been afraid of the dark, but as I clamber the rickety staircase, my imagination plays tricks on me. Flickers in the shadows catch my eye. Every creak and crack of the old house makes me jump. And a chill sinks into my bones.

The bulb outside my room swings lazily when I switch it on, as if it's been brushed by the trailing hand of an unseen spirit. My breath catches in my throat. Fear floods my body.

The bulb can't be moving. It's just in my head. Although, it's definitely cooler up here. The air so chill it brings goosebumps out all over my arms.

My hand hesitates on the handle of my door. I thought I'd left it open, but I can't be sure. I was in such a nervous state, worried about spending the evening with Rufus and Carmel, I wasn't thinking about much else.

I take a slow breath in and shoulder my way into the room, feeling for the light switch on the wall. The bulb flickers for a second and an eerie low whistle needles around the frame of the skylight as a strengthening breeze picks up outside.

I peer into the room. Everything's exactly as I left it. My rucksack in a heap in the corner. My phone charger on the cabinet by the bed. My make-up and lotions on the chest of drawers.

What was I expecting?

That all my belongings would be scattered across the room by the malevolent spirits of the dead children angry at my intrusion into their space? Green ectoplasm smeared across the bed? The furniture floating in the air?

If I think like that, I'll drive myself crazy.

Ghosts don't exist. It's just my mind messing with me.

There must be plenty of other rooms in the house where I could have stayed, so why put me up here? Are they deliberately trying to scare me? The way Carmel gleefully told me the bodies were found in the attic, I can't think of any other reason.

The best thing I can do is get to bed. I'm sure things will seem less scary in the morning after a decent night's sleep. *If* I can get a decent night's sleep.

I hurriedly brush my teeth in the bathroom across the hall, change into my pyjamas, and ready myself for bed. Unfortunately, there's no bedside lamp, so I have to flick off the main light at the switch by the door and stumble blindly across the room to my bed in the dark.

But the instant the light goes out, my heart hammers in my chest and my brain convinces me there are things in the dark that weren't there before. Like the warm, wet slickness of blood under my feet as I pad across the bare wooden floorboards. The sound of fingernails scratching at the walls. The agonised wailing of the dying.

I dive into bed with the lumpy mattress bowing under my weight. I yank the duvet over my head and squeeze my eyes shut, my breath hot and heavy under the covers. My ears pick out every little sound. Carmel and Rufus's muted voices from below. A hot water pipe clanging. The howl of the wind. The creak of branches in the woods surrounding the house.

I reach out to locate my EarPods on the bedside cabinet, hoping music will help me relax and fall asleep.

It seems to do the trick. My head sinks deep into the pillow as the calming melody of one of my relaxation playlists begins. Soon, I'm drifting off. Plunging towards sleep. My heart rate slowing. My mind wandering.

I've no idea how long passes before I'm rudely jerked awake. One of my EarPods has fallen out onto my pillow. The other is hanging loose. I sit bolt upright, my mouth dry and my pulse galloping like a stallion on amphetamines.

What was that noise?

It sounded like a scream.

'Did you hear that?' I whisper loudly.

I hear Hannah roll over and groan.

'What?' she mumbles, her voice thick with sleep.

'That noise. Did you hear it? I thought I heard someone scream.'

'It's probably just a fox or a badger,' she groans. 'It's the countryside. It's just noises you're not used to.'

It's pitch black. So dark it's like putting your face into a vat of tar. I can't see a thing. Not even my hand in front of my eyes. In the city, it's never truly dark, but out here, there's no ambient light whatsoever.

'I'm scared.'

Hannah's bed creaks as she sits up. 'What are you scared of?'

'I don't like it here. It gives me the creeps.'

'Go back to sleep,' she says.

I hear the rustle of her bedclothes and the thump of her head landing on her pillow. Soon her breathing slows and deepens. I can't believe she's gone back to sleep.

I reach for my phone to check the time, but the screen's displaying a red battery icon. It's about to die, and not charging, even though I definitely plugged it in before I went to bed. I wiggle the cable and check the connection. Still nothing. The screen goes blank and the small amount of light it was emitting dies with it.

I sit up and put the phone down. God, I'm so thirsty. The meal must have been saltier than I realised, and I drank a fair amount of wine to get me through the evening. Now I'm paying for it. I really need some water. Desperately. My throat is parched and my tongue gummed to the roof of my mouth.

I throw off my duvet and roll my legs out of bed. The floorboards are cool but smooth, and I can feel every ridge and bump under my soles.

I shuffle forwards with my hands out in front of my body, feeling my way. There shouldn't be anything between the bed and the door, but I still stub my toe on the chest of drawers, knocking one of my bottles of moisturiser over. It falls to the floor with a loud thud as I squeal in pain, hopping on one foot as I grab the other.

'I'm trying to sleep,' Hannah moans. 'What are you doing?'

'Sorry,' I whisper. 'I need a drink. Do you want anything?'

'No, just keep the noise down, will you?'

Eventually I find a wall and feel along it until I come to the door. How is it possible it's this dark? I grasp the handle and quietly attempt to turn it, conscious Hannah's already cross with me for waking her.

That's weird. It won't turn. It's stuck fast.

I try with my other hand. And then both hands. Why won't it budge? Panic blooms in my chest. In desperation, I rattle the door in its frame. Still, it doesn't open.

'Hannah,' I gasp. 'The door's locked.'

'Mmmm?'

'The door. It won't open.'

'What do you mean, it won't open?'

'It's locked. Someone's locked us in. I can't get out.'

This can't be happening. Why would Rufus and Carmel lock me in my room?

I can't deal with this in the dark. I need to see. Where's the light switch?

My hand scrubs across the wall, but I can't find it.

I work faster. Fingers brushing across the paint-work. Frantic. Panicking. Pulse racing. Wide awake. Mind racing. Terror building.

What do they think they're doing? They can't keep me imprisoned in the attic.

I freeze as a terrifying realisation hits me.

Nobody knows I'm here. I didn't tell anyone where I was going. Nobody's expecting me at work, and I doubt Frazer will wonder where I am. No one is going to miss me. And on top of that, my phone's dead.

I renew my effort to find the light and eventually my finger falls on the switch. I flick it on with my thumb.

But nothing happens.

I switch it on and off, pressing harder and harder, but still nothing.

'Hey, let me out!' I yell, hammering on the door with my fists.

'Marcella! What are you doing?' Hannah screams. 'You're going to wake up the whole house.'

'Yeah? Well, that's the idea.'

'Stop it.'

I keep banging. I can't stop myself. The thought of being trapped up here forever is too much to bear.

'Rufus! Carmel! Let me out! Unlock this door - now!'

'Marcella. That's enough.'

'You don't understand,' I howl. 'We're locked in.'

Suddenly, my big sister's at my side, grasping my fists. Holding me. Coaxing me back to bed. 'There's nothing you can do in the middle of the night,' she says.

'But they've disconnected the lights.'

'You've had a tough few days. You're exhausted. Everything will seem better in the morning, I promise. Now come on, get into bed and get some sleep. We'll sort this out tomorrow.'

She's right. There's nothing we can do in the dark. I let her lead me back across the room and into my still-warm bed.

As I sink into the mattress, Hannah pulls the duvet over my body and strokes my brow until my eyes flutter closed. I'm grateful not to be alone. That Hannah's here with me. My body relaxes. I drift towards sleep.

'It'll all seem better in the morning,' Hannah continues to whisper in my ear.

It'll all seem better in the morning.

It'll all seem better in the morning...

Chapter 14

A light knock on the door rouses me from a dream-less sleep.

'I've brought you a cup of tea.'

I prise open a sticky eye and lift my head as Carmel strides into the room carrying a mug, which she places on the cabinet by the bed, next to my phone.

'How did you sleep?' she asks, folding her arms.

I despise that sneer she always seems to wear when she's around me.

My memories of the previous night come flood-ing back as I prop myself up on my elbow, pulling the duvet up over my chest. Of waking to the sound of a scream and a raging thirst. Stumbling around in the dark. Discovering the door was locked.

'The door...' I mumble, creasing my brow. Did all those things really happen? Or did I dream it? 'It was locked. And the lights wouldn't work.'

Carmel raises an eyebrow. 'The door?'

'Didn't you hear me banging?'

'We heard you thrashing about. We thought you must be having a bad dream.'

'And the lights?'

'We had a power cut in the middle of the night, I'm afraid. It's the price we pay for living out here in the sticks. You get used to it after a while.'

A power cut? I suppose that would explain the lights and why my phone died in the night.

I snatch it up to check. The battery's on eighty-four per cent, the icon in the top corner showing it's now charging.

'What about the door? It was locked. I didn't imagine that.'

'It's an old house,' Carmel explains. 'Sometimes the doors stick. Didn't Rufus mention it? Honestly, he can be such a waste of space. There's a bit of a knack to opening this one.'

She walks to the door, pushes it closed, and shows me how you need to lift and pull it inwards at the same time to open it.

I shake my head. 'No, it wasn't stuck,' I protest. 'The handle wouldn't turn.'

Carmel laughs. Not the sympathetic response I was hoping for.

'Why would the door be locked?'

'Because... someone must have...' My words dry up. I can't think of any reason why Rufus and Carmel would lock me in my room. Maybe I dreamt it after all, although it felt so real.

'I promise, no one locked the door,' Carmel says. 'In fact, I don't even know where the key is to this door.' She checks her watch. 'Anyway, I wanted to tell you I have to head into the office this morning. Something's cropped up. Rufus will be here, though. He'll be able to talk to you about the renovations and the extension, but if you need anything from me, I'll be back later. What time were you planning to start?' She looks at me, still in bed, disapprovingly.

It's not even nine o'clock yet. I'll need a shower and a strong coffee before I'm even vaguely functional.

'I was just about to get up.'

She stares at me for a moment, then nods and walks out, pulling the door closed behind her.

I shudder, glad she's gone. She has an unfortunate manner about her that raises my hackles.

There's no sign of Rufus when I finally make it down an hour later, showered and dressed. The house is silent, and he's not in the kitchen or in the modern extension where we ate last night. Maybe he's outside.

While I wait for him to emerge from wherever he's hiding, I help myself to a coffee from a fancy machine in the kitchen, adding a splash of milk from a bottle in a ridiculously well-stocked fridge.

It's filled with all sorts of things I could never afford. Bottles of sparkling mineral water and cans of fizzy drinks. Fresh fruit and vegetables, meat and fish. Jars and pots of fancy condiments I've never heard of. And enough cheese to fill a supermarket deli counter. How the other half lives.

When there's still no sign of Rufus, I take the opportunity while I'm alone to explore the house.

On the ground floor of the old farmhouse, there are a series of reception rooms, including a large lounge with a huge TV mounted on the wall and another that's filled with books on floor-to-ceiling shelves. I've never been in a house with its own library before.

Casually, I wander from the original wing of the farmhouse into the new extension, almost tripping on an intricately woven rug in the hall, and through a glass connecting walkway. For the first time, I get a proper sense of the views across the meadow garden and beyond to a wood in the distance through the vast glazed frontage. Birds swoop and dive. Wild flowers bob and sway in the breeze. And above, fluffy white clouds drift aimlessly in a vast sky.

'Nice view, isn't it?' Rufus's voice makes me jump. He appears from nowhere and comes to stand behind me.

'Stunning,' I agree. 'You're lucky to have found this spot.'

'Carmel mentioned you didn't sleep too well last night?'

I stare into my mug, embarrassed. 'I think it was being in a strange room in a strange house. I had some weird dreams.'

'I'm sorry. I don't know what Carmel was thinking, telling you about the bodies being found in the attic. She shouldn't have said anything.'

'It's fine,' I lie. 'I panicked when I couldn't turn on the lights.'

'An occupational hazard of living in the country,' Rufus says, with a warm smile that lights up his eyes. 'We're always getting power cuts out here.'

'And then there were all the weird noises outside.'

He frowns.

'Don't laugh, but I thought I heard a scream. I'm a city girl. I'm not used to animal noises at night.'

Rufus gazes out of the window, his hands shoved into his trouser pockets. 'Did you want to start filming this morning?'

'Yes, please. Would you have time to do an interview?' I'd love to know more about how they came to buy the old farmhouse and anyway, I need to keep alive the illusion that there are actually going to be some films.

'Sure,' he says. 'We could do it in my office, if you like? I'm working on some drawings at the moment.'

'Perfect.'

He shows me a door at the far end of the room that I hadn't noticed before. Although it's not really a door at all. More like a panel in the wall you can hardly see unless you were looking for it.

He pushes it open and leads me into a minimalist office with bright white walls and a large desk. There are two computer monitors, a keyboard and mouse on the desk, but that's about it.

'Why don't we have you sitting at your desk?' I suggest.

Rufus sits and pulls up some complicated-looking designs on one of the computer monitors.

I pull out my phone, line him up on the screen and hit record.

'What made you want to take on such a massive project like this when most people would have run a mile?' I ask.

He clears his throat. Wets his lips. And barely draws breath for the next five minutes, telling me how brilliant he is for having the vision to bring the house back to life. He's clearly revelling in being the centre of attention and blowing his own trumpet.

But I hardly hear a word. I'm really not that interested, although I continue to nod my encouragement.

'I love that the house allows you to circulate freely,' he drones on pompously, 'but of course, it wouldn't have worked at all without the contrast of aesthetics, the exciting dialogue between old and new...'

'Okay, that's great for now. We can come back to the design at a later stage,' I interrupt, my eyelids growing heavy. 'Can we get a few shots of you working at your desk?'

'Oh, right. Sure,' he says, surprised I've wrapped up the interview when he was in full stride.

He turns to face the monitors and takes it all incredibly seriously, adopting a professional, stoic expression as he pretends to work.

'How long have you and Carmel been married?' I ask casually, as I circle around him, pretending to film with my phone. It's what I'm really interested in knowing.

'Too long,' he laughs.

'Really? You don't mean that?'

'I'm only joking,' he says. 'It'll be thirty years, next year.'

'Congratulations.'

'Thanks, I think.'

'Tell me, how did you meet?'

Rufus glances at the ceiling as if recalling a distant memory. 'Through a mutual friend. We'd both come out of long-term relationships and neither of us was looking for anything serious,' he says, wistfully. 'And here we are about to celebrate thirty years of marriage.'

'How romantic.'

'You think so?'

'Absolutely. It's like a fairy tale.'

He considers this for a moment and shrugs. 'I suppose so.'

'What's that you're working on?'

'This?' He nods at the screen displaying a complex three-dimensional design that looks like three shipping containers, cantilevered and offset at odd angles. 'It's a house I'm working on for a client in the Cotswolds.'

I lower my phone to look closer. I don't know the first thing about architecture or buildings, but even I can see it's an ingenious design.

'Did you always want to be an architect?' I place my hand on the desk as I lean forwards at Rufus's side.

'Since as long as I can remember. Here, look at this.' As he reaches for his mouse, our fingers touch.

It's the merest contact of skin. The slightest brush of our little fingers, but he reacts as though he's been stung, pulling his hand away in shock.

'I'm so sorry,' he says, his cheeks flushing.

I laugh. It's a bit of an overreaction. 'It's fine.'

'I didn't mean to... I was just...'

'Don't worry about it.'

He bites his lip like a little boy who's been told off by his mother. He folds his hands into his lap, his shoulders hunched.

'Let's get a few more shots, and then maybe you could give me a proper tour of the house,' I suggest.

He sighs. And then looks up at me from under the hoods of his eyes. His gaze wandering across my face. Focusing on my eyes. My nose. My mouth. My neck. He blinks rapidly and swallows.

Rufus is old enough to be my father. Could this be any more inappropriate?

And then it hits me like a cannonball in the chest. My stomach tightens and fizzes. It's all too perfect. Too easy.

I came here with a vague plan of stealing Carmel's life and Rufus has just given me an idea of how I can do it.

It would be the ultimate humiliation for her, and from the way Rufus is staring at me right now, not such a ridiculous idea.

All I have to do is seduce her husband, convince him to fall in love with me and persuade him to leave Carmel. She'd be left with nothing. And all of this would be mine.

It could be the perfect way of taking my revenge and finally getting justice for what she did to Hannah.

Chapter 15

If I'm going to seduce Rufus, I need to take it slowly. I can see he's keen, but I don't want to offer it to him on a plate. I want to make him work for it. To drive him crazy with lust until he's begging.

'I'd love to see what you've done with the rooms upstairs.' I shove my phone in the back pocket of my jeans and tuck a strand of hair behind my ear.

'Sure.' Rufus smiles and averts his gaze. 'There are five bedrooms on the first floor, plus the rooms in the attic where you're staying. Carmel wanted them all decorated in their own individual style.'

The mention of Carmel's name makes my insides squirm. The sooner she's out of the picture, the better. And then all of this will be mine. The house. The money. The lifestyle. I'll never have to work again. Certainly not as a healthcare support worker. I'll be a lady of leisure, free to fill my time as I please.

Rufus isn't actually all that bad looking for an older guy. He's certainly not unattractive. The flecks of grey around his temples and the deep-set craggy lines around his eyes are surprisingly alluring. A mark of his experience of life. He's not in bad shape either. He still has a full head of hair. And he's obviously loaded. The only thing I'd need to work on is his dress sense, which leaves something to be desired.

There'll be no more mustard-coloured cords or paisley waistcoats when I've finished with him. And I'll make sure he gets a decent haircut too, something to control those unruly curly locks.

'You're such a talented couple,' I say through gritted teeth.

'Can't take any credit for the interiors, I'm afraid,' he says.

That's something else I'm going to change. The house is beautiful, but it looks like something from a magazine shoot. It could do with some more homely touches.

Rufus leads the way up to the first floor. We start in their bedroom. It's a massive room with an equally large en suite bathroom and a bed that's fit for royalty. It's easily as wide as it is long, scattered with cushions and a woollen throw draped elegantly over the end of the mattress. I coo and fawn, telling Rufus how amazing it is, while trying not to imagine the two of them sharing the bed, a pang of unexpected jealously gnawing at my gut.

He's equally enthusiastic about the other rooms, each of which has its own distinctive style. Not that many of them are to my taste. One is decorated in lush deep red, with crushed velvet curtains and a thick pile carpet. It's hideous. Like a prostitute's boudoir. Another has a beach hut feel with faded whitewash wood panelling on the walls mixed with striped navy blues and cool greys, which is more agreeable. One of the rooms has a four-poster bed and acres of exposed wood. Another is crowded with so many houseplants it's like stepping into a jungle.

It must have taken so much time and money.

'These rooms are incredible,' I say, walking into a bedroom painted in shocking Barbie pink. I like a bit of pink as much as the next girl, but it would give me a headache sleeping in this room. It's the first one that I'm going to make over when this is all mine.

'Like I said, it's Carmel who has the creative eye when it comes to the interiors.'

Urgh. I wish he'd stop mentioning that woman's name.

'But it was your vision that created it all from the ruins of the old farmhouse.'

He bows his head graciously. 'One does one's best,' he says in a plummy accent, like he's the king or something.

I giggle like a schoolgirl. If I've learned anything in my short life, it's that men love women who laugh at their jokes, even if they're not remotely funny. Never mind putting out. Make them believe you find them irresistibly hilarious and they'll be falling over themselves to please you.

'You must have spent a small fortune.'

Rufus cocks his head to one side, chewing on his bottom lip. 'It's been worth every penny.'

I'd love to know how much they've poured into the project. It has to be easily a million, if not more. And what must the house be worth now? Double that, I'd guess. Imagine that much money. It's obscene.

The last room he shows me is the impressive family bathroom I glimpsed when I arrived. It has two basins, each with gold taps, sunk into a thick slab of white marble, a walk-in shower that's bigger than the lounge in my rented flat, and a freestanding bath with ornate claw feet. It's so regal, it wouldn't look out of place in Buckingham Palace.

'I love it,' I say, although actually I think it's a bit over the top. Chintzy. Who in their right mind needs gold taps?

'You want to see something really cool?' Rufus says, his excitement bubbling.

'Sure.'

We tramp back down the stairs to the kitchen.

'I've already seen the kitchen,' I say, shaking my head. It's too modern for me. Too many clean lines. Too many shiny white surfaces. It looks more like a science lab than a kitchen. A kitchen's a place where you should be able to make a mess and be creative. It's not supposed to be a work of art.

Rufus stands in the middle of the room, hardly able to contain himself. His grin's so wide, he looks as though he could burst.

'You haven't seen all of it.'

He presses a button hidden behind a panel on the wall. At first, nothing happens.

But then there's a low buzz, like an electrical motor whirring.

'Stand back,' he warns me, as a crack appears in the tiled floor.

I jump out of the way as the crack grows larger and a section of the floor disappears entirely, leaving a gaping hole, like something out of a James Bond movie.

As I peer over the edge into the darkness, Rufus flicks another switch, and a light comes on, illuminating a set of concrete steps spiralling down.

'Want to look?' he asks.

Curious, I follow him into a small subterranean wine cellar with a low ceiling.

There are scores of bottles of red wine stacked up in racks and six glass-fronted fridges filled with white wine and champagne.

I suck in the air between my teeth.

'Awesome, isn't it?' he says.

It is pretty cool. And there's so much wine. I bet it's not the cheap supermarket stuff either.

I pull one out and look at the label. Not that I know anything about wine. I'm more of a porn star martini kind of girl.

Rufus twitches and rushes to my aid.

'Careful,' he says. 'That one's expensive.'

The label's in French with an ink drawing of an old chateau and two peasants tending the land in the shade of two tall trees that frame the image. It's a Bordeaux from 2000. Almost as old as me. The bottle itself is dulled with dust and grime, as if it hasn't been touched in years.

'It's a Chateau Lafite,' Rufus says, as if that should mean something to me.

'Is it worth a lot of money?'

He shrugs. 'A couple of grand.'

'Two thousand pounds? For a bottle of wine?'

'It's a vintage wine.'

He eases the bottle out of my hands and replaces it in the rack.

'Is that the most expensive bottle?' I ask.

He smiles. 'No.'

There must be a hundred bottles of wine, if not more, down here. And if they're all that expensive, it makes the cellar a gold mine.

'Do you never drink them?'

'Of course,' he says. 'But there are certain bottles we keep as an investment. Our nest egg.'

'Can we try one?'

'What?'

I turn my attention to the glass-fronted fridges. I open one and pluck another bottle at random. I'm tempted to choose a bottle of champagne, but settle on a rosé.

'What about this one? It's almost lunchtime. You could tell me how to taste it properly.'

That's another thing I've learnt about men. They appreciate having their egos stroked once in a while and love nothing better than to mansplain on topics they think you couldn't possibly have any knowledge about.

Rufus looks uncertain.

'Please?' I pout like a silly little girl. Something I've picked up from those vacuous women all over Instagram.

'I suppose it wouldn't hurt.' Rufus's smile returns to his face as he takes the bottle from me. He holds it up to the light. 'Good choice.'

'Is it?'

'A Sancerre Pinot Noir. I think you'll like this one.'

He ushers me back up the stairs, letting me go first. Probably because he wants to check out my arse. No harm in giving him a bit of a show. So I sway my hips provocatively, taking the steps more slowly than necessary.

While he uncorks the bottle and finds two glasses, I draw up a stool at the breakfast bar.

He fills the glasses, the cool liquid frosting them with a light condensation.

'Cheers!'

I'm about to take a sip when he holds up a finger.

'Savour it,' he says. 'Take a little in your mouth, hold it on your tongue and breathe in through your nose, letting the wine hit your palate.'

'Like this?' I do as he instructs, trying not to giggle as I make a slurping noise and a dribble of wine spills down my chin.

'What notes do you get?' he asks.

'What?' What's wrong with just drinking it and enjoying it? Why does it have to have notes and subtle hints of raspberry and black pepper? It's another thing I'm going to have to work on with him.

Rufus tilts his head back as he sips, pursing his lips and working his jaw. If only he could see how stupid he looks.

'Can you taste red berries and floral rose?' he asks in all seriousness.

Oh, for god's sake.

'Don't be so pretentious,' I laugh. 'Yeah, it tastes nice.'

109

For a split second, he looks wounded. I shouldn't have mocked him. But then his face softens, and he grins.

'Sorry. A bit too much?'

I mimic him drinking, over-exaggerating the silly way he tasted the wine and swirled it around his mouth. 'Can you taste red berries and floral rose?' I mock, my voice a high-pitched, posh approximation of the way he speaks.

'Hey! I don't sound like that,' he laughs.

I raise an eyebrow. 'That's exactly how you sound.' I take a huge mouthful of wine and deliberately gulp it down without swilling it around my tongue. The way wine should be drunk.

'Philistine,' he scorns.

'At least I'm not a wine snob.'

'Hey!'

I splutter with laughter. 'You are! You should hear yourself. I mean, who has a secret wine cellar filled with two-thousand-pound bottles of wine, anyway?'

'It's my passion. My hobby.'

'Hobby? A man of your age should be bird watching or a taking up a nice gentle sport like bowls.'

'A man of my age?' His eyebrows shoot skywards.

I've definitely gone too far, but I can't stop laughing. My sides are aching and I can barely keep my balance on the stool.

'What the hell's going on here?' a sharp voice snaps.

Carmel stands at the door, a briefcase in one hand, scowling. Her gaze shifts from Rufus, to me, to the bottle of wine, and back again.

Her presence is instantly sobering. The grin on Rufus's face vanishes. He looks as awkward and as embarrassed as a teenager caught by his parents raiding the drinks cabinet.

'We were just...' he mumbles.

'Yes, I can see what you were just doing.' Her tone is icy.

I shrink into myself, my gaze fixed on my hands. Why do I feel so guilty? It's her fault she went out and left her husband alone with me. I'm not responsible for his behaviour.

She makes a demonstrative show of checking her watch. 'A bit early to be drinking, isn't it?'

'I showed Marcella the wine cellar and was explaining to her how to do a proper tasting,' Rufus says, his cheeks flushed and glowing.

'At eleven-thirty in the morning?'

Rufus bows his head, chastened. The poor man. Imagine being talked to like that by your wife in front of a house guest. It's no wonder he's so unhappy in his marriage. Still, it all works in my favour.

'It's almost lunchtime,' he says, but he sounds weak and defensive. He needs to stand up to her. Not let her bully him. He's a grown man, for pity's sake.

'I thought you had work to do this morning?'

'We've just finished some filming,' Rufus says, glancing at me. 'I was about to get back to it.'

I take that as my cue to leave. I don't want to get caught up in this argument. I push my glass towards Rufus and climb down from the stool, grabbing my phone as I turn to leave.

Carmel shoots me a filthy look, and it takes all my willpower not to react. Not to grin. It's a small victory in a minor skirmish. The bigger battle has yet to be won.

'Thanks, Rufus. It was an interesting interview. Maybe we can pick up again later?'

He's standing with both hands on the counter, looking despondent.

'Sure.'

I brush past Carmel with a nod and an attempt at a friendly smile.

'And maybe I can chat with you later, Carmel?' I ask.

Her faces pinches. Her eyes cold. 'Of course. Whenever you like.'

'Great. I'll come and find you.'

I walk off, heading for my room, with a smirk of delight spreading across my lips. Everything is going to plan beautifully.

Hannah is going to be thrilled.

Chapter 16

Hannah has braided her hair into two pretty plaits which hang over her shoulders. She's sitting on her bed, playing with the end of one of them, twiddling it around her fingers as she listens to me outline my plan to seduce Rufus.

'Do you really think it's a good idea?'

Why does she always have to question everything I do? It's been like this since we were kids. Her nagging voice in my ear, telling me I'm not good enough or that I'm doing the wrong thing. Sometimes I get sick of it.

'Hannah, I'm doing this for you.'

She grimaces. 'What if it goes wrong?'

'How?'

'I don't know, but I don't like it. It doesn't feel right.'

'Don't you remember what Carmel did? Do you want her to get away with it?' I snap.

I don't mean to sound defensive, but she could show a bit of appreciation.

'Does she even remember me?'

'It doesn't matter. Probably not. But what's important is what she did. How she treated you,' I remind her.

What Hannah needed after she was arrested and charged was proper support, understanding, and the right medication. Not to be branded as a danger to the public, who needed to be locked up in a secure hospital with no idea how long she'd be detained. No one was hurt in the fire, and as she said, she never meant to cause anyone any harm.

She didn't really know why she started it. Or how she found herself in the stairwell of that block of flats in Margate. Maybe if they'd taken better care of security and installed locks on the doors, she'd never have been able to get in. It wasn't really her fault.

She was ill. She heard voices in her head and thought she was doing the right thing. It's not like she went out to rob a bank or murder someone. She certainly didn't deserve to be locked up indefinitely in a psychiatric hospital with a bunch of dangerous criminals. It was the most terrifying experience of her life.

Carmel was the court-appointed psychiatrist assigned to assess Hannah's mental health. But I'm not sure she even spoke to her. I think she made up her mind about her based purely on what she'd read in the police files and happily signed the report off, condemning my sister to a place worse than hell. It destroyed her and I'll never forgive Carmel for that.

'I can tell Rufus has a soft spot for me.' I kick off my shoes and flop on my bed. 'And I think they might be going through a bit of a rocky patch in their marriage. It's not going to take much to prise open the cracks and then it's goodbye Carmel. Give it a few months, and all this can be ours.'

Hannah shoots me a weak smile. 'I don't want you to get hurt.'

'The only person who's going to get hurt is Carmel. But she's brought this on herself, so don't go feeling sorry for her.'

'I'm not... it's just...'

'You worry too much. Leave it with me. It's going to be fine.'

'I don't trust her, Mars,' Hannah says. 'I think she's dangerous.'

I snort. 'She might be cold and aloof, but she's not dangerous. I promise.'

A few hours later, and with my stomach rumbling, I venture downstairs and help myself to a cheese sandwich. There's no sign of either Rufus or Carmel, so with nothing else to do, I decide to explore outside, especially as it's a warm, bright day.

It really is the most idyllic spot. Bird song carries on the breeze and as I pick my way through the meadow garden at the front of the house, my hands trailing through the tall grass, I'm rewarded with a warm glow of contentment.

Maybe it's because I now have a definite plan and in a matter of months, this house could be mine and, more importantly, Carmel's going to find out what it's like to lose everything. To have nothing. I can tell her it's not a great feeling.

When I interviewed Rufus earlier, he was waffling on about how the old and new parts of the house spoke the same language. It sounded like a load of old twaddle to me. Pretentious architect-speak. But looking at the building from this different perspective, I kind of get what he means.

On paper, it shouldn't work. The farmhouse is a handsome historic building. It's constructed of brick and timber and blends perfectly into its surroundings. By contrast, the extension is a modern monstrosity. All reflective glass and steel beams. Flat roof and angular lines. The two parts of the building shouldn't work together. And yet, it's the contrast between them that allows them to fuse into something spectacular. Rufus is far more visionary than I gave him credit for.

I might as well film some shots while I'm out here, in case Carmel or Rufus ask to see some footage. I can hardly confess I've not shot anything. They'd wonder what the hell I'm doing here.

I take my phone from my pocket and start with a panning shot, focusing on the old farmhouse before slowly revealing the new extension. Then I try a few more angles, surprising myself with the artistic images I capture, with the sun glinting in the corner of the frame.

Tucking my elbows into my sides to steady the shot, I zoom into the extension. The camera on my phone struggles to focus for a moment, but when it does and everything becomes sharp, I'm surprised to see a silhouette behind the glass, watching me.

I lower my phone with a flush of embarrassment. How long has Carmel been there? My skin prickles with goosebumps.

I'm tempted to wave. I know she doesn't like me much, and I bet she's still cross she caught me and Rufus sharing a cosy bottle of wine earlier, but not keen on being under her scrutiny, I wander back towards the house. There's a path I noticed earlier which I fancy exploring. It appears to lead into the woods behind the property.

But I only make it as far as the drive before I'm intercepted by Carmel, who's now leaning against the frame of the front door with her hands in her pockets, as if she's been there the whole time. It's a casual pose, but she's tense. Her jaw tight. Her muscles rigid.

'Getting the footage you need?' she asks, her eyes narrowing suspiciously.

'I think so, thank you.' I smile sweetly to annoy her.

She looks me up and down, assessing me with that permanent sneer she wears whenever I'm around, like there's an unpleasant smell under her nose. But now I've caught her on her own, maybe it's an opportunity. A chance to find out more about her and Rufus. Something I can use against her later.

'Are you busy? Would now be a convenient time to grab a quick interview?' I ask. 'I was interested in finding out more about the house and what made you want to move here.'

She sniffs and scratches her nose.

'Yes, I suppose so,' she finally replies, running a hand over her hair, smoothing it down. 'Where do you want to do it?'

I look around, searching for inspiration. 'What about in the meadow with the house in the background?'

Her brow creases. 'I'd prefer to sit at the table on the patio.'

'Fine. Let's do that.' If she wants to call the shots, I'm not going to argue.

On the courtyard patio, where the old and new parts of the house meet, she pulls out a chair from the weathered wooden table and sits with the farmhouse framed neatly behind her. 'Will this do?'

I take out my phone and line up the shot. Actually, it doesn't look bad. Not that it matters.

'That works for me. You've done an incredible job of transforming the building into something amazing. What drove you?' I ask.

She shrugs. 'The need to have a place to live and a roof over our heads, I suppose,' she says curtly.

I wait for her to elaborate, but she just folds her hands in her lap and stares at me, waiting for the next question.

'Yes, but what was it specifically that lead you to buying *this* property when you must have had the choice of a dozen houses? From what Rufus was saying, it was virtually derelict. The whole place was falling down. It must have been a huge commitment.'

She shrugs and shakes her head. 'Because it was for sale.'

'That's it?'

'I don't know what you want me to say.'

I lower the phone and stop recording. 'Just try to relax, okay? Pretend we're chatting and I'm not filming.'

'I *am* relaxed.'

'What about you and Rufus? How long have you been together?'

'What?'

'When did you and Rufus meet? How long have you been married?' I start recording again.

'I don't see what that has to do with the house.'

'Context, that's all.' I peer over the top of my phone. 'You've been together for a while, haven't you? Many marriages don't last the test of time, so what's your secret?'

'I really don't think that's relevant,' she snaps. 'What about you? We've let you into our house and yet we don't know the first thing about you.'

I'm tempted to remind her she's the one being interviewed, but it's probably prudent to keep my mouth zipped. 'What do you want to know?'

'Everything.'

'Okay,' I say. 'I'm very much single at the moment. I used to work in a hospital. And I'm a twin. There, how's that?' Might as well throw in a few truths to hide the one big lie about why I'm really here.

'You're a nurse?'

'Assistant nurse.'

'And a twin. Are you close?'

'Extremely.' My throat tightens. If only she knew. 'Were you aware of the history of the house before you bought it?'

'You mean the murders?' Carmel shifts in the chair, crossing her legs. She tugs at her necklace, a string of differently sized and coloured spheres. 'Yes, we knew about them.'

'And it didn't put you off at all? I'm not sure I'd have wanted to buy a house with that kind of history.'

'You shouldn't be so squeamish.'

'I'm not squeamish, but the thought of moving into a house where a family, including six children, was murdered would make most people think twice.'

'It never bothered us.'

'But don't you sometimes find yourself thinking about what happened here?'

'Sometimes.'

'And it doesn't worry you?'

'No.'

I knew she was cold, but this is a whole different level of icy.

She continues to stare at me, blinking lazily. There's something she's not telling me. Something she's holding back. I can see it in the way her lips are pulled tight, almost as if she's clamping them closed to stop herself from blurting out the truth. And then it hits me.

'Oh my god, you bought this house *because* of the murders.'

'Why would you think that?'

I remember how gleefully she told me the story last night and specifically how the children's bodies were found in the attic where she's put me to stay. Does she have some kind of macabre fascination with the killings? I've read about 'dark tourists', those people drawn to the locations of horrific murders, like the thousands of people who turned up to see where Fred and Rose West, the serial killers from Gloucester, lived even after their house had been demolished. And, of course, you always get rubberneckers slowing down on the motorway to catch a glimpse of a fatal crash on the other side of the road. But buying a house because it was the scene of a horrific crime? That's freaky.

'I mean, it's a lovely spot and everything,' I say, 'but it was the killings that swung it, wasn't it?'

Carmel's head jolts back a fraction, as if she's surprised by my question. Her icy stare melts and a smile creeps across her lips.

She holds my gaze for what feels like an eternity. My arms, holding up my phone, begin to tremble and ache.

'We were able to get the house at a bargain price because of the murders,' she says. 'People didn't want to live here knowing about its history, but you're right, it's not the only reason we wanted it. I'd known about the house for a long time, and even though it was a wreck when we first saw it, I convinced Rufus it was the right place for us.'

'The right place? In what respect?'

'Let's say I have a unique bond with the property.'

Who has a unique bond with a house where six children were murdered?

'Meaning?'

She leans closer, lowering her voice conspiratorially. 'It wasn't just any family who owned this house,' she says. 'It was *my* family. The children who died were my cousins. And the man who killed them was my great-great uncle.'

Chapter 17

I lower my phone and stare at Carmel in disbelief.

For a moment, I wonder if it's some kind of sick joke. Whether she's messing with my head, like she was last night when she dropped the bombshell that the dead children were found in the room where I'm sleeping.

'Are you serious?' I ask.

'Oh, yes,' she replies lightly. 'My family has a dark history.'

'But why would you want to come back here knowing that?'

She stiffens. 'I told you. It was our ancestral family home and no one else wanted it, for obvious reasons.'

I can't help but think it should have been razed to the ground, not restored.

'Think of it like a memorial,' she adds. 'My tribute to them.'

It's a weird tribute. 'Right, okay.' I'm really not sure what to make of this revelation. It's an odd thing for anyone to have wanted to do.

'You might have seen the old photo at the bottom of the stairs? That's Agatha, my great great aunt.'

I nod. I vaguely recall seeing a few old photos hanging in frames on the wall. I think the one she means is a grainy sepia image of a woman with piercing, sad, black eyes and a slightly down-turned mouth. Immaculately smooth skin and a head of unkempt wavy hair.

'The dead children's mother? Didn't you say her body was never found?'

'That's right. I imagine her remains are in the grounds here somewhere.' I shudder. 'That picture was taken shortly after Edith, her youngest daughter, was born. She disappeared not long after that.'

'She looks so sad.'

Carmel shrugs. 'She had six young children and a husband who was suffering debilitating shellshock from the war. I don't suppose her life was a bed of roses, do you?'

'I suppose not.'

Carmel suddenly glances at her watch. 'I'm sorry, I have to go. I need to be on a call in five minutes.'

She jumps up and slides the chair back under the table.

'Oh,' I say, surprised at how abruptly she's ending the interview. And just as we were getting onto interesting ground. 'Perhaps we could pick up again later?' I call after her as she strides away, marching back to the house. I'm intrigued and I want to know more.

'Maybe,' she says, before vanishing around the corner and disappearing from view.

For the rest of the day, I'm left largely to my own devices. Carmel and Rufus are both caught up with work, and I barely see either of them. They don't invite me to dine with them again. And I'm glad. It was a trial last night, especially making small talk with Carmel all evening, pretending that I didn't hate her with every bone in my body. Frankly, it was exhausting.

Instead, I warm some soup and take it to my room to eat. Then I decide on an early night. After all, there's only so much scrolling through social media I can do, and the wifi here is patchy at the best of times.

I keep thinking about what Carmel told me, how she was drawn back to the house because of what happened here, not in spite of it. I can sort of understand that she'd want to save an old family pile from ruin, but who in their right mind would want to do that knowing her entire family died here? It wasn't just the children. It was their mother, whose body has never been found, and their father who shot himself with his revolver.

My family has its own chequered history, but nothing like that. I certainly wouldn't want to return here, if I was Carmel.

My second night at Shadowbrook Farm is only marginally more peaceful than my first. At least I don't wake with a raging thirst in the middle of the night to discover the power's out and my door's jammed shut. Instead, I'm tortured by vivid nightmares.

In them, the children who died horribly here drag themselves across the floor through sticky pools of their own blood towards where I lie paralysed in bed, unable to do anything but watch and wait. Their progress is agonisingly slow, drawing out my terror. And the awful wailing and groaning is something else.

Several times, I'm woken by weird noises. Bumps and bangs. Screams and howls. I'm sure it's only the sounds of the countryside. Badgers and foxes, owls maybe. But my mind does a good job of tricking me into believing it's something much more sinister.

In the morning, I'm woken by the sound of car doors slamming. Engines growling. Tyres rumbling up the drive. It's a little before eight. And when I get up half an hour later to grab myself a coffee to take back to bed, the house is empty. There's a note on the breakfast bar in the kitchen with an apology from Rufus that they've both had to go out for work and will be back later in the day. In the meantime, he says to help myself to anything I need.

It's disappointing. I was looking forward to spending more time with Rufus. Still, it can't be helped and actually it's a relief to have the house to myself. It takes the pressure off having to be on my best behaviour.

Carmel's creepy obsession with the family murders is odd, and the more I think about it, the more I'm convinced Rufus would be better off without her. At least I understand now exactly how much this house means to her. And when Rufus kicks her out to be with me, it's going to be even more sweet.

The only hiccup I can foresee is over the ownership of the property. If it's jointly owned, Carmel's going to have a claim on half of it, even though Rufus was the architect and it was his vision and hard work that's turned it into what it is now.

We're going to need a very good lawyer.

That might be the hardest part of my plan. It's not going to be difficult to persuade Rufus to fall in love with me. I think he's already halfway there. Shame he's not around this morning. I was planning on putting on another dress and one of my push-up bras. Nothing too tarty. Just something to catch his eye.

'Are you going to have a good snoop around?' Hannah asks, peering bleary-eyed from under her duvet. Her hair's plastered to her forehead, and she has a red mark down one cheek where it's been pressed into a fold in the sheets.

'Hannah!'

'If you're careful, they'll never know. And who knows what you'll find?'

'I'm not sure. What if they come back early and catch me?'

'You'll hear the cars. Come on, Mars. Don't be such a baby. You might find something useful. Have you thought about that?'

'Fine,' I huff. 'Let me get dressed first.'

'Go now,' Hannah urges. 'You might not get another chance.'

'Alright, alright, I'm going.'

Still in my pyjamas, I creep down the stairs with my heart thumping, even though the house is deserted. I've already had a good nose around downstairs, but if I'm going to find anything of interest, it's going to be in Carmel and Rufus's bedroom. I might not get another opportunity.

I pause on the landing outside their door. Am I really going to do this? It's a complete invasion of their privacy. A peek into the most intimate part of their lives.

Well, Carmel has it coming to her. She's brought this on herself.

I'm about to push open their door, to cross a line I probably shouldn't be crossing, when something makes me hesitate. A feeling I'm not alone. Of being watched.

Guilt? Or something else?

What if there are CCTV cameras hidden around the house and Rufus and Carmel are watching me right now?

I glance at the ceiling, looking for a lens or a blinking light. But there's nothing. Maybe I'm being paranoid.

The door swings open noiselessly and I step inside. I saw the room yesterday, briefly, when Rufus gave me a tour of the house, but there's something illicit about being in here on my own.

The enormous bed has been made, the cushions scattered haphazardly across the duvet. One of Carmel's dresses hangs from a wardrobe door and I catch a waft of her perfume.

I picture her here in the mornings, floating around in her underwear, choosing her outfit for the day. Her jewellery. Applying her make-up in the mirror above the dresser. Rufus bringing her coffee as she preens, looking forward to her day ahead and condemning another poor, unsuspecting victim to yet another institution where they'll suck out their dignity and humanity, while Carmel carries on with her perfect life in her perfect home.

There's a framed photograph on the windowsill. A picture of Rufus and Carmel on their wedding day. I'm drawn towards it, my bare feet sinking into the lush, thick carpet.

They both look much younger. Carmel's grey hair is a thick, chestnut brown, cut in a stylish bob. Her skin is smoother. Her face rounder. She's wearing a simple white dress with no fussy lace or a veil.

Rufus is wearing a dark suit with a waistcoat and a postbox-red tie. His hair is longer, his corkscrew ringlets thicker and darker than they are now. His face is ruddy, and his eyes are sparkling with delight. He's definitely aged better than her.

I've always dreamt of my own white wedding with flower girls and pageboys, a satin and lace dress with a long, floating train and a church packed with friends and family. Is that what it will be like when I tie the knot with Rufus? A wedding people will talk about for years to come? Or would it be more prudent, given the circumstances, to go for a low-key event? After all, I don't have much in the way of family.

I slam the photo face down where I found it so I don't have to look at it and drift into their en suite bathroom, where I find several bottles of expensive perfume on a glass shelf above the basin. I deliberate for a moment and choose a squat square bottle with a black label with gold lettering. It's French. Sophisticated. I twist off the cap and squirt a little in the air.

Vanilla and cedar wood. It's nice. Not what I'd choose, but I don't dislike it. Did Rufus buy it for her? I spray more under my chin, coating my throat. And another couple of squirts on my wrists, for good measure.

In the medicine cabinet on the wall, there are packets of over-the-counter painkillers and hay fever tablets. Indigestion pills. A bottle of sleeping tablets. Some sachets of cold and flu remedy. A thermometer in a plastic case. Nothing of any genuine interest.

I head back into the bedroom and turn my attention to the wardrobes. One is filled with Rufus's shirts, trousers, jackets and suits. The other is overfilled with Carmel's clothes. All of it expensive brands. Beautiful fabrics. Stylish cuts. Nothing from the cut-price high street stores where I shop.

In a chest of drawers, I find Carmel's underwear. Cotton knickers and comfy socks. Thick tights and sensible bras. But at the back, shoved away and forgotten, I discover something far more exotic. A flimsy black thong, matching bra and thin, black stockings with intricate lace tops. Not been worn for a while, by the look of it. Good. The idea of

Carmel cavorting around like a cheap hooker for Rufus's titillation leaves me feeling nauseous.

I slam the drawer shut, inexplicably angry. What is it? Jealousy? Disgust? Were they a cheeky Christmas present from Rufus? A gift to spice up a birthday?

I stomp across the room and collapse on the end of the bed, furious tears pooling in my eyes. Why the hell am I getting so upset? I've not even let Rufus kiss me yet.

I fall backwards with my arms stretching above my head, sinking into the deliciously soft mattress and sweeping all those stupid cushions onto the floor. It's a damn sight far more comfortable than the lumpy bed in the attic room.

On one side of the bed, I guess Rufus's side, is a pile of books on an oak bedside table. All non-fiction. On the top, with a card bookmark poking out from its pages, is a grim-looking book called *The Moors Murderers*. Not exactly what I'd call bedtime reading.

I rest my head on Rufus's pillow. I can smell his apple shampoo. The musky scent of his sweat. A smell I'm going to have to get used to.

I roll over and wiggle onto the other side. Soon to be *my* side, if I get my way. For now, it smells of Carmel. Her perfume. Her moisturiser. Nothing a sixty-degree wash cycle can't remove. Anyway, we'll probably want to buy new bedclothes. Maybe even a new bed. I don't want any reminders of Carmel when we start our new life together.

From the bed, all I can see through the window are the tops of the trees, fleecy white clouds hanging in an azure sky and the occasional fleeting outline of a bird swooping past. I take in a deep breath and let it out slowly. Imagine when that's the view I'll be waking up to.

Without thinking, I pull back the duvet and slip into the bed, sliding down the luxurious white sheet, stretching my legs and my toes. A thrill fizzes in my stomach.

I know I can't rush things with Rufus, but it could all happen ridiculously quickly. A few months? Weeks, even. This could be my bed. My life. It's an exhilarating thought. But first, we need to find a way of getting Carmel out of our lives for good.

Her bedside table is largely uncluttered. She has a lamp and a small pot of lip balm. No books. No phone charger. No clock. It's taking minimalism to the extreme.

I hang off the side of the bed and pull open the top drawer. Inside there's a box of tissues. Some hair clips. A bottle of hand cream. Disappointed, I try the bottom drawer and recoil in utter horror and surprise.

It's stuffed full.

But not with what I expected.

I sit up, the duvet falling from my chest, as I pull out what looks like a pair of black leather hand restraints and an assortment of other disgusting paraphernalia. Ropes and chains, cuffs and bonds. Paddles. Masks. Whips. Lubricants.

What the hell?

Is this really what Carmel and Rufus are into? I'm no prude, but I've never been remotely interested in anything like that. It makes my insides twist with revulsion.

The thought of the two of them, at their age, tying each other up and doing god knows what to each other, is vile. I only hope to god this is Carmel's kink, because if he thinks he's going to use any of this stuff with me, he's going to be sorely disappointed.

'What are you doing?'

My arms jerk involuntarily. The cuffs in my hand fly into the air and land on the carpet.

I scramble out of bed, stumbling, with my heart pounding. I've been rumbled. Not only caught in Rufus and Carmel's bed, but with my hand in her drawer. Could it be any more mortifying?

I didn't hear any cars pulling open. Doors opening. Footsteps on the stairs. But I guess I was so preoccupied, I wasn't paying attention.

But it's not Carmel or Rufus.

Standing at the door, staring at me with eyes narrowed suspiciously, is a small woman in a loose-fitting T-shirt and black leggings.

'Who the hell are you?' she says, her voice wavering. 'You shouldn't be in here.'

Chapter 18

How do I even begin to explain? I've been caught red-handed in Rufus and Carmel's bed. My cheeks flame with embarrassment.

'I could ask you the same thing,' I say, putting on an air of indignation. 'Who are *you?*'

'I'm Paulina. I come to clean,' she says, with a heavy accent which could be Polish or Romanian or even Albanian. She folds her arms defensively over her ample chest.

There's a bright orange bucket at her feet, filled with bottles of cleaning products and cloths. Why didn't Rufus warn me there was a cleaner coming? I could die.

'I'm Marcella,' I say, grabbing a handful of hair and gathering it into a ponytail. 'I'm staying with the Van Der Prousts for a few weeks.'

Paulina raises an eyebrow. She is extraordinarily ugly with thick plastic glasses and eyes that seem to look in opposite directions. She has a warty mole above her upper lip that's sprouting black hairs, and buck teeth that poke out between her lips even when her mouth is closed.

'Why you in their bed?'

It's a good question.

'I'm staying in the attic room, but the bed's lumpy. Carmel said I could sleep in here while they're out,' I say, grasping at the first excuse that comes to mind. At least I'm still in my pyjamas.

One of Paulina's eyes, the one that looks straight ahead, drifts to the leather strap of a wrist restraint on top of the crumpled duvet.

I wait for her to say something while my mind races for an explanation. An excuse of some kind, but thankfully she doesn't question it.

'I'm shooting a series of films about them,' I say, to distract her attention. 'For YouTube. All about Rufus and Carmel's decision to buy and renovate the house.'

Paulina nudges her glasses up her nose with a knuckle, watching me, as if she doesn't believe a word I'm saying.

'Why? She not very nice woman,' Paulina says.

'I'm sorry?'

'Carmel. She dangerous. She not treat Mr Van Der Proust well.'

Dangerous? Funny, that's the word Hannah used.

'What do you mean? How?'

'Be careful,' she says, but before I can question her further, she picks up her bucket and disappears out of the room.

I think about chasing after her, to ask her to explain what she was trying to tell me, but I have to get this room straight. Rufus and Carmel could be back at any moment. It's one thing explaining what

I was doing to the cleaner. It's something entirely different to justify what I was doing to them.

I hurriedly pack everything back in the drawer, slam it closed, and remake the bed. I scatter the cushions across the duvet and take a quick, last look around the room to make sure I've left no other trace.

The wedding photo on the windowsill. Damn!

I'm in half a mind to leave it face down, to mess with Carmel's head. But I don't want to give her any reason to suspect I've been snooping. So I set it right and slope back to my room, closing the door firmly behind me.

'Find anything useful?' Hannah asks as I slump to the floor with my back to the door.

I breathe out through my nose, tipping my head back and squeezing my eyes shut. 'No, not really.'

I'm too embarrassed to tell her what really happened.

Rufus returns home mid-afternoon without Carmel. I hear his car pull up. A door slam. His footsteps crunching across the gravel. I give it ten minutes and make my way downstairs, aiming to bump into him casually. As I descend, I run my fingers through my hair, lifting it and giving it some volume. I've put on a strappy summer dress and applied a little make-up. Just enough to highlight my lips, cheeks and eyes.

Rufus is in the kitchen, flicking through a pile of post.

'Oh, hey,' I say. 'I didn't know you were back. How was your meeting?'

He grimaces. 'Difficult.'

He looks stressed.

'I'm sorry.'

He shoots me a tight-lipped smile. 'It's fine.'

'Want to talk about it?'

'Not really. Thanks anyway.' I can see he's trying hard not to check me out, keeping his eyeline resolutely level with mine, well away from my cleavage.

'If you're not too busy, I thought we could pick up where we left off yesterday. I have a few more questions I'd like to ask.'

Rufus drops the pile of post into his briefcase and sighs. 'Yeah, sure. If you like. Give me five minutes, though, yeah?'

'We can do it later, if you'd prefer,' I suggest, sensing his reluctance. I don't want this to become a chore for him. It would be a disaster if he started to find my presence annoying.

'No, no. We promised we'd give you as much time as you need. It's the least we can do.'

I glance at my hands. I guess at some point he's going to find out the filming is a sham, and that there is no YouTube channel. I'll cross that bridge when I come to it.

'Well, as long as you're sure?'

'Of course. I'll meet you in the lounge in a few minutes. I just have a quick call to make.'

While he disappears off to his study, I rearrange some of the furniture, shifting a chair in front of the long window overlooking the garden to catch the best of the light. I pull up another chair opposite for me.

When Rufus reappears, he's shed his jacket and rolled his shirt sleeves up to his elbows. I direct him to sit and while he makes himself comfortable, I set up my camera, framing him with the light artistically hitting the side of his face. I'm getting the hang of this.

'I'd like to get to know the man behind the architect,' I say as I hit the record button. A vision flashes through my mind of Rufus in leather hand restraints being spanked by Carmel. I push it away. It's a horrible, *horrible* image.

Rufus smirks.

'What's so amusing?' I ask.

'Nothing. It's just a funny thing to say. The man behind the architect.'

'Did you always want to be an architect?'

'Not always, but probably since I was a teenager.'

'Why?'

'I suppose because I've always enjoyed thinking creatively and developing new ideas. Plus, I've always liked the idea of my lifetime's work outliving me,' he says.

'That's interesting. You think of the buildings you design as your legacy?'

'Yeah, I guess so. Everyone wants to make their mark, don't they? To be remembered for something. To go down in history.'

'Ted Bundy went down in history. It's not necessarily a good thing.'

Rufus throws his head back and laughs. I enjoy making him chuckle.

'Good point,' he says.

'Did you know about the history of the house when you bought it? About the murders?'

'Of course,' he smiles, while eyeing me warily.

'And you knew about Carmel's connection to the dead family? That's why she was so interested in the property?'

'Ah.' He grimaces. 'She told you, then?'

'She said she wanted to restore the house in memory to them. How did that make you feel?'

'I thought it was a delightful idea. A little sentimental, but you know, that's Carmel for you.'

'Do you think you and Carmel are a good fit?'

Rufus frowns. 'What do you mean?'

'You said you're a creative. And you like solving problems. Carmel's a psychiatrist, right? So I'm guessing she must have more of a scientific brain? The two of you, I guess, approach life in very different ways?'

'I wouldn't say that.'

'Do you think she understands you?'

I'm pushing my luck by asking such a personal question, but I hope, while he has a camera pointed at him, he'll answer honestly.

Rufus's eyes narrow. 'I think so. Why?'

'I'm just trying to get a better understanding of the dynamic between you.'

'It's fine. We're fine,' he says, a little too forcefully.

I don't believe him.

'Remind me how you met.' I cross my legs, making sure he gets a good flash of my thigh.

His gaze dips momentarily, but he catches himself and clears his throat.

'A friend introduced us,' he says, crossing his own legs, subconsciously mirroring me.

'And you'd both recently come out of relationships with other people?' I look over the top of my phone and raise an eyebrow.

'That's right.'

'No overlaps?' I stop recording and lower my phone, resting it in my lap. 'People fall in love when they don't mean to. Sometimes when they're already in a committed relationship. It's nothing to be ashamed of.'

'Oh, no, it was nothing like that.' His eyes open wide as he catches on. 'I'm not the cheating type.'

Well, that's disappointing. But we'll see.

'I don't think it has anything to do with types. We can't help who we fall in love with. Or when.' I hold his gaze for a second or two, and then look away, feigning embarrassment.

But not before his cheeks flush. He clears his throat and straightens himself.

'What about you?' he asks. 'Have you always been faithful to your partner?'

'I told you, I don't have one right now. My boyfriend walked out on me.'

'I'm so sorry. I didn't realise.'

'He was an arsehole.' I wipe an imaginary tear from the corner of my eye.

Rufus tugs at his bottom lip. 'So I guess you're off men for a while?'

'I don't know. I could be tempted.' I laugh.

He laughs harder.

I regain my composure and pick at my fingernails. 'Are you happy?' I ask.

His brow creases. 'Happy? Yes, I think so.'

'I mean, are the two of you happy together? You and Carmel?'

'Yes! Yes, of course we are.'

'Sorry, I'm speaking out of turn. I shouldn't have said anything. It's just that watching the two of you together, as an outsider, I feel like there's somethi ng... I don't know.'

'Missing?'

I shrug. 'Maybe.'

Rufus goes quiet. He puts a finger to his lips and looks out of the window, his gaze fixed on the whispering grasses and billowing leaves on the trees outside. His eyes become watery and I can see he's struggling to swallow.

'Rufus? What is it?'

I lean forwards and reach for his hand. He flinches, jerking his arms back as if he'd momentarily forgotten I was there.

'Nothing. I'm fine.' He forces a smile, but there's a hollowness in his eyes. 'It's just... well, Carmel and I have been going through a few difficulties lately.'

'What difficulties?' His candour takes me by surprise.

'Nothing serious,' he adds, hurriedly. And then he lets out a long sigh, his whole body seeming to deflate. 'Carmel can't have children.'

I'd assumed they had no children through choice. This is an interesting revelation.

'I'm sorry. That's hard,' I say.

'It's been really tough on both of us. I kind of always thought I would be a dad one day, but I guess it's not meant to be. I know it's not Carmel's fault, and it's too late now, anyway. Oh, god, I can't believe I'm telling you this.'

'I'm glad you did,' I say.

'Please, forget I said anything. I shouldn't have mentioned it.'

'Look, I know we barely know each other, but I want you to understand that you can trust me, okay? If there's something on your mind and you want to talk about it, I'm here for you. I'm a good listener.'

He sniffs and wipes his nose with the back of his hand. Then he looks deep into my eyes as if he's searching my soul.

'Thank you, but I feel silly now for telling you that. You won't say anything to Carmel, will you?'

'Of course I won't. It'll be our secret. But perhaps you should talk to her about how you feel. Maybe you can look into IVF or surrogacy. There must be a way?'

He shakes his head. 'No, she's not interested in any of that. She says it's just the way it was supposed to be. Although, maybe it's not such a bad thing, given how things turned out on her side of the family.'

'What do you mean?'

But before he can answer, we're interrupted by the rumble of a car outside. Rufus glances up and looks over my head.

'That'll be Carmel home,' he announces.

That bloody woman has terrible timing.

'Whatever's going on in your life, however hard everything seems, I want you to know I'm your friend,' I persist. 'You can tell me anything and I won't breathe a word to a soul.'

He shakes his head. 'I've already said too much.'

And then Carmel barrels into the house like a full-scale tornado.

'Hello?' she calls out. Her voice is like nails down a chalkboard. 'Rufus? Are you home?'

'I'm in here.' Rufus jumps out of his chair.

Carmel appears through the glass walkway, the smile sliding from her face when she sees the two of us together.

'I was just doing another interview for Marcella,' Rufus says. I'm not sure he could sound any more guilty. 'But it's okay, we were just finishing.'

She stares at me with cold, piercing eyes. I meet her stare and hold it.

'Well, don't let me interrupt,' she says.

It's too late. She's broken the spell. Just when I had Rufus opening up to me.

'No, that's okay,' I say, lightly. I stand and straighten my dress. The way Carmel's looking down her nose at me, I can tell she doesn't approve of what I'm wearing. But I didn't put it on for her benefit.

'We've finished for now. I'll leave the two of you alone to chat.'

Chapter 19

Hannah's standing at the chest of drawers, trying on some of my make-up, when I storm into the room and slam the door shut.

'What's wrong with you?' she asks, holding a bottle of eyeliner in one hand and the applicator in the other.

'That bloody woman!' I yell.

'What bloody woman?'

'Carmel. Who else?'

'What's she done now?'

'She's come back and ruined everything, just as Rufus was opening up to me.'

'What did he say?'

'He told me they can't have kids. I think it's a bit of an issue between them.' I throw myself on the bed.

'Really? That's useful to know.' Hannah returns to applying the eyeliner, pulling faces in the mirror.

'But then Carmel came back, and he clammed right up again, just as I was making real progress.'

'Keep going. You're doing great.' She gives me an encouraging smile.

I sit up and fold the pillow under my head. 'I have absolutely no intention of giving up. Don't worry.'

'Good, because it's obvious Rufus likes you.' Hannah comes and sits down on the edge of my bed.

'You think so?'

'For sure. Why wouldn't he? You're young and beautiful, and you've shown him how easy you are to talk to. How could he fail to fall in love with you?'

'But what if he doesn't?'

'You worry too much,' Hannah assures me, stroking my arm. 'It's all going to work out in the end.'

I spend the rest of the afternoon and evening in my room with Hannah. We don't hang out enough and it's good to spend time with her. When we were little girls, we were rarely out of each other's sight, but since we've grown older, I've seen less and less of her. Our lives have moved in different directions, my time taken up with boyfriends and work and social commitments, and maybe I haven't always been there for her as much as I should have been, if I'm honest.

And it's good to give Rufus some space to think about our chat earlier. To digest what I was telling him. Hopefully, he'll come around to the idea that I'm someone he can trust and open up to about his problems. In a few days, when he's had time to think about it, perhaps he'll be more willing to talk. That's what I need. If I can get him to talk about Carmel behind her back, accept me as a confidante, there's only one logical direction for our relationship to go.

Hannah yawns loudly, stretching her arms above her head. We've spent the evening talking about all sorts of things, and the time has flown. I'm surprised, when I check my phone, that it's almost midnight.

'I'm tired,' Hannah says. 'Think I'll turn in.'

Her yawn is infectious. I catch it, trying to stifle it with the back of my hand. 'Me too.'

My stomach rumbles. I only had a sandwich for dinner. Now I have a craving for something sweet. I wonder if there are any biscuits in the house? I know I'm supposed to stay in my room after nine, but Rufus and Carmel will surely be in bed by now. Probably asleep. If I'm quiet, they won't even know I've slipped out. Anyway, I'm not their prisoner. I should be able to come and go as I please.

'I'm going to grab something to eat. Want anything?' I ask Hannah as she slips into bed.

She shakes her head, her eyes already half closed.

I creep across the room, peel open the door and listen. The house is silent and in darkness. I stalk down the rickety wooden stairs, pausing briefly outside Rufus and Carmel's room, but there are no lights on, so I guess they must be asleep.

When I make it down into the hall, I breathe a sigh of relief. It's like being back at my parents' house when I was a teenager, creeping around at night, trying not to wake everyone.

A blast of cold air hits my arms, causing them to pucker with goosebumps. There's a breeze blowing through the house. Odd.

I didn't notice it at first, but someone's left the front door ajar. I know we're not in the city, but I can't believe Rufus and Carmel would have left it open deliberately. It's asking for trouble.

Curious, I put my head around it in case someone's decided to pop out for something. Maybe Rufus forgot to put the bins out? An owl hoots, its ghostly call echoing across the valley. But there's no one out there.

I shrug. Must have been an oversight. My stomach growls and I'm about to return inside when a flickering light in the woods behind the house catches my eye. It looks like someone carrying a torch.

But who the hell is out in the woods at this time of night?

Surely not Rufus or Carmel, although it would explain why the front door has been left open. What if it's a prowler, though? Someone casing the house or coming to steal the cars?

I cower behind the door, watching through a narrow crack with my pulse threading dangerously fast through my veins and my palms sweating.

It's a solitary figure, moving quickly and with purpose along the path through the woods I've been meaning to investigate. Snatching a breath I hold in my lungs, I watch as they emerge onto the drive, feet crunching on the gravel.

The torch shines directly at me and I duck out of view, not wanting to be spotted if it is intruders.

I give it a couple of seconds and crane my head around the door again.

It's definitely a man, but his loping walk looks familiar.

It's Rufus, carrying what looks like a dog's bowl in one hand.

Confused, I inch back into the house. He's never mentioned anything about owning animals before, but it's a big house in the middle of nowhere. Maybe they have guard dogs kennelled in the woods. But why feed them at this time of night? And why have neither of them mentioned it? I've not heard dogs barking either. It doesn't make sense.

Something doesn't add up. Something's off. But rather than waiting to confront Rufus about it, I sprint for the stairs and bound up them as fast as my legs will take me.

I reach the landing as Rufus steps inside and latches the door closed.

From my vantage point, I watch as he kicks off his shoes, leaves the torch on the table in the hall, and vanishes into the kitchen with the bowl.

I sprint back to my room, not wishing to be caught spying on him.

I burst in and ease the door shut, wincing as the latch clicks.

'Shhhhh. I'm trying to sleep,' Hannah murmurs from under the covers.

I'm breathing hard through my nose, my mind a whirl of confusion.

'I don't know what's going on,' I whisper. 'I've just seen Rufus coming out of the woods.'

Hannah pulls the duvet back and sticks her head out. 'The woods?' Her eyes are narrow slits, her hair all mussed up. 'At this time of night? What was he doing out there?'

'I don't know.' I shake my head, trying to make sense of it. 'It's all a bit odd.'

'Did you speak to him?' Hannah throws back the covers and props herself up on one elbow.

'No, he didn't see me.'

'It's his house. I guess he can do whatever he likes.'

'Yes, but why's he out there at night? I wonder if he's keeping animals.'

Hannah frowns. 'Animals?'

'Guard dogs or something. He had a bowl with him. But it doesn't explain why he would be feeding them in the middle of the night. I think he's hiding something from me.'

'Like what?'

'I don't know, but I intend to find out. I'm going to see where that path leads.'

Chapter 20

The Somme, Northern France
July 1916

Billy clutched his rifle to his chest, his shoulder wedged up against the bare earth, and braced himself, waiting for the guns to fall silent.

The ground shuddered and shook as if hell itself was trying to break loose of its subterranean shackles. A relentless bombardment from the Howitzers intent on crippling the German resistance on the other side of no-man's-land. Not that it made any difference. The enemy was dug in so deeply, it didn't seem to matter what you threw at them. They were always ready for the onslaught that came their way.

A skinny rat with matted fur scurried across Billy's mud-clogged boots, hunting for scraps of bully beef and crumbs from biscuits dropped carelessly from the soldiers' paltry rations. Good luck to him. Billy was used to rats on the farm. Great big juicy buggers fattened on the abundance of wheat and corn. He almost felt sorry for these wretched creatures on the front line, reduced to scavenging for whatever they could find in the dirt, blood and muck.

A shell whistled overhead and exploded with a deafening thump. The smell of damp earth, sweaty bodies, rotting sandbags, cordite, death and decay filled Billy's nostrils. A putrid cocktail he wondered if he'd ever be able to forget. It smelt like terror. No one wanted to be here, for King or country. No one out here believed the lie anymore.

Then there was silence.

Billy's heart thudded as fast and as furious as a machine gun. Up and down the line, men adjusted their helmets. Shifted the grip on their weapons. Wet their lips. Extinguished cigarettes.

An officer marched up and down, splashing through claggy puddles. Whistle between his teeth. Revolver clutched in his leather-gloved hand.

A flare went up. Bright red with a smoking phosphorous tail.

'Right, lads, this is it. Over the top!'

Whistles sounded up and down the length of the trench.

And suddenly scores of soldiers were clambering out, boots slipping on coarse wooden ladders. Bullets fizzing overhead.

No time to think. No time to be scared.

Up and over. Out into the open. Bayonet fixed.

Billy put his head down and half-ran, half-stumbled forwards, into the abyss of mud, shell holes, smoke and wire.

Alongside him, a man jerked to a halt, his head snapping back. His legs gave way, and he collapsed into a rancid puddle, with most of his face missing.

He'd known the man. Taffy. A coal miner from the Welsh valleys. A soldier with a huge heart and a wicked sense of humour. Cut down in his prime.

No time for sentiment. No time for tears. There'd be opportunity for that later. Billy had to concentrate on staying alive.

He stumbled on, almost forgetting to shoot.

He pulled up. Raised his rifle. Fired in the vague direction of the enemy lines. Reloaded. Sprinted on.

A bullet whistled past his ear. A close call. Too close.

All around him, men were falling. Bullets cutting them down like a scythe through a field of wheat.

Ahead, the flash of a machine gun, spewing out a deadly barrage of death. His stomach tightened. Of all their weapons, this was the worst. Worse than the bombs and the gas and the snipers. The machine guns terrified him the most.

The screams of men lying injured and dying rose above the sounds of battle. Some cried for their mothers. Others howled with such anguish, Billy could only imagine their pain.

He fired again. No idea where his bullet landed. Reloaded. Eyes wide. Stinging. Muscles cramping.

He pushed on. Around a vast crater so large it could have easily swallowed up two buses. Men clung to its sides. Eyes squeezed shut. Hands over their helmets. The cowards and the quitters.

He could have happily joined them. Put his head down and waited for it to be over, but he'd rather take his chances against a German machine gunner than a British firing squad.

The whine of a shell grew louder. Too late, Billy realised it was right over him. The whistle reached a crescendo. And the explosion ripped the air out of the sky. White light. A deafening crack. Billy was lifted clean off his feet.

His landing was mercifully soft, although it knocked the breath from his lungs and everything sounded dull and distant, as if someone had placed two jam jars over his ears.

He shook his head and prised open his eyes, blinking away the dirt and blood that caked his face. But he felt no pain. Either he was numb with shock or he'd been fortunate.

He rolled over, gathering his senses.

He glanced down to see what he'd landed on and recoiled in horror when he saw it was a soldier. Or at least part of one. The top part. His legs had gone and his stomach ripped apart. Blank eyes stared at him. And for a moment, Billy was convinced he was still alive.

He scrambled to his feet, wiping the blood off his hands and onto his trousers.

Someone's son. Someone's husband. But there was no time for sentimentality.

His rifle was a few feet away, next to the crater the shell had blasted into the soft French soil. Half buried in the earth. He wiped it down. Cleaned off the worst of the mud and pressed on.

Another wave of soldiers was coming from behind, faring no better. Their numbers decimated with every forward step.

Fire. Reload. March on.
Fire. Reload. March on.

Ignore the fear. Ignore the screams. Pray there isn't a bullet with your name on it today.

Through the chaos and the carnage, the coils of sharp wire and across the pitted, bomb-scarred land, Billy slowly advanced until the enemy trenches finally appeared through the smoke hanging heavy over the land like a November mist rising over the Kentish Downs on a crisp autumnal morning.

A head popped up above the parapet. Eyes filled with fear. Rifle raised. Billy's hands trembled as he lifted his own weapon. He planted his boots on the ground, jarring to a halt. Took aim. Tightened his finger on the trigger.

The soldier turned his head. Looked Billy straight in the eye. He was only a boy. Sixteen, maybe. Seventeen at most. His uniform hanging off his skinny frame.

His mouth opened in surprise.

Billy hesitated.

He was just a boy.

He swung his rifle around.

Billy pulled the trigger.

A bright red hole opened up in the boy's throat as his mouth fell open in shock. He dropped his weapon and stumbled backwards, disappearing back into the trench.

Everything around Billy seemed to slow down. Soldiers running and shouting and shooting in slow motion. The bloom of nausea swelled in his stomach and a numbness dulled his brain.

A clap on his back brought him back to the moment.

'Clear the trenches,' someone barked in his ear.

He reloaded. Followed the soldier to the edge. They peered over together. Found it deserted and clambered down. Into the dragon's lair.

Billy turned right. The other man left.

It was a miracle they'd made it this far when so many others had been cut down.

Billy moved slowly, his hob-nail boots reverberating along a wooden boardwalk, until he came to a ninety degree corner. He held his breath. He raised his rifle. He stretched his trigger finger.

He risked a glance to assess the danger. Too quick to be shot.

Nothing other than a couple of bodies.

He moved forwards, vigilant. One of the bodies groaned. He swung his gun. Almost fired. Until he saw it was the boy he'd shot. His back against a fortified wall. His hands clamped to the wound at his throat. His fingers soaked in blood.

His eyes pleaded for mercy.

Big, sad eyes, the colour of cornflowers.

Billy lowered his gun as the boy emitted a wet gurgle. He edged away as Billy approached, the heels of his boots scrapping helplessly on the planks raised above the mud.

'It's okay,' Billy soothed, putting his rifle down. He approached with his palms up. 'I'm not going to hurt you.'

The injury was bad. Really bad. The boy was dying. A long, slow, painful death.

Billy knelt at his side, peeled one of the boy's hands from his throat and squeezed it tightly. A child's hand. Delicate and soft. Not the hand of a seasoned soldier.

'Does it hurt?' Billy asked.

The boy gurgled.

Tears pricked Billy's eyes.

'I'm sorry,' he whispered, holding his hand tighter, their fingers gumming together with the boy's blood. He never imagined it would ever be like this. It was worse than hell.

The boy's eyes darted over Billy's shoulder, reflecting a glint of hope and surprise.

Billy spun around and came face to face with a long blade and a steely German soldier with a determined look in his eye.

Billy tumbled backwards, smacking his head on the dirty wooden boards as the man threw himself at him. The knife came perilously close to Billy's face as he snatched the man's wrist.

The soldier snarled. He was bigger than Billy. Stronger. Heavier. Lips back. Teeth bared. A vein in his neck pulsing angrily.

The blade inched closer to Billy's bare skin.

He glanced at the boy he'd shot. He was watching dispassionately, his eyes glazing over. His face deathly pale.

Billy had evaded bombs and bullets to get here and now he was going to be gutted like a pig at the hands of a sweaty German soldier who'd been too stupid to run when his trench had become overrun. It wasn't fair.

Billy grunted, his arm shaking with the effort of the fight. Gravity against him. Exhaustion washing over him.

He clenched his eyes shut and put in one last desperate effort to dislodge the man straddling him.

A rifle shot rang out.

The soldier froze, the strength in his arm evaporating. His eyes opened wide with shock and he fell away, the knife slipping from his grip.

Billy kicked him off, panting.

'Are you hurt?' A tall, thin soldier in a British Army uniform, caked in mud and blood, was standing with his rifle half-cocked.

Billy shook his head.

'Good job I got here when I did.' He smiled at Billy as he offered him a hand and pulled him to his feet.

'Thanks.' He should have been paying better attention. Luck, again, had been on his side.

'Come on, we've got them on the run,' the soldier said, excitement bubbling. 'This could be it. They're all over the place. The tide of the war is finally turning.'

Billy wished he shared the man's confidence. But the front line was constantly changing. A few hundred yards won here. Another few hundred yards lost there. And all there was to show for it was death and destruction.

As the soldier marched off, Billy glanced down at the young boy.

His hands had fallen into his lap, his head slumped onto his chest.

Billy dropped to one knee and closed the boy's eyes. One small dignity he could give him.

What a waste of a life.

He dug down the front of his tunic and found a metal identification tag on the end of a chain around his neck.

But there was no name on it. Only a roster number and details of his regiment.

'Are you coming, or what?'

The soldier who'd saved his life had come back for him.

'What are you doing?'

'I... I wondered what he was called,' Billy mumbled.

'Why?'

'It doesn't matter.'

'Where's the rest of your unit?'

'I don't know,' Billy said. Probably most of them were dead.

'Stick with me until we get a chance to regroup.'

'Alright.' Billy stood and adjusted his helmet, his hair salty with sweat. 'I just need a moment.'

Another shell landed close by, spraying the trench with mud.

'I'm George,' the soldier announced, as if they were meeting over a pint in the pub.

'William. People call me Billy.'

'Okay, Billy. Are you ready? Let's get after them.'

Adrenaline was still coursing through his body, but his limbs were heavy and even holding his rifle was an effort. When he made it home, *if* he made it home, he'd sleep for a week. He missed his wife. It wasn't fair that Agatha had been left to look after the farm in his absence. He smiled at the thought of her having to deal with cattle. She was terrified of the cows.

'You kill this one, too?' George nodded at the other body in the trench.

He'd fallen in a heap on the ground like a marionette whose strings had been cut.

George rolled him over with his foot.

His arms flopped lifelessly to one side and as his head fell back, Billy saw part of his jaw was missing.

The explosion took them both by surprise, the blast erupting from under the soldier's body, the stick grenade booby trap detonating with a devastating force in the closed environs of the trench.

George took the full brunt. It ripped through his flesh like talons through wet paper and snapped his limbs as if they were biscuit fingers.

Billy was sent flying backwards. He landed on his back, jarring his spine and cracking his head as earth scattered on top of him.

Darkness descended.

After the shock of the blast, there was nothing.

Only a momentary peace.

When he came around, groggy and disorientated, it took him a few moments to remember what had happened. The flash of light. The deafening bang. Being thrown physically across the trench.

He wiped the dust from his face for the second time that day and startled when he saw George close by, staring blankly at him, both arms missing and his face covered in blood.

Another life snuffed out.

Billy tried to sit up, but a searing pain radiated from his leg, the ringing in his ears muffling the sounds all around.

He glanced down at his body, his uniform filthy.

There was nothing below his knee. Only the tattered remains of his trousers and a bloody stump. Where the hell was his leg?

He screamed as his brain caught up with what his eyes were seeing, and a whole new wave of terror washed over him.

'Medic! Medic!' he yelled. 'Please, someone help me.'

Chapter 21

Shadowbrook Farm, near Wychwood
March 1917

Agatha's stomach was a broiling mass of trepida-
tion and excitement. She'd not seen her Billy for
more than a year and in recent months his letters
home had become increasingly infrequent, especially since he'd been injured. She'd heard he'd
been evacuated to a field hospital in France after
he'd attacked an enemy trench and was later sent
to convalesce at a home in Eastbourne. She could
scarcely believe he was finally coming home.

The hiss of steam and a cloud of dirty smoke
rising above the treetops heralded Billy's train. She
waited for him at the end of the platform with
her pulse racing, wondering how he might have
changed. She had no idea about his injuries. Nobody had bothered to tell her, but at least he was
alive. She knew other men from the village had
been killed in action and she'd feared she'd be made
a widow before she'd had time to come to terms

with being a wife. They'd barely been married three years before Billy had been sent across the Channel.

A door swung open as the train pulled in. After what felt like an age, Billy emerged stiffly, climbing gingerly down onto the platform with the help of a pair of crutches. A guard helped him with his kit bag, which he slung over his shoulder, and stood looking forlornly as the train puffed away.

Agatha clamped a hand over her mouth with tears pooling in her eyes. Where his left leg should have been, there was only a stump. It had never even occurred to her that he might have lost a limb. But at least he was alive, thank god.

She waved. He hobbled towards her, his movements achingly awkward, his progress desperately slow.

When he reached her, she didn't know what to say or how to react.

She leaned into him and put her hands around his frail body. She hardly recognised him. His clothes were practically hanging off his frame and his skin was grey. His eyes were sunken. His cheeks hollowed out. And he had a faraway look in his eye, as if he was present only in some place in his mind.

He didn't hug her back, but allowed her to kiss his cheek.

'I've missed you,' she said.

He grunted.

'Here, let me take your bag,' she offered.

'I'm not a bloody invalid,' he snapped back.

Somehow, he climbed into the cart without her help and settled into the seat with a weary groan.

'How was Eastbourne?' Agatha asked, flicking the reins as they set off. 'I thought you might write.'

He turned his head away and stared at the passing hedgerows.

'I've always wanted to go. I hear the air is very good for the soul.'

He said nothing.

'You'll be glad to see the farm again, I'm sure. I've had some help with the cattle, but I've learned so much while you've been away.'

She clicked her tongue to encourage the horse on as he slowed at the sight of a clump of cowslips on the verge.

'What was it like?' she asked.

'What?'

'France. The war. Was it awful?'

'What do you think?' He picked at the cuffs of his scratchy green uniform.

'I've been so worried about you. Did you hear about Lillian Radcliffe? She lost her son in Fromelles. And Evelyn Kingston, you know from Maplehurst Cottage? Her husband was shot at Verdun.'

Billy screwed his eyes tightly shut, his hands balling into fists.

Agatha glanced at him. He looked in pain.

'Does it hurt? Your leg. Is it giving you trouble?' She let her eyes drift briefly to his stump where his trouser leg was pinned up just below the knee.

'No,' he growled. 'It's fine.'

They didn't exchange another word for the rest of the journey back to Shadowbrook Farm.

Chapter 22

Shadowbrook Farm, near Wychwood
   March 1917

Billy finally relaxed a little when he was home. Agatha helped him up the stairs with his bag and then brought him a cup of tea so he could sit by the fire with his favourite view across the valley.

After ten minutes, he'd fallen asleep, his chin on his chest, snoring lightly.

Agatha propped his crutches against the wall and decided, as it was a special occasion, she'd make a cake. Nothing fancy. Just a Victoria sponge. She'd not baked a cake since they'd been married and while butter and flour were in short supply because of the war, they had plenty of eggs from the chickens.

Buoyed by the idea, she left her husband sleeping and retreated to the kitchen. It was only natural that Billy would have changed since he'd been away. Heaven knows what he'd had to endure in the war and who could blame him for being so sullen and grumpy after losing a limb? It was bound to take him time to adjust. For them both to adjust.

Agatha gathered together the ingredients she needed on the big table in the middle of the room and reached into the cupboard under the counter, looking for the cake tin she knew was in there somewhere.

Eventually, she located it, buried under a stack of bowls, pots and pans that had been shoved into the cupboard haphazardly. She knelt down and, humming quietly to herself, yanked the tin out, but in doing so managed to dislodge a large saucepan that had been stacked on top of it. It tumbled out, bringing with it Agatha's earthenware mixing bowl, which instantly shattered on the flagstone floor with a resounding crack, followed by the saucepan which thudded to the ground with a thunderous clatter.

The scream that echoed around the house was like nothing she'd ever heard before. A primal wail that bore witness to unfathomable grief and unspeakable horrors and raised the hairs on the back of her arms.

Billy!

She hurried to him, lifting her skirts as she ran.

She found him curled up on the floor behind the chair, his hands over his head, his knees pulled up to his chest, shaking violently. He whimpered as she approached.

'Billy?'

His clothes were damp with sweat, and he flinched when she touched his back. She didn't

167

know what to do or how to comfort him. So she sat on the floor with him and soothed him until he stopped trembling.

'It's okay, I'm here,' she said, over and over, like she was speaking to a child. 'It was just a pan. It fell on the floor. Just me being clumsy.'

She stayed with him like that for more than an hour, until he eventually allowed her to put her arms around him.

An hour later, she had him back in the chair with the fire stoked up and a fresh cup of tea in his hands.

Is this what it was going to be like now? Was her Billy damaged forever?

Eventually, in the weeks that followed, they settled into an easy routine, learning all over again how to be a married couple. Agatha didn't ask questions about the war and learnt to avoid making any sudden, loud noises. For his part, Billy never spoke about his time in France. Apart from the night terrors and the flashbacks, and the physical scars on his body, it was as if he'd never been away.

Even Billy's frustration with his disability soon gave way to a grudging acceptance that his leg was lost forever, and he quickly developed ways of coping. He became a master with his crutches, and sometimes didn't even use them at all, choosing to hop around the house and grabbing whatever piece of furniture was to hand for support.

Night times were still difficult. There weren't many days when Billy slept through without waking up screaming, his body drenched in sweat, his mind transported back to the horrors of the front line. He often spoke in his sleep. Garbled nonsense, mostly. A few shouted names. Often a cry of alarm or warning. Lots of tossing and turning, and thrashing of arms. He was obviously in torment, but what could Agatha do? She wasn't a doctor, and there was no way Billy would allow her to ask Doctor Peterson to make a house call to see him.

And so they carried on as if it was all perfectly normal. Billy slowly returned to the farm, taking more and more responsibility back from the help Agatha had brought in when Billy signed up, and Agatha pretended she was happy.

As the Reverend Bennett was keen to remind his flock on a Sunday morning, marriage was about supporting each other in times of trouble, and that when illness or adversity came knocking at your door, you should hold each other's hands firmly and face it together.

That was easy for him to say. He wasn't married. He had no idea how difficult it was since Billy had returned home. Billy was refusing to attend church. He couldn't see the point. She thought he might even have lost his faith.

'A loving god?' he scoffed. 'If there really was a higher power, how could he allow such cruelty? Such barbarity? I've seen the chaos and destruction of your god and I don't want anything more to do with him.'

Fine. That was his choice. His decision. She had a bigger worry swelling in her stomach. She'd never intended to fall pregnant. It had been a mistake, and a devastating shock when she found out, but she wasn't going to get rid of it. It was a new life. A bean growing inside her that deserved a future.

And anyway, she liked the idea of becoming a mother. It would give her purpose. The only problem was how she was going to tell her husband. She'd have to confess the truth. They'd not exactly been intimate since his return home and unless she claimed some kind of divine miracle, he'd find out soon enough, anyway. There was no hiding it. She was growing bigger by the day.

'Are you putting on weight?' he asked one day out of the blue.

Agatha's hands instinctively travelled to her belly and the delicious, hard ball that was forming under her skin.

She was five months gone already and had noticed some of the women at church giving her knowing looks. They must have realised and wondered what she'd been getting up to behind Billy's back.

It had only been the once. Well, maybe it happened a few times, but she hadn't planned it. She was lonely and welcomed the attention. And for all she knew, Billy was dead.

'There's something I need to tell you,' she said, finally plucking up the courage to do what she should have done weeks ago.

She sat him down at the kitchen table and chewed her lip.

He stared at her with those deep-set, dark eyes that were filled with things she'd never understand.

'I'm pregnant,' she said. 'I'm having a baby.'

He continued to stare, his expression impassive.

'It's not yours,' she added, rather unnecessarily. He'd not even attempted to make love to her since his return, for which she was grateful. It was going to take her time to get over his injuries and the knowledge that below his knee was a gnarled, scarred, angry red stump instead of a lower leg and foot. It turned her stomach.

He scratched the table with his fingernails, making a slow, rhythmic scraping sound.

'Whose is it?' he asked, deadpan. There wasn't a catch of emotion in his voice. He might as well have been asking where she'd left the broom.

'Gerald's,' she said. One of the farm hands who'd offered to help run the place while Billy was away.

'His wife know?'

She shook her head. 'I've not told him.'

'He doesn't know?'

'I don't want him to know.'

'You keeping it?'

'Yes.'

'Okay,' he said. He pushed his chair back, grabbed his crutches, and hobbled away.

Chapter 23

Shadowbrook Farm, near Wychwood
June 1917

Although Billy could be sullen and uncommunicative, he'd never raised a hand to Agatha or even threatened her with harm. Which was a minor miracle in her mind, given the violence he must have seen when he was fighting, given the nightmares and flashbacks he regularly suffered.

But that changed unexpectedly one night when she was seven months pregnant. She'd stopped going to church, as she could no longer disguise her condition and didn't want to set tongues wagging. She'd planned to wait until the baby was a few months old and let everyone know it was Billy's. Most people wouldn't guess the truth. She hoped.

She was used to the nightmares by now, waking when he woke, often by his screams or an errant arm being flung across her face in his torment. She would hold him, stroke his hair and try to soothe him back to sleep, often only to be woken again a few hours later by more of the same.

Tonight was different. She woke with a deep sense of dread and the sensation she couldn't breathe.

Her eyes sprung open to find Billy sitting astride her belly with his hands around her throat. His face contorted in a rictus grin, his eyes closed. He was pressing so hard she couldn't draw breath. Her head turned somersaults, and she had a desperate sensation of sinking deeper and deeper into the bed like she was drowning in it.

Her fear quickly turned to panic. Her lungs ached to breathe and her arms and legs were tingling. She tried to speak, but couldn't utter a sound.

She tried slapping him. Bucking him off. But he was too heavy, and he wasn't even awake. He had no idea what he was doing, but if she didn't rouse him and make him stop, she was surely going to die.

She balled her hands into fists and pummelled his shoulder, the side of his head, her blows becoming harder, more desperate. But he wouldn't let go and he wouldn't wake up.

She had to make him stop.

The baby kicked in her belly. Little butterfly strokes like fingers tapping a path down her spine.

If she died, the baby would die with her. And she couldn't let that happen.

With every ounce of strength, she tried to roll Billy off, but his muscles were rigid, his arms locked. His fingers digging deeper and deeper into her flesh.

173

Her hand flailed at her side, looking for something to use. A weapon. Something she could hit him with. Her fingers toyed over the pages of her book, a cheap romance set in the Wild West. It skittered off the bedside table and thudded to the floor. Even that didn't wake him, when normally any kind of thump or bump would send him into a frenzy of fear and terror.

She found her alarm clock. A simple piece with large numbers and two bells sitting like ears on top. She wrapped her fingers around it and swung it at Billy's head. She winced as it connected with his skull with a dull, wet crack.

The pressure around her neck instantly eased as Billy fell back onto his side of the bed, clutching his head. He yowled in pain as Agatha sat up, clutching her throat and sucking in huge lungfuls of air.

Billy rolled around in pain as she kicked her legs out of bed.

'You tried to kill me,' she croaked, her voice rasping.

Billy stared at her like she was a stranger.

'You hit me,' he said.

'It was the only way to make you stop.'

He glanced at his hands and the smear of blood on his fingers from the cut on his head.

'I thought you were...' he said, his words drifting off as his gaze wandered towards the ceiling. 'I didn't mean to hurt you.'

Agatha grabbed her dressing gown and yanked it on, pulling it tightly around her waist. 'I've put up with a lot from you, Billy,' she said, with tears running down her flushed cheeks. 'But how can I trust you if you're going to strangle me in my sleep?'

'I didn't mean—'

'I think you'd better sleep in the other room,' she said.

'Aggie, please. It won't happen again.'

'Just go,' she cried, turning her back on him and wondering if life would ever be the same for them again.

Chapter 24

Shadowbrook Farm, near Wychwood
   August 1917

Agatha was in the kitchen preparing lunch when she was startled by a knock at the door. They hadn't had many visitors since Billy's return, and even those who'd come to see him didn't return after receiving a less than warm welcome. And so Agatha and Billy had become increasingly isolated from the community and the village. It didn't help that Agatha wasn't even going to church. Not while she was pregnant.

She wiped her hands on her apron and went to the door, curious to see who it could be.

'Gerald,' she gasped.

He was standing at the door with his hands in his pockets, grinning like a mischievous imp in a dark fairy tale. He whipped off his cap to reveal a mop of hair like straw, sticking out at all kinds of odd angles.

'What are you doing here?' Agatha whispered.

'I came to see you.' The grin on his face slowly faded as he noticed the swell of Agatha's stomach. She was eight months pregnant and there was no way of hiding it. 'You're pregnant.'

'What do you want, Gerald?' she snapped. He was the last person she wanted to see. At least he'd had the decency to keep a low profile since Billy had returned home, but she couldn't understand why he was here now. He'd clearly not heard about the baby. So what else?

'I've not seen you at church for a while. I wanted to check on you.'

'I'm fine. I'm cooking lunch, so I can't talk right now.'

'I heard Billy's not the same man he was.'

'There's nothing wrong with Billy.'

'Not what I heard,' Gerald said. 'I heard he's damaged. Not well.'

'Who told you that?'

'People talk, don't they? Where is he, anyway? I'd love to see him and give him my best wishes.' The impish grin was back. A sly, nasty smirk that turned Agatha's blood cold. Whatever had she seen in him?

'He's repairing a fence down in the bottom field. He'll be back for his lunch at any moment, so you'd better scarper.'

'Aren't you going to invite me in?' Gerald asked, leaning against the doorframe.

'No! Just go before he finds you here.'

Gerald feigned a look of hurt. 'Don't be like that. I'm sure he'll be pleased to see me and to talk about

177

everything that happened on the farm while he was away. How I looked after his precious herd.'

Agatha's jaw tightened and her eyes narrowed. 'He knows about us,' she said. 'I confessed my sins.'

Gerald's eyebrows shot up. 'Really?'

'So don't threaten me.'

'I've missed you.' He lunged at her, planting his mouth on hers, his hands grabbing her hips.

She pulled away in disgust, shoving him roughly in the chest.

'Don't touch me!'

'Come on, you were happy to play around while the cat was away. Billy's not going to find out.'

'Go away, Gerald.'

She tried to close the door, but his boot was across the threshold in a flash, trapping it open.

'If Billy finds you here, he'll kill you.'

Gerald laughed cruelly. 'From what I've heard, he can't even stand up straight. Has he got any other physical problems? Anything I can help you with?'

Agatha's stomach churned. 'He's lost a leg, that's all. At least he did his bit in the war, for his country and the King. What about you, Gerald? What have you done?'

Gerald forced his way inside the house, causing Agatha to fall back, edging away from him. She didn't like the look in his eye. She should never have encouraged him. Now he wanted to make trouble.

'You see, you weren't complaining about me popping around before, when Billy was away and you was lonely, was you?'

'Please, Gerald.'

He loomed over her, backing her into a corner in the kitchen until she had nowhere else to go.

'Is it mine?' he asked again, prodding her stomach with a finger ingrained with dirt.

'Of course not.' She stared him in the eye, daring him to contradict her.

'You're huge, Aggie. I reckon at least eight months gone. Billy's only been back four months.'

'It's Billy's baby. He's the father.'

'I don't believe you.' He loomed over her, his breath hot and sour, the stench of stale sweat radiating from his clothes.

Her fingers closed around the handle of the knife she'd been using to peel the potatoes.

'I don't care what you believe. Get out of my house.'

'Come on, one kiss.'

He lunged at her again, planting his lips on hers, but this time she couldn't push him away. He was too forceful. Too insistent. He pressed his groin into her and snatched a handful of her skirts, pulling them up over her thigh.

Her grip tightened on the knife. She'd kill him before she let him touch her again.

'Get off me,' she screamed as his mouth moved down the length of her neck.

'What the hell is going on here?' Billy appeared out of nowhere, moving remarkably quickly for a man with only one leg.

In the blink of an eye, he'd crossed the kitchen and was hauling Gerald off Agatha by the scruff of his neck.

He threw him over the table, his crutch clattering to the floor.

'You stay away from my wife, you hear?' he screamed.

And then he punched Gerald square in the face. It made an ugly, dull thud.

'Stay away,' he repeated.

And then punched him again. And again. And again.

Until there wasn't much left of Gerald's face other than a bloody pulp.

'That's enough,' Agatha screamed, as she watched Gerald's body turn limp.

She pulled her husband away, and Gerald slumped to the floor.

'You'll kill him,' she yelled.

'He'll be fine. Now get him out of here and if I ever see him in this house again, I *will* kill him.'

Chapter 25

It's no good. I can't sleep. I'm too tightly wound up. Knotted with anxiety. I keep thinking about Rufus prowling around outside in the woods, wondering what he was doing. Where he'd been. I suppose it's possible he couldn't sleep either, and went for a walk to clear his head. But what about that dog bowl? I still haven't heard any barking, so maybe it's something else. Perhaps he was feeding deer? Or badgers? Whatever it was, it's all a bit odd.

It makes me question what I'm doing here in this house. I never set out to seduce Rufus and steal Carmel's perfect life, but it's the only way I can think of to make her pay for how she treated Hannah.

I can tell Rufus is totally into me and I'm sure it's not going to take much to encourage him to make a move on me. You only have to watch the way Carmel treats him, how she talks to him, and how he looks at me, to see he'd be much better off without her. With me.

And then this all becomes mine. No more sleeping in the attic room with the ghosts of a murdered family. No more Carmel and her bitchy comments.

Just me and Rufus living a life of freedom and luxury.

Although, what if he won't act on his impulses? What if he's one of those men who would never dream of cheating on his wife, no matter how badly she treats him? No matter how many times I prostrate myself on a plate for him? I guess men like that do exist. Let's hope Rufus isn't one of them.

Both sides of my pillow are hot and damp under my head, and I've rucked up the thin cotton sheet under my legs in a messy tangle. I can't find a comfortable position and although my eyes are heavy with tiredness, sleep feels desperately out of reach.

'Hannah? Are you awake?' I hiss.

She snores lightly and rolls over, turning her body away from me.

I guess not.

I have a hollow, sunken feeling in my stomach. I need to eat something. Ice cream. Chocolate. A bag of popcorn. Anything sweet.

And if I can't sleep, what's the point of staying in bed, getting more and more wound up?

It's almost four in the morning. The screams, screeches and bangs I've become used to around the house have all quietened down now and there's a thick silence that hangs like smog.

I slide out of bed and crack open the door. Then, using the torch on my phone, I light a path down the stairs. Along the landing. Past Rufus and Carmel's room. Down the main staircase and into the kitchen, wincing with every creak and groan under my feet.

I head straight to the freezer. It's mostly filled with little transparent bags of frozen meat and fish. More food than Rufus and Carmel could ever eat in a month. But buried in the top drawer, I find a tub of an expensive vanilla ice cream. It's not going to help me sleep, but it's always been a wonderful comfort food when my mind's in turmoil.

I spoon out three large scoops into a bowl and sit at the breakfast counter with only the glow from my phone piercing the darkness. Casually, I flick through my social media feeds, pausing to smile at a video of a dog that's adopted a cat as if it's its own puppy, swamping it under its body as it curls up in its bed.

A dull thud makes me jump.

I freeze, my spoon halfway to my mouth.

It sounded like a chair toppling over in a distant room. Or someone sitting on a bed, kicking off a shoe.

My skin prickles as blood rushes in my ears and my heart hammers like a drum in my chest.

Silence again.

My phone grows dim and then the screen switches off, leaving me sitting in pitch blackness. Is someone else up? Or did I imagine it?

The noise sounded as if it had come from under the house, which was weird. Unless it was an animal outside. Something snuffling around on the patio and knocking over a plant pot, perhaps?

I flick my phone back on and see by the faint light that my ice cream has started to melt, a yellowy milk creating a sea around three ice cream islands.

'I didn't expect to find you up. Can't sleep?'

I jerk violently, almost falling off the stool at the sound of Rufus's hoarse whisper.

I clamp a hand to my chest, as if I can physically still my racing heart. Rufus emerges from the darkness of the hall and strolls into the room.

'Jeez, you frightened the life out of me.'

'Sorry. I didn't mean to make you jump,' he says, raising a hand in apology.

He flicks a switch on the wall and lights under the cabinets come on, filling the room with a soft hue. He's wearing a loose white T-shirt and a crumpled pair of boxer shorts. He's not in bad shape at all. Certainly, no sign of a middle-aged paunch, and he has reasonably muscular thighs and calves. It's a pleasant surprise.

'I didn't hear you,' I say, although the thud I heard must have been him.

He shrugs. 'Carmel's a light sleeper, so I've had to learn to be quiet. What you eating?'

I show him my bowl. 'I can do you some?'

He shakes his head. 'I'll just have a taste of yours.'

It's a little presumptuous, but I don't protest as he grabs a spoon from a drawer and leans over me to help himself to what's left of the melting mess. A smile creeps across my lips, hidden by the darkness. There's something curiously intimate about the proximity of his body. The way he's helping himself to my ice cream. The fact that Carmel is in blissful ignorance, asleep upstairs. I couldn't have planned it better, although ideally I'd have put a brush through my hair if I'd known I was going to bump into Rufus.

He doesn't step back as he puts the spoon to his mouth, but keeps his body close to mine, his chest pressing into my shoulder.

Is he doing it deliberately?

'Good?' I ask, a shiver snaking down my spine.

He mumbles his appreciation. 'Mmmm, so good. Do you usually eat ice cream at this time of the morning?' He laughs.

I will him to keep the noise down. I'd hate for us to wake Carmel.

'Sometimes. What about you?' I think about him marching back through the woods with that dog bowl. I'm tempted to ask him about it, but I don't want him to think I was spying on him.

'I only came down for a glass of water,' he says. 'But I could get used to this.'

He looks down at me and I shudder under the intensity of his gaze, his warm body pressed against mine.

'You should try it more often. It always tastes better when you know you're not supposed to be eating it.'

I'm trying to be flirty, but was that too obvious?

'I'll have to take your word for it.' Finally, he steps away and rests against the counter, licking his spoon clean. 'How's the filming coming along? Are you getting everything you need?'

'It's early days. But yeah, I'm getting there,' I lie. 'It's interesting finding out more about you and Carmel.'

Rufus stops licking his spoon and cocks his head to the side. 'Really? I thought you were interested in the house. Not us.'

'You *are* the house. Everything about this place is an extension of your personalities.'

He contemplates this for a moment, wrinkling his nose.

'That's interesting. I hadn't thought about it like that.'

'Although Carmel's a bit of a closed book, isn't she? I don't think she likes me much.'

'She's a private person, that's all. She's never liked talking about herself.'

'Tell me,' I ask. 'What do you really think of me being here?'

He looks taken aback by my question, but it's a chance for him to tell me what he really thinks, with no danger of Carmel overhearing.

'I don't know. It's... interesting.'

'Interesting?'

'I mean, the project's interesting.'

'But you've opened up your home to a stranger and agreed to let me film your lives. You must have had some reservations?' I suggest.

'I guess I'm vain.'

'You don't strike me as the vain type.'

Rufus clears his throat and crosses his legs. 'I'm proud of what we've achieved and I suppose I want people to see the house and appreciate what we've done.'

'You want people to admire you?' I suggest.

'No!' he snaps. 'Well, maybe a little. Appreciate. Not admire. That's okay, isn't it? I've poured my heart and soul into this house. It's not a crime to want to show off a little.'

'And Carmel? She's always been one hundred per cent behind the project?'

'It was her idea to buy the house. If anything, it was her vision,' he says, reminding me of Carmel's macabre obsession with the property and how keen she was to return it to its former magnificence in tribute to her murdered family.

'But you're the architect.'

'I couldn't have done it without her. She was my... inspiration.'

I nod slowly, concealing my irritation. I hate that he holds her up as some kind of muse. 'Did you always see eye to eye on the rebuild?'

'Not always, no, but it's all about compromise, isn't it?'

'If you say so. I guess the entire project must have put a strain on your relationship then?' There must be cracks in the marriage. In fact, I know there are. If only I can get him to admit it.

'No. Not really.'

'Not really?'

He sighs. 'All couples go through their ups and downs. We're not any different. Look, we're not perfect, okay? But this house was a joint project. It's every bit Carmel's vision as it is mine.'

'You're the architect,' I remind him.

'And Carmel has a wonderful eye for decor. We complement each other.'

Yuck. Not the answer I was hoping to hear.

'Where did you go tonight?' I ask.

His eyes open wide. 'When?'

'I heard you come in late. I thought you were always in bed by nine.'

'I went for a walk,' he blurts out. 'Sorry if I disturbed you.'

'It was gone midnight.' I raise an eyebrow.

Rufus holds my gaze for a second or two before hanging his head. 'Okay, Carmel and I had a bit of an argument earlier. I went for a walk to clear my head. Okay?'

'About what?'

'It doesn't matter. It was nothing.' He shakes his head sadly.

'I've noticed Carmel can be quite mean sometimes. I've seen the way she treats you and the way she talks to you.'

Rufus's body stiffens. 'I don't think... no, I wouldn't say that.'

'You deserve better.'

'It's just the way she is.'

'But you shouldn't have to put up with it!'

'We're fine. Do you want some more?' Rufus points to my empty bowl.

'No, thanks. I guess I'd better get back to bed. It'll be light in a few hours.'

'Yeah,' Rufus agrees, checking the time blinking on the front of the oven. 'I have to be up in an hour.'

He drops his spoon into my bowl. I push my stool back and hop down, intending to carry the dirty dishes to the sink.

But Rufus stops me. He grabs my wrist and holds it tight.

'Rufus? What are you doing?'

He looks pained. As if he's struggling with some awful agony. He stares into my eyes and butterflies dance in my stomach. His gaze grazes across my lip.

He pulls me closer until I can smell vanilla on his breath. The tips of our noses are millimetres apart. His breathing is fast and ragged. He closes his eyes. Dips his head. Our foreheads touch.

'Marcella,' he whispers.

And then his lips are on mine. Firm and insistent. His coarse stubble scratching my chin. Pressing his body against mine.

I sink into him, my lips locked on his. I couldn't have planned this any better if I'd tried.

The kiss only lasts a few seconds. Rufus wraps his hands around my back, his fingers splaying across my spine, his desire growing more urgent.

I pull back and gently push him away.

'Rufus,' I gasp, feigning a look of shock and embarrassment. I deliberately don't look him in the eye.

He lets me go. Takes a step back. His eyes opening wide. 'Marcella,' he chokes. 'I'm so sorry. I didn't mean...'

'It's okay,' I assure him.

'I don't know what came over me.'

It's a struggle to keep the smile from my lips. 'You don't have to apologise.'

'I was out of line. Please, don't say anything to Carmel. I beg you.'

'Why would I say anything to Carmel?'

He turns away, his hand on his forehead. I don't want to make it too easy for him, but I don't want him to have any regrets, either.

'I'm flattered. Really, I am,' I say with a coy smile. 'It's just you took me by surprise.'

'You don't hate me?'

'Hate you? Of course I don't hate you.'

I reach up on tiptoes and peck him on the cheek, my palm flat against his chest. 'But I should get back to bed.'

I pull away, holding his gaze.

'Yes, you're right. Sorry again.'

'There's nothing to apologise for. Goodnight, Rufus.'

'Goodnight.'

I turn and shimmy out of the kitchen, giving my hips a little extra wiggle, and finally allowing a smug, self-satisfied grin to spread across my face.

Poor Carmel. She has no idea what's about to hit her. She's about to lose everything, starting with her husband, and there's nothing she can do about it.

Chapter 26

I can't help humming to myself as I pull a brush through my hair and check my appearance in the scratched mirror above the chest of drawers. I've put on some make-up and thrown on another clingy dress that extenuates all my curves.

'What are you so happy about?' Hannah moans from under the covers.

'Nothing.'

I've slept in later than I'd planned, but I've woken feeling fresh and alive, all my plans slowly falling into place. If all goes well, I won't be staying in this dingy room for much longer. I'll have the run of the entire house. And it can't come a moment too soon.

'Fine. Don't tell me,' Hannah says, poking her head out. Her hair's an unruly mess.

'What are you planning to do today?'

'I don't feel too good. I'm going to stay in bed.'

I roll my eyes. That's so typical of Hannah.

I'm still humming to myself as I bound down the stairs with my phone in one hand. I'm going to ask Rufus for another interview, so we can be alone together again. I'm curious to see how he'll follow up on last night's kiss.

I head for his study, skipping through the lounge with barely a glance out of the long windows streaked with rain. But he's not there. I hope he's not had to go into the office again. I can't bear the thought of spending the day alone. Or worse, with Carmel. It makes my guts knot.

'Hello? Rufus?' I call out as I trot back into the old farmhouse, praying I don't bump into her.

I poke my head around the kitchen door and hear movement coming from the utility room.

Rufus is piling heaps of dirty clothes into a washing machine, scooping them out of a basket and shovelling them in hurriedly.

'Hey, there you are,' I say.

Rufus reacts like I've sneaked up on him and yelled 'boo' in his ear. He straightens up and yelps.

I laugh. 'That gets you back for making me jump in the kitchen last night.'

He scowls at me and slams the door of the washing machine closed.

'What are you doing prowling around the house?' he snaps.

'I wasn't prowling.' I don't like his tone. Is he regretting what happened last night? 'I was going to make some brunch. You want anything to eat?'

He shakes his head. 'I need to get back to work.'

He flings the basket onto the counter and marches out of the room, forcing me to step out of his way.

'Are you angry with me?'

'What?' He stops and turns. 'Of course not.'

'There's no need to be embarrassed, you know.'

His body softens as he exhales. He looks down at his feet. 'Look, about last night—'

'It's fine.'

'No, it's not. I shouldn't have taken advantage. I don't know what I was thinking.'

'Honestly, Rufus. It's nothing.'

'I hope you don't hate me.'

'Hate you?' I gasp. 'No, of course not. If anything, I was... flattered.'

He looks up, surprised. 'You were?'

'Of course I was. But, you know, you're married.' I hold up my left hand and wriggle my ring finger.

Rufus lets out a long, lingering sigh. He has big bags under his eyes and he looks unusually pale.

'You won't say anything to her, will you?'

'Carmel? Of course I won't. Where is she, anyway?' I ask, lowering my voice.

'She had to be in court this morning.'

The muscles in my face tighten. Carmel never appeared in court during Hannah's case. Never gave evidence. Her testimony was never cross-examined. The judge was happy to accept her report without question.

'Does that mean we're home alone?' I run a hand over the back of my neck, rotating my head and exposing my throat like a playful kitten.

Rufus's eyes roam hungrily over my body and any thought I had that he might have lost interest in me are instantly dismissed. He wants me more than ever. This is going to be as easy as finding a grain of sand on an empty beach.

His cheeks flush and he clears his throat, unable to hold my eye. 'She'll be back later.'

'If you're not too busy, I'd love to grab another interview. I'd like to find out about your childhood and what influence that had on your career.'

'Yeah, sure,' he mumbles. 'When? Now?'

'Unless you have something else on?'

He glances at his watch and runs his fingers through his thick mop of curly hair. 'Why not? Where do you want to go?'

I know exactly where. 'What about the lounge overlooking the garden?'

It's somewhere we can get comfortable, and who knows, maybe pick up where we left off last night. With Carmel out for the morning, anything could happen. I'm certainly glad I chose this dress. He can't stop snatching glances at me when he thinks I'm not looking.

Rufus leads the way and I ask him to sit on the big, grey L-shaped sofa. He's already more relaxed than when I surprised him in the utility room. He even cracks a few jokes at my expense, which I laugh at with a forced bonhomie.

I pull up a padded footstool and sit opposite him. I frame his head and upper body on my phone and press record. Rufus sits up with the assumed stiffness of a decorated colonel on military parade, hands in his lap.

I giggle at the silliness of his pose. 'I just want to check the sound. Can you tell me what you had for breakfast?'

'Roger that,' he says in an affected public school-boy accent. 'For breakfast this morning, one had a slice of granary toast with a poached egg and a good dollop of hollandaise sauce.'

I screw up my nose in disgust. 'Yuck. Really?'

'No, I had a bowl of cornflakes.'

We both laugh.

'Idiot,' I giggle.

'Hang on. Who are you calling an idiot? I'm supposed to be your interviewee. You can't talk to me like that.'

'Start behaving like an interviewee then.'

'Oh, I love it when you get cross,' he grins.

'Stop it. Come on, be serious.'

'I am being serious.' He pulls a stupid face, baring his teeth and rolling his eyes, which only makes me laugh harder. 'Anyway, what about you?'

'What about me?'

'Tell me about your breakfast. How do you like your eggs in the morning?'

I lower my phone and slap him on the arm in mock horror. 'Rufus!'

'What?'

'Behave yourself.'

He throws his arms up in mock innocence. 'I don't know what you're talking about.'

Our eyes meet and our gaze lingers for longer than it should. Rufus wets his lips and blinks three times.

'Are you going to take this seriously or not?' I ask, adopting a matronly tone with him as I raise my phone again.

195

'I know. Why don't I interview *you?*' He snatches my phone right out of my hand and holds it out of reach.

'Rufus!'

'Come on. It's only fair. Let me ask you some questions,' he says, grinning. He aims the phone at me, peering at the screen with his neck craned.

'Don't be silly.'

'Tell me about your family,' he says. 'Do you have any brothers or sisters?'

My mood instantly deflates. I suppose at some point I'll have to tell him about Hannah, but there's no reason he has to know that she's the reason I'm here. About the devastating impact Carmel has had on our lives.

I launch myself off the footstool, hoping to catch him by surprise, my hand grasping for the phone. But he's too quick for me and falls back onto the sofa with my mobile held high above his head.

I collapse onto him, our bodies tangling, and our faces inches apart.

His laughter fades as he stares into my eyes and I know this is the moment everything is about to change. All my hopes and dreams are about to come true. This is the moment I finally bring Carmel to her knees and destroy everything she holds precious.

Our lips meet for a tentative kiss. A gentle caress.

Rufus drops my phone on the floor and wraps his arms around me, one hand on my back, the other in my hair.

Our kiss becomes more passionate, our mouths crashing together. I press my body into his and his fingers find their way under my dress.

I gasp with pleasure, throwing my head back and squeezing my eyes shut.

'Are you sure about this?' he whispers.

'Yes,' I moan, kissing him again.

There's no way to stop this now. We've gone too far. Crossed too many boundaries. This is happening, and it's exactly what I want.

Chapter 27

Rufus peels himself off me with a grunt, his chest heaving and his skin glistening with sweat. Hurriedly, he gathers up his clothes and pulls on his boxer shorts without even looking at me. I watch him as he moves, bending and ducking to retrieve trousers, shirt and socks flung across the room in a flurry as we gave in to our passions, not caring about anyone or anything in that moment.

'Rufus? Are you okay?'

I prop myself on my elbows, suddenly feeling exposed and vulnerable, conscious that anyone walking past the vast picture window would have had a pretty good view of what had just gone on between us. I draw my knees up to my chest, trying to cover my nakedness.

Rufus perches on the edge of the footstool to pull on his socks, his shirt flapping open. It all happened so quickly, but it was amazing. Furious. Desperate. Animalistic. It was everything I hoped it would be, and more. It didn't last long, but Rufus certainly knew what he was doing. He was like a man possessed and we were two spirits conjoined as one in that moment.

Except now he's grown cold. Why won't he look at me? Is it something I did? Or is he embarrassed? Ashamed? Guilty?

Following his lead, I scoop up my own clothes, pull on my underwear and wriggle my dress over my hips.

'Please talk to me,' I plead as I flatten down my hair. 'What's wrong? Was it something I did?'

Rufus stands to button up his shirt, his breath coming back under control. His fingers are trembling. His face flushed. His expression taut.

'I'm sorry. That should never have happened,' he mumbles, staring at his fingers as they button up his shirt.

'What? No. It was amazing.'

'I took advantage of you,' he says.

'You didn't take advantage of me. If I didn't want it to happen, I'd have told you.'

Finally, he glances at me as he stops fiddling with his shirt. 'Really?'

'Yes, really. It was incredible.'

I move towards him, hopeful of rekindling the mood. I don't want it to be like this. I want him to hold me. And kiss me. Tell me he cares for me and that I'm the most precious woman he's ever been with. And in time, I want him to tell me he loves me. But most of all, I want him to tell me he doesn't want to be with Carmel anymore.

He shakes his head with a sadness in his eyes.

'No, I'm sorry. This was a terrible mistake.'

'What? Don't say that.'

This isn't how I planned it. But it's my fault. I've rushed things. I should have been more patient. Now I've given him what he wants and if I'm not careful, he's going to discard me and pretend it never happened. My throat tightens as a bubble of tears floats to the surface.

I snatch his arm as he turns away. I want him to look at me. To see me. But he wrests free of my grip, ripping one of my nails.

'What's wrong? Why are you being like this?' I wail.

He turns on me with such a fierce, dark look in his eye, I physically recoil. For an instant, I fear he's going to hit me.

'Don't touch me,' he screams.

'I'm not going to tell Carmel, if that's what you're worried about.'

His eyes are as black as a starless void. He grabs both my arms so tightly it hurts.

'If you breathe a word of this to anyone...'

'I won't,' I croak. 'I promise.'

'Especially to Carmel.'

'I wouldn't do that. I'm not stupid.'

He lets me go, shoving me away. I stumble but catch my balance as he turns his back to me, his head in his hands. He paces up and down, banging his forehead with his fist.

'Stupid! Stupid! Stupid!' he rants to himself like a man swirling in a tempest of madness.

It's a complete overreaction, but if he's this wracked with guilt and self-loathing after sleeping with me once, I still have a lot of work to do to convince him to leave Carmel. Maybe this won't be as easy as I thought. It's going to take time, and time isn't on my side. I've told him I need a couple of weeks, three at most, for the filming. And then I need to leave.

'Rufus, please calm down.'

He spins around, his eyes flaming. 'Calm down? You have no idea what you've just done, do you?'

'Me?'

'Yes, you. Coming onto me like that. You know I'm married.'

My mouth opens, but I can't find the words. I can't believe what I'm hearing.

'You kissed *me!*'

'Only because you led me on and now look what's happened.'

'I didn't plan this,' I lie. 'It was something that just happened. We acted on our impulses. We couldn't help ourselves.'

'No, no, no.' Rufus resumes pacing up and down, his shoulders hunched and his head bowed.

'I'm sorry if you feel this is my fault,' I say through clenched teeth. 'But please, don't take it out on me.'

'This is a mess. What the hell are we going to do?' he rants to himself under his breath.

'Look, nobody needs to know what happened. It can be our secret.'

'And if Carmel finds out?'

'How? I'm not going to tell her. And unless you tell her or you have security cameras hidden around the room, she's not going to know.'

He glowers at me, anger simmering. Maybe he does have cameras secreted in the walls. I wouldn't put it past him.

'You don't know what Carmel's like,' he says. 'She's going to know and then...'

I take a deep breath. 'Maybe, you know, it's not such a bad thing if she finds out?'

He stops pacing and stands as still as stone, staring at me in disbelief.

'Are you out of your mind? You have no idea what's going on here, do you?'

'Look, I like you, Rufus. I like you a lot. I don't regret for a second what just happened. I enjoy your company. You make me laugh. You make me feel good about myself. Yes, you're married, but I think you're making a mountain out of it. I want to be with you, okay? I have... feelings for you. And I think you might be feeling the same way.'

'Shut up!' he screams so loudly it makes me jump. 'Don't say that.'

I shake my head in disbelief. What the hell has got into him?

'Rufus, please—'

'Leave.'

'What?'

'You heard me. I want you to go,' he says, folding his arms across his chest.

'Go where?'

'I don't know. Home. Anywhere. Just not here. Leave this house,' he says, his foot tapping furiously on the tiled floor.

'B... but the filming,' I stammer.

'I don't give a flying fuck about your film. Just get out!'

The tears I'd been struggling to hold back now come hot and fast. This can't be happening. He can't seriously be throwing me out.

'But why?' I sob. 'I want to be with you. And I know you feel the same way.'

'No,' he yells. 'I don't. I'm sorry, but it's for the best. Go.'

'Please, we can work this out. We can talk to Carmel together. I'll be right by your side. It won't be that bad, I promise.'

'You still don't get it, do you?'

'Get what?'

'She's dangerous. More dangerous than you could ever imagine. And if she finds out, she'll...'

His chin sinks onto his chest and his shoulders sag.

'She'll what?' I ask. He's being such a drama queen.

He draws in a deep breath, filling his lungs. When he glances at me, his eyes are red and his face pale.

'You should never have come here. It was a big mistake. Your life is in danger, Marcella.'

'What?'

'Get as far away from here as you can, because when Carmel finds out what's happened, she's going to kill us. She's going to kill us both,' he says.

Chapter 28

I turn and run from the room with tears streaming down my face. I've never been so humiliated in all my life. I bound up the stairs without a backwards glance and don't stop until I make it to my room. I slam the door and throw myself on the bed.

I thought I'd played Rufus perfectly. I never imagined he'd reject me so cruelly afterwards. It was bad enough that he was so cool and off-hand with me, but to throw me out of the house?

Carmel's hold over him is obviously much stronger than I realised. But why's he so terrified of her?

'What's with the tears?' Hannah asks. She's wearing one of my dresses, a loose-fitting cotton sleeveless dress with spaghetti straps, twirling around in it so the skirt flies up above her knees like she's in an advert for a holiday in the sun. Annoyingly, it looks better on her than it ever did on me. 'Let me guess. Rufus?'

I roll over onto my back with my hands folded over my stomach. 'How did you know?'

'What happened?'

She listens patiently as I tell her about seducing Rufus and how, as soon as he was done, his whole demeanour changed.

'It was like sleeping with Jekyll and Hyde. One minute he was all over me and the next he was ordering me to leave.' A fresh wave of tears catches me by surprise. Hannah hands me a tissue.

'What are you going to do?'

'I'm staying. I came here to get even with Carmel, and that's what I intend to do.'

Hannah grins. 'I love it when you get all determined.'

'I'm doing it for you, remember?'

'I know. And I'm grateful.'

'Men are pathetic. You think he'd happily pull out his own fingernails to be with you over her. You're far prettier, younger and way nicer.'

'I mean it. He doesn't deserve you.'

'I'm not doing it for him. I'm doing it for us. I just want Carmel out of the picture,' I say, imagining warm summer days entertaining friends on the patio outside. Rufus at the barbecue. A glass of champagne in my hand. Carmel, meanwhile, holed up in some grotty bedsit by the sea, out of sight and out of mind.

'So what next?' Hannah asks.

A sudden steely determination rises from deep in my gut. I'm not giving up on Rufus that easily. 'He'll come round. I won't give him any choice.' I stare at the ceiling, the paint yellowed with age, and run my tongue over my teeth. 'Every chance I get to be with him on his own, I'll remind him what he's missing. What we could have together.'

Hannah crosses her legs and knits her hands over her knee. She's wearing my perfume as well as my dress.

'And how long's that going to take?' she asks.

'I don't know.'

'There is another way you could hurry things along.'

I raise an eyebrow. 'Oh, yeah?'

'You could tell him you're pregnant,' Hannah smirks.

'Hannah! I couldn't. That's an awful thing to suggest.' But it's not a bad idea. 'And anyway, it's a bit soon. We've literally only just had sex.'

'Okay,' she shrugs. 'You know best.'

The thing is, I'm not sure if I do.

Hannah's rooting through my bag, looking for more of my clothes to try on when there's an unexpected knock at the door. I'm still lying on the bed, wallowing in self-pity and thinking things through. Hannah freezes. We stare at each other in alarm.

'Who's that?' she mouths.

'Quick, get under the bed,' I hiss, jumping up.

'Marcella? Are you in there?' It's Rufus, his voice muted.

'Just a minute.'

Hannah drops everything and scurries across the room. The old floorboards creak as she contorts her body under the bed and I yank the duvet down on one side to conceal her.

'Don't make a sound,' I whisper with a finger to my lips. 'I'll get rid of him.'

Rufus has changed his shirt, and his hair is damp. I assume he's taken a shower to wash away the scent of me. It makes me feel grubby and used all over again. I peer at him through a crack in the door.

'Hi,' he says. At least he has the grace to look embarrassed.

'Hi.'

'Um, can I come in?'

'Sure.' I glance over my shoulder to check Hannah is out of sight before opening the door and inviting him in.

'I thought I heard voices,' he says. 'Were you talking to someone?'

'I was on the phone to a friend.'

'Oh?'

'It was nothing important.'

He stands in the middle of the room, not sure what to do with his hands, his expression souring. 'Did you tell them you were here? Filming with us?'

'No, she's an old friend I haven't seen for years. She just wanted a catch-up, that's all,' I lie.

'Right.' The tension in his body melts. 'And nobody else knows you're here?'

I frown. 'No. Why?'

'No reason. I just wouldn't want rumours starting. You know what people are like and you're, you know, a young, attractive woman...' He stumbles over the words, his cheeks reddening. He chews his lip and glances at his feet.

'Was there something you needed?'

'I wanted to apologise for losing my temper earlier. I'm sorry. I was confused and, well, you know, it was wrong what happened. It was a mistake.'

'Was it?'

'Come on, Marcella, please. I was weak and, of course, any man would be flattered to think he had a chance to be with you, but I'm married. You know that. I made a commitment to Carmel and—'

'But she doesn't love you.'

'Don't say that.'

'She doesn't love you or respect you like I do,' I say.

'Don't.'

'We could be happy together.'

Rufus shakes his head, but there's a pensive sorrow that lingers in his eyes.

'We could build a life together,' I continue. 'We could be happy.'

I reach for his hand, but he pulls away. 'No, we couldn't.'

'Why not? I know you have feelings for me. And I know how I feel about you. We're destined to be together.'

'Don't say that,' he snaps, his anger rising once more.

'It's true.'

'I meant what I said, Marcella. Pack your things and leave. It's not safe here. You have to go.'

'No,' I protest. 'I'll only go if you come with me. Leave Carmel and be with me.'

'Don't be ridiculous. I can't do that.'

'Why not?'

'You know why not. This is my house. I've put everything into making it my home. I can't just walk out and leave Carmel.'

'I don't see why not,' I say.

'Because she's my wife!'

'Divorce her. Be with me.'

He laughs cruelly and slaps a hand to his forehead. 'I hardly even know you.'

'That didn't stop you from sleeping with me.' I lunge forwards, reaching up on the tip of my toes to kiss him. I know it's not going to take much to bend his will.

But he pushes me away violently and I fall back on the bed, cracking my head on the wall. Not that he notices.

'Why won't you listen to me?' He's shouting again now.

'I thought you had feelings for me?'

'I do, Marcella. And that's why you need to leave. It's not safe.'

'Why? You keep saying that, but I don't understand. What am I supposed to be afraid of? Carmel?'

I laugh as I climb off the bed, smoothing down my dress.

Rufus stares at me without a trace of humour. He really is totally under her thumb.

'You don't know her like I do,' he says.

'What's the worst she could do? Sure, it might get ugly. She'll probably lose her temper. Maybe even throw some stuff and bad-mouth you to her friends. But so what? Isn't that worth it for the life we could have together?'

I can see he's wavering. He's imagining a life without Carmel. With me. Someone he thinks genuinely loves him. Who desires him. Who won't rule his life and make it a misery.

'We can't do this,' he says. 'Maybe in another life. But not this one. And if you really care for me, like you say you do, you'll leave. Go somewhere far away and never try to contact me again.'

'Is that what you really want?' I ask.

'I don't want you to get hurt, Marcella. You don't know the half of what you've got yourself involved in. You're better off without me.'

'Fine. If that's what you really want, I'll go. You'll never see me again.' And suddenly I'm crying again. A flood of tears that cascade down my cheeks. Tears of frustration. Of humiliation. Of anger.

It's futile continuing to argue, and I won't debase myself by begging. If he wants me gone, I'll go. He's used me and now he wants to wash his hands of me. And if I can't change his mind, I'll find another way of getting to Carmel. This isn't the end.

'Thank you.' He breathes a sigh of relief and the lines of anxiety furrowed in his brow iron themselves out. 'But you need to hurry. It's best you're gone before Carmel gets back.' He checks his watch. 'She could be home at any time. I need to go out on a site visit, but promise me you'll be gone when I get back.'

'Alright,' I sniff. 'I get the picture.' He's still worried I'm going to say something to Carmel. It's tempting, but it's too risky. It would be my word against his. I should have thought about setting up a camera. Or recording our conversation. That's the kind of evidence I'd need to make her believe me. Without that, I'm just a fantasist chancing my arm.

He turns to leave, the floorboards creaking under his feet. 'Marcella,' he says, as he reaches the door.

'What?'

'I'm sorry.' He hesitates as if he has something else to say, but then clamps his mouth shut and stalks off.

I bang the door closed behind him, wait until I hear his footsteps on the staircase, then stamp my foot on the floor in frustration.

Hannah pokes her head out from under the bed. 'Well, that certainly told him. What are you going to do now?'

'Shut up, Hannah!'

Chapter 29

I shove all my clothes and dirty laundry in my bag in a furious hurry, angry that Rufus has used me, outplayed me, and cast me aside like a broken promise. I don't even know where I'll go. There's no point going back to the flat. I'm due out in a few days, and I don't have enough money to put down a deposit on somewhere new. I don't even have any real friends I can turn to for help. But I've promised Rufus I'll leave. For whatever reason, he's not willing to leave Carmel, and that leaves me with very few options.

With one last look around the room, I storm out with my bag over my shoulder. Although I have no regrets that I won't be sleeping in the creepy attic room for another night.

I heard Rufus leave a short while ago. The growl of his car. The hum of its tyres rolling up the drive. And now the house is silent again. I'm alone, and the temptation to cause havoc is overwhelming.

Just imagine the damage and destruction I could wreak if I left the taps running in their en suite bathroom. Or turned their fridge and freezer off at the plug. Or emptied all of Rufus's expensive bottles of wine down the drain.

But what's the point? It might make me feel better for a short time, but I have bigger plans. A ruined freezer full of food is going to be an inconvenience to Carmel at best. It's not going to make up for what she did to Hannah.

As I trudge wearily past Rufus and Carmel's bedroom, resisting the temptation to sneak in and pour bleach in their bed, I deliberately scrape my bag along the walls, hoping to leave an indelible mark. A reminder of me.

I bump my bag petulantly down the stairs into the hall. The house smells of lavender and beeswax polish. A comforting smell. A far cry from the stink of cooking fat and damp that used to linger in our old flat.

For all its extravagant splendour, the craziness of the old melded with the new, I'm going to miss the house. I'd already started imagining my life here with Rufus. How I'd change the colour scheme. Update the sofa with something more comfortable and less fashionable. Buy a bigger TV. But for now, that remains a pipe dream. If I can't persuade Rufus to leave Carmel, none of this will ever be mine. It's not fair. What's she ever done to deserve it?

I take one long, last lingering look around, my heart heavy. I doubt I'll ever own anywhere quite like it. How would I begin to afford it?

But there's no point dwelling on it. I need to focus on Carmel and think of another way to settle my score with her. Find another weak point to exploit. A vulnerability. I thought it was Rufus, but I was wrong. There has to be something else. I'm sure there is. I just need the time to think and to plan.

I'm halfway along the hall, checking the bus times from the village on my phone, when the front door flies open. Carmel barges in, key in one hand, brief-case in the other. She's flustered. Her face red. Her cheeks puffed out.

We both freeze.

She glances at my bag and looks me up and down with a frown.

'Marcella? Are you going somewhere?'

She sounds surprised.

'I... I'm...' I stammer, not sure what to say. Rufus is going to be furious I've been caught before I've had the chance to make my escape.

'You're not leaving, are you?'

'I was going to write a note,' I say. The way she's staring at me makes me feel about two-feet-tall. It galvanises my determination to do everything I can to bring her down.

Carmel's eyebrows shoot up. 'I don't understand. I thought you had several more weeks' filming to do? You can't have finished already. You've barely started.'

'No, the thing is... the film's not really working out as I planned. Sorry if I've wasted your time.'

Carmel puts her briefcase down by her feet and closes the door, trapping me like a rabbit confront-ed by a hungry wolf. Instinctively, I glance up the stairs, looking for a way out, imagining making a run for it. Up to the attic room and locking myself in.

'Really? You've not given it much of a chance.'

'No, but—'

'I'm sorry, you can't go. Not yet. I'm sure it's just a creative block. We can work through it together, can't we?' Her smile is unnervingly warm and friendly.

It instantly puts me on my guard. It's not like her. She's never shown the slightest semblance of amiability before.

'I... I guess,' I mumble.

What do I do now? She's not going to let me leave, although I'm surprised. The way she's treated me from the moment I arrived, I'm staggered she's not ushering me out of the door with fireworks and ticker tape.

'Good. That's settled then.'

'I don't want to be any trouble. I've taken up enough of your time.'

'Nonsense. You'll stay as long as it takes to finish the filming. Rufus and I won't hear of you going. Anyway, he'll be devastated if you leave without saying goodbye. Now go and put your bag back in your room.' It's an order, not a request.

'Are you sure?'

'Of course I'm sure. I'm not letting you go until you've got everything you need. Stay for as long as you like. Now, while you're upstairs, I'll put the kettle on, and then why don't you join me for a cup of tea? We can chat through why you think the film isn't working,' she says.

It's the first time I've seen this softer side of Carmel. It makes me uneasy. What's brought about the sudden change? And more to the point, how's

Rufus going to react when he gets back and finds I'm still here?

Who cares? I can deal with him. Carmel's warming attitude towards me is a new opportunity I can't resist.

'I'd like that, thank you.'

Chapter 30

Over tea and cake in the lounge overlooking the meadow garden, with a strengthening spring sun warming our faces, Carmel and I discuss my spurious filming project. What I hope to achieve. What barriers I perceive are in my way. She even offers some suggestions for filming and topics about the house build I should explore.

But the conversation swiftly moves onto other things. Notably, how Carmel and Rufus nearly ended up in the divorce courts, she says, because the house took so long to complete and they were effectively living on a building site. Interesting. She tells me how the stress took its toll on them both, especially as they were both holding down demanding full-time jobs at the time.

'You're a psychiatrist, aren't you?' I ask.

Carmel smiles over the top of her teacup, her lipstick smudged on the china rim. 'That's right.'

'The thing is, I've never really understood what a psychiatrist does. Or how they're different to psychologists,' I say.

Carmel's cup rattles as she places it on its saucer. 'Most people don't grasp the difference. They think we're all the same. But basically, psychologists are concerned with the normal function of the brain. How we think and act. What drives us to do the things we do. Whereas psychiatrists are more concerned with mental health issues.'

'Is that why you were in court today?'

'I'm often in court. A large part of my job these days is preparing psychiatric reports for defendants where their mental health might be an issue in their offending,' she explains.

'Oh, I see,' I say, feigning ignorance. I know exactly what she does. How easily her words can condemn someone to a life of misery. They call it a hospital, but it's not like any hospital I know. It's all heavy locks, bars on the windows and a nighttime of anguished screams and demonic wailing. It's far, far worse than prison.

I nod, as if it all makes sense. 'So, say someone started a small fire in a block of flats because they'd heard voices in their head telling them to do it, it's your job to decide if they're actually crazy or not?'

Carmel's superior smile is nothing short of patronising. 'Actually, we don't refer to people as being crazy or insane. That's quite outdated language. But yes, if someone committed arson and was hearing voices, a psychiatrist would normally be asked to assess their mental health to help the court decide on sentencing.'

'That's what happened to my sister.' The words slip from my mouth as if they have a mind of their own. They're out before I can hold them back.

'I didn't know. I'm sorry.' Meaningless platitudes. She doesn't even look as though she means it.

'She didn't mean any harm, but they caught her with a pile of newspapers and a cigarette lighter, building a small fire in the stairwell of some flats in Margate,' I say.

I've heard the story from Hannah so many times, I can picture it in my mind almost as clearly as if I'd been there. The stink of stale urine. The echo of children's voices up the stairs. The electric spark of the lighter. Smudged black newsprint on Hannah's hands. The first coil of acrid smoke. A tentative flame that blazed and flared as it consumed the crumpled edges of an old copy of *The Sun*.

'Right,' Carmel says. 'Then it's likely she was assessed by a psychiatrist, like me, to determine her state of mind.'

*It wasn't someone like you. It **was** you. You didn't even know her, but your words, your stupid report, sealed her fate and doomed her to a life not worth living.*

'They sent her to a psychiatric hospital on the other side of the country,' I say, my jaw aching as I grind my back teeth, the muscles balled like rocks.

'That makes sense. That's all perfectly standard.' Carmel's lips are curled into a sickly smile I'd love to carve off her face. She has absolutely no idea what she's done, which makes it worse.

'Hannah hated it. It wasn't good for her. The staff treated her worse than a dog. She couldn't sleep. She wasn't eating. It was no life at all.'

'But it was probably the best place for her to be.'

219

I want to take Carmel's cup and smash it into her head. For an instant, I imagine what it would be like to do it. Mushing up her immaculately made-up face into a stew of blood and gristle. Shards of china cutting and ripping her skin. Slicing through her nose. Her lips. Her eyes. The gurgle in her throat. The spray of blood across the back of the expensive sofa.

'... not unusual, I'm afraid.'

I blink, tuning back into Carmel's whiny voice, pushing the image of her mutilated face out of my mind.

'What?'

'I was saying, it's not unusual for patients to feel distressed when they're first admitted to hospital, but the staff really do know what they're doing,' Carmel says.

'I don't think you understand,' I say, gripping the arms of my chair so tightly, my knuckles lose all colour. 'That place destroyed her. It didn't make her better.'

'It would have been worse for her in prison, I'm quite sure.'

I shake my head, my back teeth grinding against each other. 'She begged me for help, but there was nothing I could do. I couldn't get her out. Nobody could. And so she did the only thing she could think of.'

Carmel's smile slips and her eyes darken.

'What happened to her?'

I shrug. 'What do you think? She was so desperate, the only control she had left was to take her own life. She killed herself because of that place, and that's why I can never forgive the people who put her there.'

Chapter 31

I've never really talked to anyone about Hannah's death and the planet-sized hole it left in my life. As a twin, she was more to me than just a sister. She was a part of me. A core essence of my being. Although we never dressed alike, wore our hair the same, or finished each other's sentences, she was the yin to my yang. And when she died, a part of me died with her. She was supposed to be my teammate for life. The one person who truly understood me. And it was all taken too soon. I doubt I'll ever get over her death. But then, I'm not sure I want to.

There's only one person I blame, and she's being so blasé about Hannah's death and her role in signing her death warrant, it makes me more determined than ever to right the scales. I need her to pay for the death of my sister at such a young age. And she will. I just don't know how yet.

'She was only twenty-three,' I say, my words as sticky as honeyed glue in my tight throat. 'She had her whole life ahead of her.'

'I had no idea,' Carmel says, her smile fading under the shadow of fake concern she's putting on.

'I don't suppose the psychiatrist who condemned her to that hospital even knows what happened to her.'

'Had she shown any suicidal tendencies previously?'

'None,' I say, spearing Carmel with a hard stare.

'That's desperately sad, but despite everything, it sounds as though the hospital was probably the best place for her, no matter how much she disliked being there. If she was a danger to other people, the court would have had no choice,' she says.

I came to the house with a deep-seated hatred for Carmel but with every word she vomits out, my contempt for her burns fiercer.

'She never hurt anyone. She didn't mean to cause any trouble. It was the voices. They were telling her she had no choice. The court should have let her off with a warning. Instead, they chose to send her to that hellhole to die.'

Carmel grimaces. She clearly disagrees. 'The system isn't perfect, but we're all doing our best. I know it's hard to hear, but everyone involved in your sister's care would have had her best interests at heart. Her death was an unfortunate tragedy.'

I'm going to enjoy destroying her. Whatever it takes, I'm going to make her pay so badly, she'll be begging me to stop. An unfortunate tragedy? Is that what she thinks? Does the woman have a caring bone in her body? I really can't understand what Rufus sees in her. She's a poisonous, sour, dried-up old hag. How he could ever choose her over me is beyond comprehension.

'Listen, would you care to eat with us tonight?' Carmel asks as casually as if we'd just been chatting about the weather. 'It would be a good opportunity for us to get to know you better, and to make sure we've finally changed your mind about leaving.'

'Sure. Why not?' What the hell?

'Great. I was going to make a lasagne. Perhaps you could give me a hand in the kitchen and we could have a little girl time together.'

I force my lips into a smile, but can't make it reach my eyes. I'm too angry. Too tightly wound up. I can't think of anything I'd less to do, but I'm not stupid. It's better if I keep her on side for now.

'Absolutely. I'd be happy to help.'

Carmel has me chopping onions and frying mince in a large pan while she concentrates on a béchamel sauce, blending flour, butter and milk over the stove at my side. Her proximity sends a shiver of disgust down the arch of my back, but I pretend to be happy in my work.

I've almost forgotten I'm not supposed to be here when the front door crashes open and I hear Rufus toss his house keys on the side table in the hall.

'Something smells good,' he calls out. His shoes thud onto the floor as he heels them off.

His face when he walks into the kitchen and sees me chopping tomatoes is a priceless picture I'd love to frame.

'Hello, darling,' Carmel says, abandoning her pot to greet Rufus with a chaste peck on the cheek. 'How was your meeting?'

He stands motionless in the doorway with his gaze fixed on me, staring in disbelief. 'What?'

'I thought you had a site meeting this afternoon. How did it go?'

'Fine,' he says, his eyes boring into me.

I'm not sure how well I disguise my smirk of delight.

'Hello, Rufus.' I smile sweetly, my face a picture of innocence. 'Carmel's invited me to eat with you tonight. I hope that's okay? I can eat in my room if you'd prefer?' I point towards the stairs with my knife.

'Don't be ridiculous,' Carmel says, returning to the stove to save the sauce from ruin. 'We've been through this. You're dining with us tonight. No arguments.' She glances at Rufus over her shoulder. 'I caught her earlier trying to sneak away.'

'You did?'

'But I managed to persuade her to stay.'

I raise my eyebrows in a 'there-was-nothing-I-could-do' kind of way. He glowers back at me.

'It would be lovely to have you dine with us,' he says, without much feeling. Is that sweat on his forehead?

'Well, if you're sure.' I can't help myself.

'Marcella's helping me cook a lasagne. We should open a bottle of wine as we have a guest. Can you choose something suitable?' Carmel asks.

'Sure. Marcella, why don't you help me if you've finished here.' Rufus flicks the switch on the wall and the hidden hatch in the floor slides open.

'I don't know anything about wine,' I protest.

'I'll teach you. Come on.'

I wipe my hands on a tea towel, toss it on the side, and watch Rufus cautiously as I approach. He stands to one side and invites me to descend into the wine cellar ahead of him.

It's much cooler down here. The air drier. As I descend, the last thing I see is the back of Carmel, piecing together the lasagne in a large rectangular dish.

Rufus follows close on my heels. Too close. I feel his breath warm on the back of my neck and sense his simmering irritation.

The moment I reach the bottom of the stairs, he snatches my wrists and presses me against the wall.

'What are you still doing here? I told you to be gone before Carmel returned.'

I wince as a sharp snag of pain radiates up my arms. 'I tried,' I gasp. 'But Carmel came home earlier than I thought. She wouldn't let me go.'

'Fuck.'

He releases my arms, spinning away on his heel and chewing one of his thumbnails. He thumps his fist against one of the wine racks, causing the bottles to rattle.

I rub the feeling back into my wrists, keeping a wary distance from him, although it's hard in such a confined space.

'It's not my fault,' I say in a low whisper.

'Why couldn't you have listened to me? Why couldn't you just leave when I asked you to go?'

'I told you, I tried.'

'You didn't try hard enough.' Spittle flies from his mouth and hits me on the cheek. It's like being stung by a live electrical wire. I jolt my head back. Wipe it away with my thumb. Rufus's face has turned a worrying shade of puce.

'I don't understand what you're so angry about. Why don't we just tell her about us?'

'Keep your voice down,' he commands, shooting a glance upwards. Carmel's so close I can hear her clattering dishes, opening the oven door and chopping a salad on a board.

'I'm serious,' I continue, in a vain hope that I can still change his mind. 'Let's go up there and tell her right now. It'll be okay.'

He glares at me as if I've lost my mind. 'Are you fucking insane?'

'She doesn't love you. You deserve better.'

'I was thinking a nice Merlot,' Carmel shouts from above.

'Good idea,' Rufus yells back. He grabs a bottle by its neck and holds it at his side.

'I don't know why you don't just grow a pair and ask her for a divorce. You don't even have to tell her about us for now, if you don't want to. But she's crushing you, Rufus. Can't you see? Whatever the two of you had, it's gone.'

'You don't know what you're talking about,' he says, placing the bottle on the bottom step.

'Leave her. You deserve to be happy.'

Rufus darts across the tiny room with the speed of a striking cobra. He wraps his hands around my throat, snatching my breath. Pinning me against the wall. Lifting me off my feet. At first, I'm too shocked to react. Then, instinctively, I grab his thick wrists and try to prise them off. But he's taller and stronger and has surprise on his side. I can barely breathe. My swollen lungs burn as I fight desperately to suck in some air. My head feels as though it's going to explode.

Rufus presses his face into mine, so close I can smell the tartness of his coffee and garlic-tinged bad breath. His nostrils flare. His eyes are as black and as piercing as a serpent's glare.

'I'm not asking her for a divorce.' The words hiss from his mouth like hot steam.

'Everything alright down there?' A shadow appears at the top of the steps as Carmel looms into view, wringing her hands in a tea towel.

Rufus releases his grip on my neck and springs back as if he's been burned by my touch.

'Everything's fine,' he says, stepping into Carmel's view and picking up the wine bottle. 'I think this one will go perfectly with lasagne.'

Chapter 32

The meal passes awkwardly, with Rufus prodding at his food, sullen and sulky, while Carmel is chirpy and chatty, blissfully unaware of what happened in the cellar earlier between me and Rufus. He barely says a word all evening, while occasionally glowering at me. Carmel, on the other hand, is the most animated I've seen her since I arrived, chatting about everything and anything, as if we're old friends.

'What the hell do you think you're playing at?' Rufus snaps at me when Carmel collects our dirty plates at the end of the meal and disappears with them to the kitchen.

'I don't know what you mean,' I smirk, enjoying his discomfort. It's small compensation for his attempt to strangle me.

My throat's still sore and my voice a touch gravelly. I hope the bruises come up overnight. Guilty marks imprinted on my skin to remind Rufus of what he did. I'm sure Carmel's bound to notice. And then what will I say?

'I don't know what you think you're playing at, but it's going to get you killed.' He picks up his glass and pours what's left of his wine down his throat, before topping it up, finishing the bottle.

'Are you threatening me?' I press my palm to my chest in mock horror.

He clenches a fist tightly and points an accusing finger. As if that's going to intimidate me.

'Please,' he says. The softening of his tone is unexpected. 'Walk away while you can. I'm pleading with you.'

No. I'm enjoying myself too much. Especially now Rufus has taken to begging.

'Why would I want to leave? Carmel and I are getting on so well tonight. Have you noticed? I think we could be good friends.'

'Stop it,' he barks.

'And good friends tell each other everything. What do you think she'd say if I told her about us?'

'Don't,' he growls.

'I might not be able to help myself. It might just slip out.' I hold Rufus's penetrating stare.

He jumps up suddenly, rucking up the tablecloth, threatening to send our glasses flying. He slams his hands on the table and leans over it, on the edge of losing it completely.

I recoil, my spine pressing into the back of my chair.

'I really wouldn't do that if I were you.'

Over his shoulder, I spot Carmel returning to the room. She's prepared a cheeseboard and a basket of biscuits.

'Rufus?'

His head snaps around and the tension seeps from his body. 'We're out of wine,' he mumbles. 'I was going to fetch another bottle.'

'Not for me,' I say, pushing my chair back as I stand. 'I'm going to grab an early night.' I affect a yawn, stretching my arms above my head. I've had enough excitement for one evening. It's time to regroup and plan my next steps. And besides, I think I've put enough worries in Rufus's head for one evening.

'Sleep well,' Carmel says, catching my yawn. 'And let's have no more talk of you sneaking away.'

Rufus storms out of the room with the empty wine bottle as Carmel places the cheeseboard in the centre of the table.

'I won't,' I promise, before hurrying away and racing upstairs.

I don't want to bump into Rufus again tonight. I certainly don't want to be on my own with him. He's shown his true colours this evening and I don't trust him not to try to hurt me again. I'll need to keep my wits about me from now on.

I slip into my room and dig out my pyjamas, which are crumpled at the bottom of my bag I've not yet had the chance to unpack. The familiar chill in the room settles in my bones and I shiver. The light flickers and my pulse quickens. Maybe I'll talk to Carmel in the morning about moving out of the attic and into one of the rooms below, now she seems to have warmed to me.

I'm not sure what's changed, but her attitude couldn't have been more different this evening.

Maybe she's worried she was driving me away. Or perhaps she'd been having a bad week. Things on her mind. Work worries, maybe. Whatever it was, it's a welcome change. Not that it's altered my attitude towards her. She has Hannah's blood on her hands, and I'm not going to let her get away with it, no matter how nice she is to me.

I slide under the duvet, pull it up to my collar, and let my head sink into the lumpy pillow. I've been trying to get to Carmel through Rufus, but it's possible our burgeoning friendship, in her eyes at least, could present a new opportunity.

There must be a way I can exploit our newfound closeness. Everyone has their secrets. Maybe if I can unearth hers, I can use it to my advantage.

As Carmel and Rufus's bedroom door bangs shut, I lie in the darkness listening to the sounds of the house. The whisper of wind through the leaves in the trees. The creak of contracting wood in the roof trusses. The steady pulse of blood in my ears.

Carmel inviting me to eat with them is a clear sign she's beginning to trust me. And if she trusts me, she's more likely to offer up some information I can use against her. A wound I can prod. Forget Rufus. This is a much better angle of attack.

Another sound drifts into my consciousness. A steady, rhythmic creaking, accompanied by an occasional thud. Like a ball being tossed against the side of a house.

Or a headboard banging against a wall.

Oh god.

The creaking gets faster.

More intense.

A scream. A moan.

I think I'm going to be sick.

The thought of Rufus and Carmel having sex makes me cringe. I'm reminded of the whips and restraints I found in Carmel's bedside cabinet. How disgusting. I try to think of something else, but the image of Rufus bound and gagged, his arse being spanked by Carmel, won't go away.

I curl up into a ball and fold the pillow over my ears, clamping it against my head with my hands. But all I can think about is what's going on in that room.

His sweaty body toiling away. Carmel sprawled out. Legs wide. What the hell is he doing? Surely her shrivelled-up old body and sagging breasts can't be a turn on for him. It's a disgusting thought. Don't they realise I can hear everything?

'What is that noise?' Hannah asks, sitting up in bed.

'Use your imagination. What do you think?'

'Ugh. Really?'

'I know. It's gross. How could he? With her?'

'Are you jealous?' Hannah asks, an eyebrow shooting up.

'No!'

'Sounds like you are.'

'I'm not,' I protest. 'She's welcome to him as far as I'm concerned.'

'I think you're annoyed because he chose her over you. Because he's gone back to her even though you offered it to him on a plate,' she taunts.

'Shut up. You don't know what you're talking about.'

I don't know why I'm so angry. I don't want Rufus. I have no interest in him. Not anymore. He was a means to an end, that's all. If he'd rather be with Carmel and share his bed with that washed-up old crone, that's his choice. I don't want anything to do with him.

'Have you worked out what you're going to do now?' Hannah asks, rolling her legs out of bed and perching on the edge of her mattress.

'Not yet,' I answer defensively. 'If I can't get to Carmel through Rufus, I'm going to have to find something else on her I can use as leverage.'

'Oh.'

'What?'

'Nothing.'

'No, come on. If you've got any bright ideas, let's hear them.' It's all very well her sitting there passing judgement on me, but she's not exactly helping.

'It's obvious, isn't it?'

'Is it?'

Hannah sighs and rolls her eyes. 'I really must have taken all the brains before Mum popped you out,' she says.

'Whatever. Spit it out, Han.' She's always been like this, thinking she's better than me just because she was born three minutes before me.

'If you really want to destroy Carmel, to make her suffer, you have to take something from her she cherishes. Something irreplaceable,' Hannah says, as if I don't know that.

'I've tried. I thought if I seduced Rufus I could persuade him to leave her.' I sit up, glad the sound of Rufus and Carmel's lovemaking has finally ceased. It didn't take long.

Hannah shakes her head, her hair flying wildly. 'Never mind seducing him. Kill him.'

'Kill him! Jeez, Hannah. What the fuck?'

She shrugs and falls back into bed, picking at her fingernails. 'Why not? That would really hit her where it hurts.'

'But... but that would be murder,' I gasp.

'Have you forgotten what she did to me? She killed me the moment she signed her name on that report and had me sent to that hospital. What's the difference?'

'I know, but—'

'Don't tell me you're scared,' she says in a mocking sing-song voice.

'I'm not scared.'

'So what's stopping you?'

'How would I do it?'

'You could poison him,' Hannah suggests.

'With what?'

'I don't know. Rat poison? There must be something in the house you can use.'

'I'm not sure. I wouldn't know how much to give him or how.'

Hannah tuts. It's dark, but I can imagine her rolling her eyes. But it's easy for her. She's not the one who has to do it.

'Or you could stab him. I bet they've got some expensive kitchen knives you could use. You might even be able to make it look like an accident.'

I shake my head. I don't think I could. I'm not brave enough. It was bad enough when I accidentally tripped up Daisy Jennings in the playground at school when we were seven. She cut her head open and there was blood everywhere. She needed stitches in hospital, and even though I never meant to do her any harm, I felt guilty for weeks. I don't think I could knowingly stick a knife into anyone. Not even Rufus.

'Maybe I could push him down the stairs?' I suggest. I think about the steep stone stairs that coil down into the hidden wine cellar below the kitchen. A quick shove or an outstretched foot might be all that it takes. And I could definitely make *that* look like an accident.

But it's not a long way to fall. Unless he hit his head, he'd be unlucky to suffer as much as a sprained ankle.

I squeeze my eyes shut and push the image of Rufus's body lying at the foot of the stairs, his eyes staring blankly, out of my mind.

'I'm not going to kill him, Hannah.'

'Why not?'

'Because I'm not, okay? Anyway, I've got a better idea. If Rufus doesn't have the balls to leave Carmel, then I'll just have to tell her about our affair. Let's see how long their marriage lasts after that.'

'And what if she doesn't believe you?' Hannah asks. 'You don't have any proof.'

'I'll find some. Anyway, she thinks we're friends now. Trust me, she'll believe me.'

'That might work,' Hannah sighs. 'Or, you could just kill Carmel.'

Chapter 33

I'm not killing anyone.

Although the idea is tempting.

No, I'm not a murderer.

I wouldn't even know where to begin planning something like that. It takes a certain kind of twisted mind. An emotional detachment and I don't have the stomach for it.

I can't deny it's fun thinking about it, though. Even if Carmel has fallen out of love with Rufus, his death would be devastating for her. I can almost picture her face, twisted in horror, as she finds his lifeless body. The disbelief. The shock. The abject misery.

I'd love to see how she copes with the gut-piercing pain of losing someone close. It could never compensate for Hannah's death, but it would be something. A shift in the scales, if nothing else.

I'm not going to do it, of course. The risks are too high, even if I had it in me to pull it off. I'd have to make it look like an accident. But how? I've seen enough episodes of CSI to know it's not easy to cover up a murder and make it appear non-suspicious. Inquisitive minds and forensic testing make it virtually impossible these days. And there's no way I'm going to prison, even if it means getting even with Carmel. There has to be a better way.

Unless, of course, I could frame Carmel for Rufus's murder.

Now, *that* would be perfect.

Oh my god. Why didn't I think of it before?

Because I'm not a killer. I'm not going to murder anyone.

This is Hannah's doing. She's put the idea in my mind, like a pumpkin seed pressed into a pot of soil, and now my brain's nurturing it. Encouraging it to germinate and take on a life of its own.

Imagine if I could pull it off, though.

Carmel would suffer not only the agony of her husband's death, she'd lose everything. Her freedom. The house. Her reputation. Her job, probably. Who knows, maybe even her sanity. It would be almost too much to bear for anyone, and would more than make up for the death sentence she unjustly handed down to my sister.

All I'd have to do, after killing Rufus, of course, would be to convince the police that Carmel flipped out when she discovered Rufus and I were having an affair. I'd tell them I'd heard an argument raging. Things being thrown. And discovered his body in a pool of his own blood.

I spend so long thinking about it as I get ready for bed that I even dream about it, waking in the small hours of the morning, dripping with sweat, and my heart thundering.

For an instant, I'm convinced it's real. That I *have* killed Rufus. That my hand's still clutching a bloody carving knife. Rufus's body, face down on the kitchen floor. A crimson pool spreading slowly beneath him, running along the grout lines. His shirt stained with blood.

The guilt and panic hit me like a high-speed train.

My eyes spring open. I'm not in the kitchen. I'm in bed, in the room in the attic. I'm not standing over Rufus's body. And he's not dead. I didn't kill him. Thank god.

The relief is a comforting blanket.

And yet it all felt so viscerally real. My dream so convincing. A sign I'm capable of killing him? Or a sign that I'm not?

It takes me ages to get back to sleep. Every time I close my eyes, I see Rufus lying there. Not moving. Ragged knife holes in his shirt. Adrenaline forges through my veins like acid. I can't slow my heart-beat.

Even when I drag myself out of bed and into the shower the next morning, the dream is at the forefront of my mind. It's all Hannah's fault. She was the one who put those crazy thoughts into my head. But I'm not the murdering type. I guess that's why my dream has disturbed me so profoundly.

I need to get some air. To get out of the house for an hour. It's become claustrophobic. The walls closing in on me. I need some space to think. To breathe. But I don't want to face either Carmel or Rufus. Not until I've straightened out things in my head and worked out what I'm going to do next.

I creep out of my room and down the stairs, but thankfully don't bump into anyone. As I reach the hall, heading for the front door, I hear Rufus's voice. It sounds as if he's on the phone in the new part of the house. His voice grows louder and fades away, as if he's pacing up and down. Good. It means he's distracted.

The sun makes a brief appearance from behind fast-moving fluffy grey clouds as I pull on a pair of trainers and inch open the door. The air tastes earthy with the hint of moss and lichen blooming in shaded corners. Gingerly, I close the door behind me, wincing as the latch clicks shut.

It's as if I've stepped into another world. The tension in the back of my neck and shoulders eases like a retreating spring tide and the pressure on my chest loosens, allowing me to breathe. Living in the house with Carmel and Rufus has taken a bigger toll on my mental health than I'd realised.

I've been playing a role since I knocked on the door and talked my way into becoming a house guest. Pretending to be something and someone else other than myself. A method actor immersing myself in a challenging part. I thought it would be easy. An escape from my own reality, even. But it's hard. Much harder than I ever imagined.

Even in my room, with Hannah, I'm constantly on guard. Ready to switch back to the pretend Marcella at a moment's notice. But out here, in the fresh air, I'm free.

Just an hour or so. That's all I need. Like pressing the reset button on my mind. And then I'll go back and pick up where I left off. Hopefully, I'll have a chance to work on Carmel again. Forging those bonds between us. Building her trust until she gives me something I can use against her. For now, I'm just going to enjoy being me.

I'm naturally drawn towards the woods and the trail where I saw Rufus that night he was out late. I never did get to the bottom of what he was doing or where he'd been. And somehow, with everything else going on, it's slipped my mind until now. It seems a perfect opportunity to go exploring and to find out.

The path is far more substantial than I'd imagined. It's more than a meandering trail. It's a well-defined track, topped with a dressing of wood chippings, not dissimilar to something you might find in a public park. It obviously leads somewhere. Why else would they go to the trouble?

With a quick glance back at the house, I enter the woods, following the track. It's edged with lengths of decaying tree branches, angled haphazardly. It's obviously taken time and effort to construct.

I march on with birdsong ringing in my ears and the strongest rays of the sun filtered out by the thick canopy above. The further I walk, the gloomier it becomes. And within twenty metres or so, the house is no longer visible. I could be in the middle of nowhere. It's actually incredibly peaceful, with nothing in sight but rows and rows of tree trunks and a tangle of squat bushes and clumps of ferns.

Something small and agile scratches around in the undergrowth to my left and as I glance down, worried it might be a mouse, or worse, a rat, I spot something I wasn't expecting.

Kneeling, I brush away a carpet of dead leaves and uncover a light. It's no bigger than a ping-pong ball. Half buried in the ground. Another few metres further on, I find another. And another. Marker lights, like Catseyes on the road, I'm assuming. Lights to illuminate the path in the dark, which suggests Rufus might be a frequent late-night visitor. Maybe he *is* keeping dogs out here.

The path winds onwards for another few hundred metres, slowly climbing, before abruptly ending at a clearing where the ground turns rocky underfoot. Ahead is a stony cliff face, no more than five or six metres high. A vast seam of rock protruding out of the earth where a few hardy, clinging plants grow out of its cracks and a green haze of moss hangs to some of its more shadowy parts. But what's most striking is a rectangular concrete porch built into the rock. Even odder is the heavy steel door that's set into it.

My feet grind to a halt as I take it all in. It's obviously some kind of entrance. But to what? An underground network of tunnels? A cave? But why put a door there at all? I can't make sense of it.

I'm drawn closer, my curiosity piqued. Is this where Rufus came from the other night? In which case, what's behind the door and why was he here in the middle of the night? It's not the sort of place you would keep animals. There'd be no light or ventilation for them. So what then?

I try the handle, but it's locked. And it's so heavy, it doesn't even rattle in the frame.

There's an electronic keypad next to the door. I stab at a few numbers, but it just bleeps and the door remains resolutely locked. There's no way I'm getting inside without the code.

It could be anything. A birthday. An anniversary. Or a random set of numbers. There are probably millions of possible combinations and almost no chance of guessing.

It doesn't stop me trying, plucking numbers out of the air.

Each time, I'm frustrated by a loud bleep and a door that remains locked and unmoving.

'What are you doing?'

Rufus's voice is like an electrical bolt through my body. I jump as if a thousand volts have passed through my bones.

'Nothing,' I reply guiltily, stepping away from the keypad.

Rufus emerges from the path from the house, his brow hooded.

'You shouldn't be up here,' he says.

'What's behind the door?'

'Nothing.'

I raise an eyebrow. 'You don't set a steel door into a cliff to hide nothing.'

'Storage. That's all. Nothing for you to worry about.'

'Storage?' My eyebrow shoots higher.

Rufus sighs, like he's dealing with a petulant child who won't take no for an answer. 'It's where we keep chemicals for safety. Fertilizer. Weed killer. That kind of thing.'

'You built that,' I say, hitching a thumb towards the door, 'to store chemicals? Show me?'

'What? No. Don't be ridiculous.'

'Were you spying on me? How did you know I was here?'

Rufus pokes his tongue into the side of his cheek. 'I heard the door. I looked for you in the garden, but when I couldn't find you, I guessed you might have gone wandering. Poking your nose into places it doesn't belong.'

'What were you doing up here the other night?'

'What?'

'I saw you walking back to the house through the woods. You'd been here, hadn't you? Why?'

He laughs as if amused by my creative imagination. 'I told you. We'd had a row, and I came out for a walk to clear my head. That's all.'

He steps forwards. Drawing closer.

I edge away, fearful. My throat's still painful from where he strangled me in the cellar last night. If he attacks me again, here in the woods, no one's going to hear me scream.

'Don't touch me.' I raise a hand, warning him off.

'Marcella, please.' He reaches out. Tries to take my hands. His manner calm. His demeanour relaxed. Not like last night, when he couldn't keep his anger under control.

I absentmindedly touch my neck. The bruises didn't come up, but the skin is still sore to touch.

'I'll scream.'

'No, you won't. Just listen to me. You have to leave. This is your last chance,' he says, his eyes doleful.

'I'm not going anywhere. Carmel doesn't want me to go.'

'No, of course she doesn't,' he says, bowing his head. 'Why do think she's being so nice to you?'

'What do you mean?'

'You really think she wants to be friends?'

I shrug. 'Yeah, why not?'

'Come on, Marcella. Wake up. Time is running out. I don't know how much longer I can protect you. Go while you can. The last bus into town leaves at seven. Make sure you're on it.'

I shake my head. I don't know what game he's playing, blowing hot and cold like this, but I came here with a purpose. And I'm not going anywhere until I've settled my score with Carmel.

'Still worried I'm going to tell wifey about our little rendezvous?' I sneer.

He stamps his foot and yowls in frustration.

'I'm asking you to leave because I care about you. Why can't you understand that?'

'Care about me? Huh! Is that why you had your hands around my throat in the wine cellar last night?'

'I'm sorry. I was angry. And afraid. I was out of line.'

'I'm here to stay, whether you like it or not, so you'd better get used to it.' I've had enough of his mind games and manipulation. He's tried every trick in the book to make me pack my bags and leave. He must be absolutely petrified that I'm going to tell Carmel what's been going on between us. But I'm not going. Not when I'm so close to finally avenging Hannah's death.

'Fine. It's your funeral, but don't say I didn't warn you,' he growls, his face clouding. 'You do what you want. I can't force you. But I'm telling you now, if you're not on that bus tonight, you'll never get out of here alive.'

Chapter 34

As if I was going to fall for all that nonsense about my life being in danger and needing to be on the last bus out of the village or I'd die. Honestly, what kind of gullible idiot does Rufus take me for?

I lie on my bed staring at my phone above my face until eventually my arms ache. The minutes tick down with the rapidity of a somnolent sloth, until finally, the time ticks past six-forty. It's too late to leave now. I'd never get my stuff packed, out of the house and into the village before the last bus. I guess I'm stuck here for at least another night.

At seven o'clock on the dot, I toss the phone aside. It bounces on the mattress towards my feet. Rufus's silly deadline has come and gone, and here I am. Still very much alive.

It's pathetic, really, how he's been trying to scare me into going. Carmel didn't frighten me off when she put me in the attic room where those children were murdered and Rufus isn't going to scare me off now.

They really are an odd couple. And frankly, they probably deserve each other.

'I guess we're staying then?' Hannah says.

She's lying on her back on her bed, mimicking me. Fingers laced. Hands resting on her stomach. Eyes roaming across the stained ceiling.

'We're not going anywhere. Not until I'm done with Carmel, anyway.'

Hannah lifts her head and rolls her face towards me. 'What if they weren't threats?' she says with a grin of devilment. 'What if Carmel really is evil, and she's on her way up here right now with an axe, ready to chop you into tiny pieces and bury you in the garden?'

I laugh. 'Or what if she's a witch, and she's going to cast a death spell on us?'

Hannah giggles with delight. 'Or turn us into frogs and cook us in a stew?'

We both roll about laughing.

'Well, whatever Carmel has in store for me, I'm doomed. It's gone seven and the last bus has left. So unless you fancy walking, we're stuck here for at least another night,' I say, my sides aching from laughing too hard.

Hannah screws up her nose in disgust. 'I'm happy to stay,' she says. She never was much of a walker.

'Good. And I think tomorrow I might have that chat with Carmel and tell her how Rufus came onto me while she was out. And that we had sex on their sofa. Let's see what she has to say about that.'

'*If* you make it through the night,' Hannah laughs again.

We spend the next few hours chatting. Discussing important stuff like where I'm going to live when this is all over. What I'm going to do for a job. How

I'm going to find a man stupid enough to want to marry me and have babies with me. I don't have any sensible answers for any of her questions.

Eventually, Hannah yawns and stretches her arms above her head.

'Think I'll turn in,' she says, crawling under the covers. 'Can you kill the light? It's too bright in here.'

'I'm not going to bed yet.'

'Why not? Aren't you tired? Or are you worried about Carmel?'

'Very funny. And no, I'm not tired. It's only nine o'clock and anyway, I have something planned.'

Hannah looks wide awake suddenly as she props her head up on her hand. 'What?' she asks eagerly.

I tell her about the path I found in the woods earlier and the locked door set into the rock.

'It's where Rufus went when I spotted him out late the other night,' I explain. 'I want to see if he goes back there again tonight. And if he does, I'm going to follow him. And then I'm going to find out exactly what's behind that door.'

Chapter 35

A few hours later, as I'm struggling to keep my eyes open and my mind keeps wandering off towards sleep, I hear a noise which makes me sit up and snatch a held breath.

I heard Rufus and Carmel retire to bed earlier. Their bedroom door clicking shut. The rush of water in the basin. The toilet flushing. But now someone's moving around again. They're trying to be quiet, but in the silence of the night, there's no mistaking it. A creak of floorboards. A door opening and being gently closed.

I ease myself off my bed and hurry across the room. I crack open the door and put an ear to the gap.

This could be it. Rufus off again on another late-night jaunt. Except this time he's not going to be alone. I'm going to be following him to see exactly what he's up to.

Footsteps scuff across the landing and plod down the stairs. I grab my trainers and sneak out, waiting until I hear the front door rasp open and snap shut before following.

In my hurry, I stub my toe as I trip lightly down the attic stairs and have to clamp a hand over my mouth to silence my howl of pain, hopping up and down on one leg.

And then I hear a sound I wasn't expecting.

The low thrum of a car engine. Followed by the crush of gravel. The murmur of a vehicle driving away from the house.

I freeze, still on one foot, gripping the other in my hand. Where's Rufus going in his car at this time of night? I check my phone. The screen blinks on, casting a bubble of light all around me. It's past midnight.

Now what do I do? The bed in Carmel and Rufus's room creaks. Sheets rustle. There's a low murmur. Carmel is still asleep, I guess. Does she have any idea Rufus has gone out? I doubt it.

I retreat back to my room, but leave the door open.

Now I really need to stay awake. I can't follow Rufus, but I can spy on him when he gets back. Maybe it'll throw up some clues about where he's been and what he's been up to.

I have to stay alert.

But I last for maybe thirty minutes. Forty at most, before my eyes grow heavy and my head falls back against the headboard.

I'm woken by the sound of my own snoring and I jerk awake, blinking in the dark. I hear a dull thud outside. Followed by another. Car doors opening and closing?

Instantly, I'm wide awake with my heart racing.

Everything goes quiet except for the thread of adrenaline racing through my veins, throbbing at a frantic pace. My whole body is rigid with tension, my muscles coiled to react.

I cock my head and close my eyes to listen.

A key scrapes in a lock. The front door hisses open. A grunt. A scuff of shoes. And, if I'm not mistaken, something being dragged along the floor. Something heavy and unwieldy. What the hell?

A cool breeze wafts into my room. A light flicks on downstairs, its residue glowing faintly at my door. My phone tells me it's well past two in the morning. Rufus has been gone for an awfully long time.

Slowly, carefully, I swing my legs off the bed and place my feet on the floor. The floorboards groan unavoidably as I stand. In this part of the old house, everything aches and moans with age.

Hannah remains asleep, breathing heavily through her nose. Just as well. I wouldn't want her making a noise and asking awkward questions right now.

I'm across the room and at the door in five soft paces. I squeeze through the gap, out onto the landing, and tiptoe down the stairs.

Whatever Rufus is doing, he's making a meal of it, huffing and puffing like a steam train.

I scurry across the landing and peer over the banister, looking down into the hall below.

I catch a yelp of shock and surprise in my throat before it reaches my mouth. It comes out as a strangulated murmur of distress.

Rufus is not alone.

He has a woman with him.

Dragging her body along the ground, his hands under her armpits. Her head is lolling on her chest and her limbs are all floppy and limp.

Is she dead? I can't see any injuries or any blood, but why's she not moving? Resisting?

And then she groans, her lips twitching as if she's trying to speak but is so heavily sedated, she doesn't know where she is or what's happening.

What the fuck is going on?

My instinct is to rush downstairs and confront Rufus. To ask whether the woman needs help. But I can't move. My arms and legs are frozen, impervious to the messages coming from my brain.

My mind races, whirling with questions, a tumult of confusion and fear.

Who is she? Where did she come from? Why is she unconscious? And where's he taking her?

My last question is answered first as he lowers the woman to the ground, taking care she doesn't bang her head. It's a surprisingly compassionate gesture.

Her long, blonde hair fans across the tiled floor, a huge hooped earring bent at an awkward angle. She's wearing tight-fitting jeans with a thin, see-through green top over a black bra. One of her shoes, a strappy sandal, is missing. She looks about my age, although her make-up is smudged. Eyeliner streaking down her cheeks. Lipstick faded and smeared across her chin. And as I look more closely, I see the beginnings of a purple bruise rising across her forehead.

Has he done this to her?

My initial shock gives way to a swelling anger as a tide of queasiness rises from my stomach.

Rufus steps out of view for a moment. Unusually, he's dressed all in black. Dark trousers. Dark, long-sleeve top. And his mop of curly hair is all flattened as if he's been wearing a hat.

Or a hood.

This can't be happening. This is so fucked up. What am I supposed to do?

A familiar low, whirring sound starts up. Like a small electrical motor. The same sound I heard the first time Rufus showed me the hidden wine cellar under the kitchen floor.

His arm darts back into view. He grabs the heavy woven rug in the middle of the corridor and pulls it to one side.

To my amazement, the floor beneath it is opening up. A sliding hatch revealing a dark hole under the house. Another hidden cellar. One I had no idea was there.

It only takes a few seconds to open fully. It's not a wide entrance. Smaller than a standard door, but easily big enough for Rufus to fit through.

He steps back into view and slides his hands under the woman's arms again. He pulls her, twisting her around with her feet trailing lazily behind her.

He backs up to the hole in the floor, watching his feet as he steps backwards and down a set of unseen steps.

The woman's body follows, disappearing into the depths like she's being swallowed by a giant anaconda.

Her feet vanish last, bumping down the steps with a hollow thump.

And then she's gone.

Chapter 36

St Mary's Church, Wychwood
August 2, 1925

The church was airless and the stifling heat had rendered most of the Sunday morning congregation either restless or sleepy. The Reverend James Bennett ploughed on, regardless. He had an important lesson to impart on the virtues of forgiveness and reconciliation, although it was clear he didn't have everyone's undivided attention this morning.

There was no sign of Agatha or the children again. It had been weeks since he'd last seen them, and before that, their attendance at church had been sporadic at best. He'd been meaning to pop over to the house to check on them all, but since his last encounter with William, when he'd executed a cow right in front of him, he'd found excuses not to visit. Too many reasons why he couldn't spare the time.

He was also troubled by the inappropriate feelings he'd developed for Agatha. Time and distance would put paid to that, he'd told himself, and so he was in no rush to see her again.

And yet her absence from church left him uneasy. It wasn't all that long ago she'd turned up at the vicarage sporting a hideous black eye and a suspected broken rib at the hands of her violent husband. He really should check on her.

'Lovely service, Vicar.' Ted Holloway grinned broadly as he shook the Reverend Bennett's hand, revealing the absence of most of his upper teeth. 'Very 'formative.'

'Thank you, Ted.' The Reverend Bennett gripped his gnarled, old hand, leathered and calloused from years of tilling the land, firmly. 'I'm glad you found it useful.'

Ted stifled a yawn. The vicar had watched him nod off at least twice during his sermon, his eyes drooping and his head falling onto his chest at all the good bits. Typical. At least he was here.

'See you next week then.' Ted slipped his cap back onto his head.

'Ted, have you seen William and Agatha recently? Agatha's not been to church for a few weeks and I was wondering if you'd seen them around the farm?'

Ted was one of William's trusted farm hands and had helped Agatha look after the place while William was away fighting.

Ted hesitated and scratched his head under his cap, a greasy strand of hair poking out over his ear. 'To be honest, I haven't,' he said, 'now you come to mention it. I haven't seen Billy in days. Or any of them kids.'

A pang of worry catapulted through the vicar's chest.

'When was the last time you *did* see them?'

'I dunno. Last week some time?'

'Last week?'

'That's right.'

'Not even William?'

'Nope.'

Agatha's words of warning rang through the vicar's head.

I worry that one day he might actually kill me.

A cold shiver ran down the length of the Reverend Bennett's spine, despite the heat, and brought a belt of sweat to his brow.

As the remainder of his congregation filtered slowly out of the church and dispersed to go about their business, the Reverend Bennett remained distracted, thanking everyone for coming but not really listening to anything anyone had to say.

When the last worshipper had gone, he hurried into the vestry, threw off his stole and surplice and grabbed his hat.

'Off somewhere?' Albert, the verger, asked as the vicar brushed past.

'I'll be back shortly,' he called over his shoulder.

When he arrived at Shadowbrook Farm, the Reverend Bennett was dripping with sweat, his feet swollen in his shoes and a painful blister on his heel. But he didn't care about any of that. Worldly discomforts, that's all. He had only one thing on his mind, and that was to confirm Agatha was safe and well.

As he pushed open the gate and let himself in, the first thing the vicar noticed was an eerie quiet about the place, as if all the birds and animals had given it a wide berth. He glanced to the heavens and said a silent prayer.

'May God grant me strength and wisdom to comfort those in sorrow and bring His peace to this troubled home,' he mouthed to himself.

There was probably a perfectly logical explanation for Agatha and William's disappearance. Maybe they'd been called away for some reason. Or were taking a holiday. He'd heard Brighton was lovely at this time of year, although pricey for a family with six children when the only income they had was from the farm.

He approached the house slowly, his feet dragging, comforting himself with the knowledge that the Lord was looking over him, and trusting that everything would be fine.

It was a handsome farmhouse constructed in red brick and with Kentish peg tiles. Bigger than most of the houses around here. William had been lucky to have inherited it, along with thirty acres of land, from his parents.

The door to the property was ajar.

'Hello? Is there anyone home?' The vicar craned his head around the door.

Flies buzzed incessantly in the hall, a maddening swarm that wouldn't stay still.

An awful stench was coming from somewhere inside. Rotten. Stinking. Like cabbages left out in the sun. And something else, sweet and sickly. Like the smell of death.

The Reverend Bennett covered his mouth with his sleeve and stepped inside.

'Hello? Anyone here? Agatha? William?' he called.

He swatted the flies away from his face with his free hand and tiptoed into the kitchen.

Food had been left out all over a big wooden table in the centre of the room. Half-eaten apples. A loaf of bread curling at the edges. Plates and knives. Cheese. Tomatoes. Slices of pie. A mug of tea, half drunk. It seemed to be at least the partial cause of the smell. More worryingly, several chairs had been knocked over, as if there had been an altercation or the family had left in a hurry.

The vicar's pulse quickened and a cloak of doom descended over his shoulders.

He eased the kitchen door closed and ascended the stairs. The sickly sweet smell that clawed in his throat and made him gag was worse the higher he climbed.

First, he checked each of the rooms the children shared. But they were all empty, their beds made and their shoes lined up by their doors.

But at the end of the landing, one bedroom door was ominously shut. He hesitated outside the room, listening. He heard only silence and the raging of his poor heart.

He knocked and waited.

'Hello? Anyone in there?'

When there was no reply, he eased open the door.

The smell hit him like a wall of putrid rot and sourness, decay suffocating the air. Like walking past a dead badger in the hedgerow, but ten times worse. His eyes watered and his delicate stomach heaved as the air came alive with the buzz of a thousand flies.

Peering around the doorframe, he saw William lying motionless on the floor at the end of the bed, staring at the ceiling, his eyes glassy and dull. Next to his body lay what looked like the revolver he'd used to euthanize the distressed cow in the barn a few weeks earlier. A puddle of blood had congealed into a dark brown mess around William's head and seeped into the floorboards. Between his eyes was a small, black hole, no bigger than a farthing.

The vicar gasped, his legs like water. He clutched the door for support and clasped his hands together in supplication.

'Oh dear Lord, may you have mercy on his soul and guide this troubled spirit, taken in despair,' he whispered.

There was nothing to be done for him. William had obviously been dead for a while, his life taken by his own hand. But where were the children and their mother?

He stumbled back towards the stairs, but as he hurried along the landing, keen to get out and into the fresh air, he noticed another staircase leading up into the attic. He hesitated. What if Agatha was hiding up there with the children, unaware her husband was dead? Or worse, what if he'd imprisoned them? Or hurt them?

With leaden legs, he climbed the creaky staircase up into the darkness. It opened up into one large space, stuffy with heat and rank with the same stench of death he'd encountered below.

As his eyes gradually adapted to the shadows, and the shape of the room revealed itself to him, his knees gave way and he crumpled to the floor.

Lying in front of him, one next to the other, their arms at their sides and their legs out straight, were William and Agatha's six children. None of them moving. All of them dead.

The Reverend Bennett threw his head back, looked up and wailed a piteous, heart-wrenching scream of anguish and despair.

Chapter 37

St Mary's Church, Wychwood
September 11, 1925

There wasn't an empty pew to sit on or an inch of floor where mourners could stand as six tiny coffins were carried into the church. It was heaving at the seams, fuller than the Reverend James Bennett could ever remember since he'd taken up his role in the parish as the entire village, shocked at such a terrible tragedy, had come to pay their respects to the murdered children.

News of their deaths had spread around the village like a shockwave. Six tiny stones dropped into a still lake, rippling out to the water's edge.

The police investigation had been rapid and conclusive. The children had all been killed by their father, who was not of sound mind after the trauma he'd suffered in the Great War. He was mentally and physically scarred by his experiences in the trenches of France and, struggling to cope with peacetime life, had often been prone to bouts of anger and uncontrolled violence.

After suffocating each of the children and lining up their bodies in the attic, the investigation confirmed William had taken an old service revolver and shot himself once in the head. He, along with his children, had been dead for at least four days before the vicar made his gruesome discovery.

'We gather here today in the midst of profound sorrow and anguish, to bid farewell to six precious souls whose lives were tragically cut short,' the Reverend Bennett began as a solemn silence descended on the congregation, punctuated only by the sound of tears as some were unable to control their emotions.

'We cannot comprehend the depths of pain and grief that have enveloped this community, but let us find solace in coming together to support one another during this harrowing time. Let us not forget the joy these young souls brought to the world, the laughter that echoed in their innocent hearts, and the precious memories they leave behind.'

They hung on his every word, even as his voice wavered, his words choking in his throat.

And then they carried the bodies out and they were finally laid to rest together in a family grave in the churchyard, where only weeks earlier they'd all been happily playing in the early summer sunshine.

'Into the arms of eternity, we commit these precious souls, entrusting them to the eternal embrace of our loving Creator,' he intoned as the coffins were lowered one by one, and a tight circle of mourners gathered around to watch.

Nobody seemed to notice the freshly dug, unmarked grave at the far edge of the churchyard where William's body had been quietly committed to the ground in a low-key service a few weeks earlier. The Reverend Bennett hoped that by giving him a proper Christian funeral, his soul might yet be saved, although he doubted many in the community would share his view. However, he drew the line at allowing his body to rest with the children he'd slain.

Eventually, it was all over. People slowly dispersed. The Reverend Bennett had made it through the service, even though his heart was breaking.

One of the last to depart was the village constable, Walter Cooper. Cooper had been the first to attend the scene when the Reverend Bennett had raised the alarm and had seen for himself the horror of what William had done to his own children.

He approached the vicar and gave him a solemn nod. 'A very good service, Reverend.'

'One I hope I never have to repeat.'

'It's a sorry business, that's for sure, but at least the little ones are at peace now.' His eyes were rimmed red and moist with tears.

'Any news on Agatha?' the vicar asked hopefully.

She'd not been seen since the bodies of her husband and children were found, her disappearance unfathomable.

'I'm afraid not. We're still working on the theory that William murdered her first and disposed of her body somewhere, before returning to the house to kill the children, and then himself,' Cooper said.

The vicar nodded. He didn't want to believe it. He preferred to imagine that somehow, against the odds, she'd managed to escape.

'I see,' he said. 'I wish I'd done more now when she came to me for help.'

'You can't blame yourself. William wasn't right in the head ever since he came back from the war.'

'But she warned me. She said she thought he might kill her one day.'

The constable shrugged. 'It's not your fault. Are you coming to the Crown?'

'I might pop my head around the door later,' the vicar said. His presence would be expected at the wake, even if the last thing he felt like doing was being around other people.

'Right-o. See you in there a bit later then.'

Inside the church, Albert was bustling around tidying up. As much as the Reverend Bennett enjoyed seeing the building filled with worshippers, he enjoyed it most when it was empty, when he could take a moment for himself to reflect. Today was definitely one of those days. He loved the majesty of the church. The impressive vaulted wooden ceiling. The beautiful stained-glass windows with their depiction of Christ on the cross, the ascension and the saints and martyrs.

He took a moment at the altar and bowed his head before the cross, remembering the children and lamenting their loss. Arthur, Stanley, Frederick,

Alfred, Dorothy and little Edith, who was only three years old when she died. God bless them all.

With a heavy heart, he retired to the vestry and removed his ceremonial robes, then jotted some thoughts down in his notebook. Some reflections on the day and a note to himself about how he would reflect on the loss at Sunday service.

Footsteps tripped lightly on the tiled floor in the nave. Not Albert. A woman's footsteps. Someone who'd missed the service and come to pay their respects? Curious, he poked his head out of the door. Sure enough, there was a woman in black seated at a pew by the rear entrance. Her head was bowed and the brim of her hat concealed her face.

She knelt and prayed.

He should leave her in peace, but there was something about her that snagged his attention. He couldn't take his eyes off her. Who was she?

After a few minutes, she stood and shuffled into the aisle.

She glanced up briefly and the Reverend Bennett caught the glint of her eye. There was something achingly familiar about her.

'Hello?' he called out.

Her head jerked back, surprised by his voice.

'I'm the Reverend James Bennett, vicar here at St Mary's,' he said, striding towards her with a friendly smile, hoping not to scare her off.

She didn't reply. Instead, she turned suddenly and hurried away.

'Wait!' he called after her.

But she didn't slow up. If anything, her pace quickened.

And as her skirt billowed around her legs, the Reverend Bennett saw something that made him snatch his breath. A small lesion. Possibly a birthmark. A distinctive shape, like a dragon.

'Agatha?' he shouted. 'Is that you?'

But she was already halfway out of the door, heading into the churchyard.

The Reverend Bennett wasn't usually a man taken to running, but in that instant he made an exception, rushing to catch her. Was it really her? Had she come back for her children's funeral? Or was it a vision? His hope and desperation playing tricks on his mind.

'Wait!' he yelled breathlessly.

When he reached the churchyard, he spotted her threading her way through the graves, towards the fields at the far end of the village.

He ran like a man possessed, his chest tightening and the muscles in his legs burning. He wasn't going to lose her. Not until he'd satisfied himself it wasn't her.

'Please, wait,' he said, finally catching up with the fleeing woman and snatching her elbow.

She spun around and lifted her head.

'Agatha!' the vicar gasped. 'It *is* you! I thought you were dead.'

Her eyes were wild with panic, her face as pale and as smooth as alabaster.

'Where have you been?' he asked, his lungs heaving as he caught his breath.

'I wanted to pay my respects,' she said. 'Please don't tell anyone I was here. No one can know.'

'I don't understand. We all thought you were murdered by William and that he buried your body before...' He glanced down at his feet.

'No,' she said.

When he looked up again, she'd regained her composure, but was edging away from him, into the shadows of the trees.

'You have to go to the police.'

'I can't. I'm sorry.'

'Why not?'

She shook her head and sighed. 'You know why.'

'I don't, Agatha. Come back to the church and talk to me. I've been so worried about you.'

The vicar's mind was a whirlpool of questions. 'Did he hurt you?' he asked.

'Please, let me go.'

'I can't stop you from leaving if that's what you really want, but I don't understand what's going on.'

She let out a long, slow breath and chewed her lip. 'You've always been most kind to me,' she said. 'I suppose I owe you the truth, as hard as it will be to hear.'

'Truth is the guiding light that leads us to understanding, healing and redemption.'

'Hmmm,' she said.

'Whatever it is you have to say, you can trust me.'

'Are you sure you want to know? You can't tell a soul if I do.'

'You have my word and God will be my witness.'

'If you breathe a word of what I'm about to tell you, I will find out,' she said with an unnerving calm. 'And when I tell you what really happened in that house, you'll understand why I had to disappear. Why I had no choice.'

Chapter 38

With my legs threatening to fold and my whole body trembling, I stagger back along the landing towards my room. I can hear myself mumbling, incoherent nonsense babbling under my breath, my lips with a life of their own.

In the moment I watched Rufus drag that poor woman into the hidden cellar under the hall, I had a flash of clarity so shocking I can hardly believe it's true.

It couldn't be, could it?

Could Rufus be responsible for all those women missing in the city?

Was the woman I saw tonight just one of many he's abducted from the streets and brought back here to the house?

If so, where are all the others? Has he killed them? What about the locked door in the woods? Is that where he's keeping their bodies?

It takes all my self-control not to purge my dinner over the landing floor, and I only just make it to the bathroom in the attic in time. I hunch over the toilet bowl with my abdominal muscles cramping, and let it all out. And then collapse on my haunches, replaying what I've just witnessed over and over in my mind.

I've been wrong all along. While I've been so focused on Carmel and how I could destroy her life, I should have been looking at Rufus. He's the truly evil one. And yet he had the gall to warn me that Carmel was dangerous.

None of it makes sense. If he's been abducting women and bringing them here, why would he invite me into the house in the first place, and risk being caught? And why has he been so desperate for me to leave?

The only thing that's clear in my mind is that I can't stay. Rufus was right. It's not safe for me. But not because of Carmel. I need to get the hell out of here. I'll walk back to Canterbury if I have to.

I drag myself to my feet, using the wall for support, and creep back to my room. I ease the door shut and switch on the torch on my phone.

'Hannah!' I hiss in her ear, shaking her awake. 'Hannah, listen to me.'

She rolls over, her eyes screwed tightly shut, her arm up to her face against the bright light. 'Mmmmmmm?' she groans.

'We have to go.'

She cracks open one eye. 'Go where? Mars? What is it?'

I press a finger to her lips, shushing her quiet. 'Keep your voice down. It's Rufus. He's the night stalker, the guy who's been abducting all those women in Canterbury. He's been bringing them here and... and... I don't know what he's been doing to them.'

Hannah frowns and swallows, shaking her head. 'Slow down. What are you talking about? What time is it?' She pushes herself up, so she's half-sitting and half-lying.

'It's almost three in the morning,' I whisper, checking my phone. 'Listen to me. I've just seen Rufus dragging a woman into the house and—'

'What?'

'Shhhh. Keep your voice down. He had a woman. She was unconscious, but I think she's alive. He put her in a secret cellar under the hall.'

'What woman?'

'I don't know. That's not important. Come on, we need to go.'

'It's the middle of the night.'

She rubs an eye with two fingers. It makes a sickening crunching sound.

'We can't stay,' I tell her.

'Where would we go? Why don't we stay until the morning and leave first thing?'

'Are you insane? What if he comes up here and tries to kill *me?*'

'I think if he'd wanted to kill you, he'd have done it by now. You've given him enough opportunity.'

That's true, but I still don't like the idea of staying under this roof a second longer than I have to. 'Do you think I should phone the police?'

Hannah sucks in her lower lip and bites on it. 'Are you certain you saw what you think you saw? It was a definitely a woman?'

'I think so.'

'You *think* so?'

'No, I did. I'm positive.' She's making me question myself, but I didn't imagine it. There *was* a woman. She was wearing a loose blue top. Or was it green? Dark hair. No, blonde.

I'm not thinking straight. My mind's a muddled mess of panic and near hysteria.

'Do you think Carmel knows?' Hannah asks. 'Could she be part of it?'

'God, no. He sneaked out while she was asleep. Maybe he drugs her so she doesn't wake up. I don't know. I should tell her, shouldn't I?'

'Probably.' Hannah scratches her head.

'Okay, I will. As soon as I've called the police.'

I flip my phone over and unlock it. But I'm stopped from dialling by Hannah's hand, which falls lightly on top of mine.

'Are you sure about this? Are you certain what you saw? What if it's something entirely innocent? And then if the police come racing here with blue lights flashing and sirens blaring, you're going to look pretty stupid.'

I shake my head. 'Innocent? He was dragging an unconscious woman into the cellar. There can't be anything innocent about that.'

'Alright, alright.' She holds up her hands in submission. 'I still think you shouldn't do anything rash. Why don't you wait until the morning and speak to Carmel before you rush into anything?'

'What? No, I have to tell someone.' I can't believe she's suggesting I wait. I shrug her hand away.

'All I'm saying is that it's late and things might look different in the morning. Trust me. I'm your big sister, remember?'

Only by three minutes.

'But—'

'Look, if you're still sure of what you saw in a few hours, then call the police. All I'm saying is, sleep on it, okay?'

I shake my head, the sting of tears of frustration and fear looming in my unblinking eyes.

A few hours? I suppose I could wait, although I know what I saw. And if it's what I think it is, Rufus needs to be stopped. They might even be able to save that woman in the cellar.

'Try to get some sleep,' Hannah soothes, rolling over and yanking the duvet over her shoulder.

Fine. I'll give it until sunrise and then I'm calling the police, whether Hannah thinks it's a good idea or not.

Of course, I can't sleep.

Every little noise, every scratch, bump, groan, scuff, pop and bang, is Rufus creeping up to the attic to come for me. To kill me in my bed. He tried to warn me, but I wouldn't listen. And now I'm here at his mercy.

By six, the first light of a new day is chasing away the heavy darkness of the night, creeping in through the window in the ceiling. But my eyes are already wide open. Every time I tried to close them, my heart would start racing, and they'd pop open again, scanning the room. Looking for danger. Expecting to see Rufus looming over me, his head hooded. His face masked.

I haven't changed my mind. In fact, the last few long hours have convinced me I have no other choice. I need to call the police.

My arm snakes out from under the duvet, hunting for my phone, but instead finds a glass of water I'd left there from the previous night. I sit, my mouth dry, and pick it up. Thousands of tiny bubbles are clinging to the inside of the glass and the water has grown stale and tepid.

I take a sip. Swill it around my mouth and swallow it with a grimace. Then I put it back, my hand trembling, my eyes fixed on the door, not really watching what I'm doing. I feel for my phone. Use one hand to unplug it, thumbing out the lead, hurrying now I've finally come to a decision. To do the right thing. What I should have done hours ago.

The bed creaks as I sit up and somehow the phone slips through my fingers. It falls straight into my glass of water with an ominous plop.

'No, no, no,' I gasp, jumping into action in a panic.

I tease the phone out with my fingers and hold it away from the bed as water drips out of its casing.

Warily, I check the screen and let out a sigh of relief, as it's still working. The screen brightens, screaming at me that it's 6:03am. It's still so early. Not too early to call the police, though. I should have done it hours ago.

Hannah's breathing is slow and deep. I've no idea how she's managing to sleep.

I swipe at the screen, half expecting nothing to happen. To my surprise, the lock screen vanishes and my home screen appears. I pull up the keypad and dial three nines.

The call takes several seconds to connect, but eventually a ringtone warbles in my ear.

I haven't rehearsed what I'm going to say. I only hope it doesn't come across as too fantastical. They might not even believe me, I suppose. I bet they get loads of crank calls making all sorts of wild allegations, especially when there's a serial killer on the loose.

'Emergency. Which service do you require?'

The relief at hearing a friendly voice at the other end of the line is like a ray of sunshine breaking through storm clouds.

Although the way the woman's voice is distorted, gurgling as though she's underwater, is slightly disconcerting.

'Thank god,' I breathe heavily. 'Police, please. Hurry, it's urgent. There's a woman in the cellar in the house.'

How weird does that sound? Like something out of a cheap thriller.

My gaze flickers to the door again. At least if Rufus bursts in now, I've made contact with the police. They'll hear my screams and I'm sure they'll be able to locate my phone and tell where I'm calling from.

There's a worrying silence on the other end of the line.

'Hello?' I croak. 'Can you hear me?'

'Emergency, which service?' the woman repeats, her voice even more garbled.

'Hello? Hello?'

Panic surfaces from my chest like molten rock spewing from a volcano. She can't hear me.

I bang my phone with the palm of my hand. If there's water in the microphone, perhaps that will clear it.

I put it back to my ear. The woman's talking again.

'... any kind of danger and can't speak right now, make a sound using your keypad,' she's saying.

'I'm here,' I hiss. 'I can hear you. Why can't you hear me?'

I press a load of random keys, desperate to let her know that I urgently need help.

'I can't hear anything,' the woman says. She falls silent. I imagine her sitting in front of a computer screen in a room full of other people, a headset on, listening intently. Trying to establish whether the call is genuine or whether I've dialled by mistake.

'He has a woman in the cellar,' I wail. 'I think he's going to kill her. I think there may be others.' My voice trails off as despair slowly strangles the fragile flicker of optimism I'd had a moment ago.

The line clicks dead in my ear.

The woman's gone.

I drop my phone in my lap. A patch of damp seeps into the duvet.

What the hell am I going to do now?

Chapter 39

There is only one Plan B. I need to tell Carmel what I saw and hope she believes me.

Rufus must have been drugging her. How else could he possibly be getting away with what he's doing without her finding out? He told me she was a light sleeper. That's why I wasn't to make any noise at night and to be in my room by nine. But was that all lies? A way to guarantee I stayed in my room and didn't stumble across him bringing a victim back to the house in the dead of night?

I have no idea how Carmel will react when I tell her, but I have to try to make her understand. As much as I hate her, she deserves the truth. And anyway, I need to use her phone to call the police.

The alternative is to sneak out of the house on my own, walk to the village and knock on some doors to ask if I can use a phone, hoping they don't think I'm deranged.

The decision is taken out of my hands when I hear voices coming from below. Rufus and Carmel chatting. It sounds perfunctory. Like they're discussing something inconsequential. The type of conversation I've heard them exchange a dozen times since I've been here.

Warily, I peel open the bedroom door and, swallowing down my apprehension, creep to the top of the stairs to listen.

Rufus is outside their bedroom wearing a smart jacket and trousers, a crisp white shirt, and a tie. Carmel's wrapped in a silk gown, her face fully made-up.

He tells her he'll be back by five. She offers him a cheek. They exchange the briefest of kisses. And then he's off. Marching down the stairs and out of the door.

His car door thumps closed. The engine growls into life and he drives off. It's the most ordinary morning scene. Something that's probably being repeated in houses up and down the country. Except this is no ordinary couple and no ordinary house.

As far as I can tell, Rufus could well be a serial killer, abducting women and bringing them back here for... I don't know, his pleasure, I suppose. I don't want to think too hard about what he's doing with them.

Of course, I have no way of being sure what's going on, but by sheer bad luck, it looks increasingly likely that I've stumbled across a psychopath and invited myself into his home.

If I'm going to speak to Carmel, it has to be now. I can't put it off, no matter how difficult it's going to be. Where do I begin? By telling her the truth of what I saw last night, I suppose.

I wait, crouching in the shadows, until she reappears from her room, dressed. She floats across the landing and skips down the stairs.

It's now or never. I take a calming breath, swallow and follow her.

She's in the kitchen, by the kettle.

'Carmel, can I have a word?' I say, my husky voice almost unrecognisable to myself.

She turns and smiles like she doesn't have a care in the world. 'Morning, Marcella. Of course. What's wrong?' She has no idea I'm about to detonate a bomb that's going to blow up everything she thought she knew. 'Want a coffee?'

I shake my head. I have no appetite and even the thought of drinking anything makes my stomach turn.

'There's something I need to tell you,' I say, scratching at the floor with my toe. 'Something that's going to be hard to hear.'

She takes her hand off the kettle and turns to give me her full attention. 'You're not thinking about leaving again, are you? We talked about that.'

'No, it's not that. It's about Rufus.'

'Oh?' She crosses her arms over her chest, eyebrows raised.

'I heard him last night.' I glance up. She's watching me attentively. 'He went out when you were asleep. In his car.'

Carmel frowns and her lips curl as if she's suppressing the urge to smile. As if she thinks it might be a wind up.

I carry on, undeterred. It's inevitable she's not going to believe me. Not at first, anyway.

'I don't know where he went, but he came back a few hours later.' I hesitate, playing with the words in my head. Reordering them. Reframing them. Trying to make what I have to say less blunt. 'And when he came home, he had a woman with him.'

Carmel's eyes open wide with shock. 'He what?'

'She was unconscious. He was dragging her. I think he might have abducted her and I think he's done it before.'

There. I've said it. It's out there.

'What on earth are you talking about, Marcella?' She shakes her head and smirks.

'I'm sorry. I know it sounds unbelievable.'

'Is this your idea of a joke? Because I don't find it very funny.'

'It's not a joke.' The pressure of the emotion builds in my throat like an expanding balloon. 'I think Rufus might be responsible for all the women who've gone missing in Canterbury recently.'

She stares at me as a treacly silence falls between us. Her eyes narrow until they're nothing more than slits. Her body is as still as an ice carving.

'Don't be so ridiculous,' she hisses.

'I watched him drag her inside. I know what I saw.'

'Oh, really?' she says, anger brewing. 'And where is she now then? This woman he *dragged* into the house?'

'I know it sounds crazy, and I didn't expect you to believe me but...'

'Why are you doing this?'

'What?'

'Why are you saying these things? We trusted you when we invited you into our home and you repay us by spouting nonsense like this? Why? Do you get off on it? Does it give you a thrill?'

'No!'

'Then what? I can't think of any other reason you'd say such spiteful, hurtful things.'

'Carmel, please—'

'No,' she fumes, springing forwards and jabbing a finger at me. 'Let's get a few things straight, young lady. While you're staying under our roof, you don't get the right to cause trouble. And if this is some pathetic attempt to get attention or to drive a wedge between Rufus and me, you're going about it all the wrong way.' She hesitates, straightening her back, blinking as if she's just been struck by the truth.

'Oh, my god. That's it, isn't it? You have a crush on him. God, he's old enough to be your father, you silly girl. You might be young and pretty, but do you honestly think he'd leave me for you? By coming up with this bullshit?'

'It's not bullshit! I'm telling you what I saw.'

'It's pathetic.'

'You have to believe me. We need to call the police. I tried last night but my phone...'

Carmel glowers at me.

'I dropped my phone in a glass of water.'

'I'm disappointed,' Carmel continues, lowering her voice. It's almost worse than when she was shouting.

My mind rolls over and over. I have to convince her I'm not making it up.

'I can show you.'

'Show me what?'

'I can show you where he took her. He's built a secret cellar under the hall.'

'Marcella!'

'Come on.' I turn on my heel and hurry out of the kitchen, along the hall, and skid to a halt where the rug has been put back in place.

I glance around, looking for the switch I know is here somewhere. Rufus was out of sight when he opened the hatch, but he didn't go far. There's a painting on the wall. Something colourful and abstract. A slash of oil splatters across a large canvas. It's not unattractive, although it's not to my taste. I bet it's massively expensive.

I'd not noticed before, but it's hanging slightly off the wall, and there's a small gap behind it, just big enough for a hand. Carmel stands in the kitchen doorway, glaring at me.

'Well?'

There's nowhere else the switch could be. I tease my hand behind the painting, careful not to knock it off, and feel along the wall with my fingers. They brush through a dusty cobweb as they sweep up and down. I'm sure it's here. It has to be.

And then I find it. A plastic rocker switch. I press it and jump back, waiting to see what happens. An electric hum begins almost instantly.

My heart skitters.

At first, nothing happens. Just the low drone of an electric motor.

Carmel leans against the doorframe and crosses her arms over her chest, watching me with a look of bemusement.

The rug twitches, and I yank it out of the way. Beneath it, a hole is opening up in the floor. A slab of tiles folds back under itself. A set of steps emerges, winding down into the darkness.

I glance at Carmel and we stare at each other in disbelief.

'Did you know this was here?' I ask.

Carmel slowly pushes herself off the doorframe and stands up straight, studying the emerging opening with incredulity. Jaw slack. Eyes wide. She shakes her head.

'This is where he took her,' I say, with a quiver in my voice. For all I know, she's still down there.

The electrical buzzing stops, the hatch wide open. Cool air drifts up from below. But that's not what makes the hairs on the back of my arms lift. It's the sound. Something moving. A groan. A grunt.

Carmel paces towards me, her gaze fixed on the hole in the floor.

'I... I had no idea,' she stammers.

Thankfully, the torch on my phone is still working. I flick it on and angle it down the steps into the darkness, fearful of what I'm going to find. But I can't see anything beyond the bottom of the steps and a few inches of a smooth concrete floor.

All the colour has drained from Carmel's face.

I swallow a lump in my throat. The last thing I want to do is to go down there, but I know I have to do it. If that woman is here, she needs our help. I need to set her free.

'Call the police,' I mumble.

But Carmel continues to stare at me in shock.

'Carmel!' I snap. She jumps. 'Call the police.'

'What? We don't know what's down there.'

For pity's sake. My feet are as heavy as lumps of lead as I make my way down and eventually get a better view of the hidden room.

It's a much bigger space than the wine cellar. About the size of my old flat. A concrete bunker with nothing in it apart from a chair, and on it, the blonde woman I saw Rufus dragging into the house last night.

Her hands are bound behind her back, her feet tied to the chair legs, and she has a gag in her mouth. As I point the torch at her, she squints and turns her head away, revealing a horrible purple bruise on her forehead and a trail of blood down one cheek.

She tries to speak. To shout. Rocking the chair back and forth in a panic.

'It's okay,' I soothe, rushing to her. 'You're okay now. I'm here. We're going to get you out.'

But she doesn't calm down. Her bloodshot eyes are wide with fear and she continues to rattle the chair back and forth, trying to free her arms.

Behind me, I can hear Carmel's heavy breath. Now she has to believe me.

'Carmel, call the pol—'

But as I turn my head, my fingers working at the ropes around the woman's wrists and ankles, my words are cut short.

Carmel's looming over me. Her face twisted. Her arms raised.

She has something in her hands.

I can't make out what it is before it comes crashing down on my head.

There's a lightning bolt of pain.

And then nothing.

Chapter 40

Oh my god, my head.

It's throbbing like a sledgehammer pounding against solid steel while the muscles in my neck twinge stiffly with the rip of whiplash. I roll my chin off my chest and grind my teeth against the searing pain.

Where am I?

I try to lift a hand to check my skull for damage, but my arm won't move. I can work my fingers and my wrist, but my arm's strapped down. My other one too. And my legs.

What the hell?

I force my eyes open, but there's not a single speck of light. Panic blooms in my chest. I'm in complete, thick, crushing darkness.

And then it comes back to me in a blinding flash.

The blonde woman in the cellar. The angry bruise on her forehead. Hair matted, face bloodied, bound and gagged in a secret cellar. Carmel following me down the stairs. Turning to see her standing over me, a weapon in her hand.

She did this to me. She attacked me.

Did she know all along that woman was down here? Did she know what Rufus was doing and has been turning a blind eye all this time?

I'm so confused.

I'd scream if I could, even though I know it's useless. I'm in a concrete bunker below a house in the middle of the countryside with no neighbours around for miles. The chances of anyone hearing me and coming to my rescue would be as good as none, even if there wasn't something wet and soft in my mouth. Material of some kind. A cloth? A sock? Wedged between my teeth. Stopping me from making a sound. Forcing me to breathe through my nose. It's tied around the back of my head, so I can't even spit it out.

I'm going to suffocate.

My breathing becomes faster and more laboured as I snort desperately through my nostrils, unable to draw in enough air. My head spins.

Carmel's done this. She's tied me up, gagged me and left me here.

Is she coming back? Is she going to kill me?

And where's the blonde woman who was here before? Is she still down here?

With every last gram of my willpower, I force myself to stop panicking. To slow my breathing. And to listen.

If she's still in the cellar, I'll be able to hear her, even if I can't speak to her.

Listen.

But there's no sound at all. Only the rapid thread of my own pulse and the air hissing through my nostrils.

This is hopeless. I'm as good as dead.

Why didn't I just get the hell out of here last night when I had the chance?

Hot, desperate tears of self-pity flow down my cheeks. What have I done to deserve this?

I should never have come after Carmel. She almost destroyed my family before, and now she's going to finish the job.

I have absolutely no idea what time of the day or night it is, or how long I've been unconscious. All I know is that I can't stay here. It'll drive me insane, if they don't kill me first. But I can't see any way of escaping.

I have only limited movement in the chair, and although I can rock it back and forth by shifting my weight, what good is that going to do? I might even end up toppling over and banging my head again. And, although the thought of knocking myself out is appealing, I can't take the risk. I have to stay alert and wait for an opportunity.

Surely Carmel or Rufus will come for me soon, and if I can talk to them, maybe I can blag my way out of this mess.

Seconds pass like minutes. Minutes pass like hours. My arms and shoulders ache. My head hurts. My mouth's dry and the darkness is a malevolent vice, slowly throttling my will to stay alive.

I drift in and out of sleep. Each time I doze off, I jar myself awake as my chin falls onto my chest and rolls around my shoulders, stretching the muscles painfully.

I have no idea how long I've been trapped down here when I hear the buzz of the electric motor and a thin finger of light opens up in the ceiling above. It's so bright, I have to squint.

Through narrow slits, I see a pair of legs descending the stairs.

The smell of Rufus's aftershave, a hint of citrus and bergamot, gives him away.

He approaches me like I'm a wounded animal, liable to lash out and bite. He keeps his distance, circling me, his lips pressed tightly together.

'Why did you have to go poking your nose around in things that aren't your concern?' he says, shaking his head.

I watch him warily. He's not the man I thought he was. He's far more dangerous. I guess appearances really can be deceptive. I didn't have the faintest clue what he was really like. Not even an inkling.

'And now see the trouble you've caused? Carmel is furious.'

I'm not sure who she's furious with. Me for catching him? Or Rufus for getting caught?

'Why didn't you go when I told you?' He stops pacing and stands directly in front of me. 'I warned you, didn't I? I gave you plenty of opportunity and you ignored me. Thought you knew better.'

I snort, keeping my gaze directed at him. I have no idea what he's planning to do with me. He's not carrying a knife or any kind of weapon that I can see, so maybe he's just here to talk. And if he removes the gag, perhaps there's a chance I can persuade him to let me go. I'll promise him anything. That I won't go to the police. That I won't tell a soul.

He lowers himself onto his haunches and draws a slow, languorous circle on my knee with his finger. It makes my stomach tighten and my skin prickle.

'I didn't want you drawn into any of this,' he says, screwing up his face in disgust. 'I care about you, Marcella. I thought we had something.'

I try to speak, but my voice gets swallowed in the gag, and the only sound that comes out is a distressed gurgle.

He shushes me quiet like I'm a toddler on the verge of a tantrum. I plead with my eyes, fluttering my lashes and making them as large and doe-like as possible.

'You want to beg me to let you go, don't you?' he says with a sympathetic smile.

I shake my head. It's a mistake. A blaze of pain strikes behind my eyes like a thousand nails being fired inside my skull. I throw my body forwards and back, rocking the chair in frustration.

'Hey, stop that.' Rufus scowls and casts a furtive glance over his shoulder. 'She'll hear us.'

Has he promised Carmel not to come down here to see me? It gives me a glimmer of hope and I cling to it tightly. It's something, at least. If he's willing to go behind Carmel's back, then maybe he still feels something for me.

I stop rocking and use my eyes again, begging him to remove the gag.

'Look, I only popped down here to check on you. Don't make a fuss,' he says.

I nod, hoping to convey my compliance. I let my head drop, my chin falling to my chest, dejected.

'Alright,' he says in a low whisper. 'I'll take it out, but you have to promise you won't scream. If Carmel hears you, she'll kill us both.'

I nod again, my eyes wide.

'Okay, I'm trusting you.' He reaches around the back of my head, his fingers working at the knot. He yanks the gag out of my mouth and relief floods my body as I cough and splutter, taking deep lungfuls of air.

'Thank you,' I gasp, my throat sore and my voice weak.

'Are you thirsty? Hungry?'

'I could use some water.'

'I'll bring you some.'

'Thank you.' I force a smile and make it reach my eyes.

'I never wanted this to happen. You know that, right? This was your doing.'

I nod again. He's totally delusional, but arguing with him while I'm tied up at his mercy isn't going to help.

'Where's the woman?' I ask, rotating my head, looking around the cellar now there's some light coming from above and my eyes have adjusted to it. There's no one else here, just as I thought.

His Adam's apple bobs as he swallows. He looks away. 'What woman?'

'What have you done with her?' I try to keep my voice level, even though I'm trembling with fear and not really sure I want to know the answer.

'Why? What does it matter?'

'Is she dead?'

He stands suddenly, his body rigid. He sniffs and wipes his nose with the back of his hand.

His whole demeanour has changed in the beat of a hummingbird's wing.

'You don't need to worry about her,' he snaps.

'Where did you find her?'

He turns from me and marches away, into a dark corner of the room, scuffing his feet on the bare concrete floor.

'Marcella, don't,' he warns me.

'Did you drive into Canterbury and take her?' I ask. 'How many others have there been?'

'You don't understand. You don't know what you're talking about.'

'Where are the others? Are they dead?'

'Stop it.'

'You know they'll catch you in the end? They always do.'

'They have no idea,' he says, striding back towards me.

'How do you do it? Do you talk to them? Win their trust first? Or do you grab them from behind when they least expect it?'

'Does it matter?' he says, frowning. 'And why do you care?'

'Do you get a thrill out of it? Does it turn you on, knowing they're completely powerless?' I ask.

I've gone too far. He launches himself at me and snatches my face, his fingers digging into my chin. His face is so close that when he speaks, droplets of spittle fly onto my cheek and into my eye.

'Shut your mouth,' he says. 'Just shut your dirty fucking mouth.'

I hold his gaze, even though he's so close he's an out-of-focus blur. But I refuse to be cowed.

'I didn't ask for this,' he continues. 'This isn't what I wanted. This isn't who I am.'

He releases my jaw, snapping my head painfully backwards.

'Then who are you, Rufus?'

He throws his arms up in despair, tears wetting his eyes. 'I don't know, but I never asked for any of this.'

'Then stop. Go to the police and tell them what you've done.'

He laughs cruelly. 'The police? Are you insane? Do you have any idea what they'd do to me? I'd lose everything I've worked so hard for.'

He is delusional.

'They can help you,' I suggest, softening my tone. 'And no one else has to get hurt.'

'They can't help me.'

'I get it. The voices. They tell you to do things, don't they? Things you wouldn't normally dream of doing.'

Hannah told me about it once, how the voices in her head were so mean to her all the time, always telling her how worthless she was. How it had started as random noises, like someone running across the roof, and that over time, the noises became more human. Like a bully sitting on her shoulder, commenting on everything she did, encouraging her to do things. To start the fire in that block of flats.

'Voices?' Rufus scowls. 'What voices?'

'It's nothing to be ashamed of. It's something that happens to lots of people.'

Things are starting to make sense. Maybe Rufus was one of Carmel's patients. I suppose it's possible she was treating him or encountered him during a court case. But if that's true, she's not done a great job on managing his condition or his auditory hallucinations, as I learnt they're called. In fact, I wonder if he's being treated at all.

'I don't hear voices,' Rufus says.

Well, they often say that.

'What are you going to do to me?' I ask. 'Let me go. I won't tell anyone.'

'It's too late for that. I gave you the chance to run, and you came back. You only have yourself to blame.'

'So you're going to kill me?'

He sighs. 'I have to go. I'll bring you some water later.'

'Tell me,' I demand. 'What happens next?'

He grabs the gag from the floor and tries to force it into my mouth. But I twist my head and clamp my mouth shut, squealing as he snatches my head in his powerful hand.

'Don't make this any more difficult,' he hisses in my ear.

'I don't want to die,' I wail.

He doesn't stop. He continues to wrestle with my head, straddling me.

'Keep still,' he demands.

'I love you, Rufus. I want to be with you.'

'It's too late for that,' he growls.

I pull my head backwards, slipping out of his grasp. I have one last card to play.

'Don't hurt me, please,' I cry. 'I'm pregnant, Rufus. I'm having your baby.'

Chapter 41

My words are like a magic spell that causes Rufus to freeze on the spot. He stops trying to fight me and stares into my eyes as if he's not sure he's heard me correctly.

'Pregnant?'

'With your baby,' I repeat.

'B... but how?'

I raise an eyebrow.

'But there was only that one time.'

'Once is all it takes.'

Rufus backs away from me, his face contorted in confusion and shock.

Then his brows knit together in a concerned frown. 'How can you be sure? Have you taken a test?' he asks breathlessly.

'No, but a woman knows these things. I'm carrying your child. There's no doubt about it.'

Rufus chews on his lip, uncertain. He has to believe me or I'll never get out of here alive.

'I... I can't believe it.'

'Wonderful, isn't it?'

He puts a hand to his mouth as he starts to cry, his shoulders rising and falling in a torrent of emotion.

I can't believe he's actually falling for it. What is it with some men? They're so gullible.

'I've always wanted to be a father,' he mumbles.

'I know. And now we can be a family. Just the three of us.'

His tears subside and his smile grows as wide as the Forth Road Bridge. 'I can't believe it,' he repeats.

'What do you think we're having? A girl or a boy?'

'Oh, I don't know. I don't mind, do you?' He rushes over to me and rests the flat of his hand on my belly, which is most definitely not swelling.

'I'd like a little girl,' I say. 'And call her Rose.'

'Rose? No, I don't think so.' His face darkens.

'Or whatever you want to call her,' I add rapidly.

'I've always liked Juliet.'

'Juliet it is then,' I say, working a smile. Trying to convince him I'm as happy as he is.

But then he springs away from me, retreating towards the stairs with a flicker of concern rippling across his face. 'What about Carmel?' he gasps. 'What am I going to tell her?'

'It's time for the truth, Rufus. Tell her you're leaving her and that we're going to be together.'

'But I can't.' His broad smile has vanished, and a look of sheer terror takes its place.

'Of course we can. We'll tell her we're in love!'

'You can't let her know you're pregnant,' he says. 'It'll kill her.'

'We'll have to tell her at some point.'

He shakes his head. 'No. We can't.'

I'm not going to argue with him, especially over a phantom baby, but it's pathetic the hold she has over him. He needs to grow some balls and learn to stand up to her.

'Untie me.'

Rufus is looking off into the distance, lost momentarily in his own thoughts. It's almost as if he's forgotten I'm here.

His attention snaps back to me. 'What? No, I can't. Not yet.'

'Rufus, please.'

'I'm sorry. I can't let you go.'

'You can't keep me here,' I say, my panic rising again. I ball my hands into tight fists, struggling against the coarse rope binding my arms to the chair. 'Not in my condition. You wouldn't want anything to happen to the baby, would you?'

But he's in a world of his own. Lost in his own panic. He doesn't hear a word I say.

'Rufus? Listen to me,' I beg. 'Untie me and let me go.'

'She's going to kill me. She's going to kill me,' he repeats over and over to himself.

'Please, let me go,' I wail.

But he's already heading for the stairs, his back to me, shoulders hunched. Head down.

'Rufus!' I yell in anger and frustration. I don't care whether Carmel hears me or not. I can't spend another minute in this windowless cell, tied to a chair, not knowing what's going to happen next.

I watch helplessly as his body and then his legs disappear out of view. I hear a click and a buzz. The hatch slowly slides closed and the light coming from above dims.

He's actually leaving me. He thinks I'm pregnant with his child and he's abandoning me.

Bastard.

At least he's forgotten to put the gag back in my mouth.

I open my mouth, fill my lungs and let out a blood-curdling scream.

Chapter 42

I took a risk telling Rufus I was pregnant, but it's completely backfired. I thought it would be a sure-fire way of winning him around, to convince him to let me go, but what if he confesses to Carmel? Instead of saving myself, I may have sped up my execution.

My only option now is to find a way out of here. If I could loosen the ropes around my wrists, then maybe I could free myself and work out a way of opening the hatch. It's my only hope. I don't want to die. I'm too young. And I'm scared.

'What are you doing down here?'

'Not now, Hannah. I'm kind of busy.' I rotate my wrists, clenching my fists, trying to work the ropes loose. But they're coarse and tied tightly. They cut into my skin and won't budge. In fact, the more I struggle, the tighter they become.

'It's so dark,' she says. I can tell from her voice that she's circling me. Watching me suffer and judging me for being so stupid. For trusting Carmel when I should have made a run for it and for not raising the alarm when I saw Rufus dragging that woman into the house. Even though *she* told me not to!

'Yes, I had noticed. Why don't you make yourself useful and help me?'

'You know I would,' she says. She's directly behind me now. 'But I wouldn't want to break a nail.'

'Fat lot of use you are.'

'Don't be like that.'

She's irritating me now. Always the smartarse with the wisecrack. I could do without it, unless she's going to help. 'You know this is all your fault.'

'Don't blame me,' she says. Now she's leaning over my shoulder, whispering into my ear, thin strands of her hair tickling my cheek. 'I didn't ask you to come here.'

'You didn't try to stop me, either. I was doing it for you, remember? But I wonder now why I bothered.'

'I told you, you should have killed Carmel while you had the chance.'

'Hannah, will you just shut up! Please!' My voice echoes off the walls and reverberates around the empty cellar. 'I need to concentrate.'

A sharp needle of pain draws my attention back to my arms. A trickle of something warm and wet rolls across my wrist. It's no good. I was hoping I could pull my hands free, but the ropes aren't giving a millimetre. And they're cutting my skin to shreds. I should have known. Rufus has clearly had a lot of practice tying secure knots.

How many other women have there been, bound and gagged in this chair? The news was reporting seven, or was it eight, women had gone missing in recent months. Was Rufus responsible for abducting them all? And was this where he brought them? Where he killed them?

I'm so thirsty, my tongue's swollen and sticks to the roof of my mouth. As much as I don't want to see Rufus again, I could really do with something to drink. I keep thinking about ice-chilled glasses of water. A can of Coke, so cold there's condensation running down it. Running cold water taps with a never-ending supply of liquid. Fountains. Waterfalls. I'm already light-headed and weak. If I don't drink something soon, I'm not going to have the energy to keep fighting. And I don't want to give up. I'm not a quitter. I'm not going to let them get away with killing me.

But as time ebbs away, weakness takes its toll. My mind plays tricks on me. At one point, I'm convinced I hear my mother calling my name. That she's upstairs, looking for me, sneaking around and wondering where I've gone. And then there's the scratching and the snuffling. Furry creatures prowling around the cellar, sniffing out food. Around my feet. Up my legs.

I squeal in terror, shaking my legs. Rattling the chair. Almost toppling over.

But there's nothing there.

I'm still alone.

And I wonder if this was Rufus and Carmel's plan all along. Did I willingly fly into their web when I invited myself to stay? Were they always planning to abandon me here in this cellar to die? A long, drawn-out suffering. Letting my body slowly shut down through a lack of food and water.

What a cruel way to go. A horrible place to meet my end. Just me and my thoughts. My body growing weaker. All hope evaporating.

Will they leave me here to rot? Will my body shrivel up and gradually decay until there's nothing left but bones and teeth?

I shudder. I can't fight it. So what's the point prolonging the agony?

And then, as I'm on the verge of giving up entirely, a strip of light opens up in the ceiling. The electric motor buzzes.

I lift my head, cannonball-heavy, and squint to see who's coming. Maybe Rufus has remembered to bring me that water he promised. Or maybe they've come to kill me.

Footsteps tap down the steps.

Rufus comes into focus through the blur of my tired eyes. There's another figure behind him. Carmel?

'What's going on? Did you bring me some water?'

He doesn't say anything as he draws closer. He has something in his hand. Through the narrow slits of my eyes, I watch as he lifts it to my mouth.

'Drink,' he says. 'It'll make you feel better.'

I drink so eagerly from the plastic bottle that it spills down my chin and drips over my chest. It's so cold it burns my throat, but it tastes so good.

'Take it easy,' Rufus warns.

I hate him for what he's done, but in that moment, I'm so grateful I could hug him.

When the bottle's empty, he wipes my mouth tenderly with a handkerchief.

'Thank you,' I croak.

'How are you feeling?'

I blink several times as my eyes slowly adjust to the light. Rufus is standing in front of me with a worried expression on his face and his hands on his hips.

'How do you think I fucking feel?' I spit.

Carmel steps out of his shadow. I fix her with a hard stare.

'You knew what he was doing,' I hiss.

'Of course I knew.' She shrugs.

'And you don't care?'

She laughs with mocking glee. 'You have no idea.'

'So why don't you tell me?'

'In good time. Untie her,' she instructs Rufus, pointing a vicious-looking carving knife at me. 'And don't try anything stupid.'

Rufus drops to his knees and works at the knots around my ankles first. And then my wrists. The relief at being free, of finally being able to stretch my legs out, is almost as satisfying as the water.

'Get up,' Rufus grunts.

I try to stand, but my legs are weak and I stumble, losing my balance. My stomach flips and I'm almost sick.

Carmel stands back, watching me warily.

'Where are you taking me?' I ask.

Rufus pulls me roughly back to my feet and guides me towards the stairs. Pushing me. Forcing me forwards.

Is this it? Are they taking me somewhere to kill me?

'Please,' I wail. 'I don't want to die.'

'Stop your whining,' Carmel shouts, 'and do as you're told.'

I dig my feet into the ground, using every ounce of energy I have left to resist climbing the steps. I've spent the last few hours desperate to get out of the cellar, but now I'd give anything to stay. It has to be better than what's waiting for me up above.

'Please, Marcella,' Rufus says. 'You're only making things harder for yourself.'

'What about our baby?' I gasp, my free hand shooting towards my stomach. I rub and cradle it like I've seen the pregnant women around the hospital doing, as if they're showing off about how fertile they are. As if anyone cares.

Rufus freezes. He looks at his wife, aghast. Eyes wide. So maybe he hasn't told her about us after all.

She stares back at him in disbelief, her eyebrows shooting up.

'Didn't you tell her?' I turn my gaze to Carmel with a smug grin. 'I'm pregnant with your husband's baby.'

The shock on Carmel's face is priceless, but it doesn't last long. Her lips turn up in a wicked grin that could sour milk.

'Is that right?'

'Didn't he have the balls to tell you? We've been sleeping together behind your back from the day I moved in.'

'Pathetic.'

'Rufus loves me. And I love him.'

Carmel throws her head back and laughs so loudly, Rufus and I both start. 'In love? Oh, come on.'

Rufus glances at the ground and shuffles his feet awkwardly.

'Oh,' she says. 'So it's true? You *have* been shagging our house guest behind my back, after all?'

'Carmel—'

'Save it,' she snaps. 'We'll talk about this later.'

'It's not what—'

'Not now, Rufus.' She glowers at him. 'You know, you really are pathetic.'

'Don't speak to him like that,' I say.

'He's my husband. I'll speak to him how I damn well like. And as for you, I should have known. Coming here, dressing like a tart and throwing yourself at Rufus. Don't you have any shame?'

My cheeks burn. 'It wasn't like that.'

Carmel raises the knife, pointing the tip at my face, and steps closer. 'And even if you did throw yourself at him, there's no way you could know if you're pregnant,' she says, casting a sideways glance at Rufus.

'I'm having his baby,' I repeat.

She shakes her head. 'Nice try, but I don't think so.'

'You've never had children. You wouldn't know what it feels like to have a baby growing inside you.'

Even in the faint light coming from above, the reddening of Carmel's face is apparent. Her features twist in fury, her nostrils flaring and deep lines furrowing her brow. I've touched a raw nerve.

309

'Shut up, you stupid little girl,' she screams, her voice deafening in the confines of the concrete cellar. 'How dare you!'

'He's leaving you, Carmel,' I say, struggling to keep my composure. 'We're going to be a family.'

'Is that right?'

'Tell her, Rufus. Tell her what we've been planning.'

He finally glances up and stares at me blankly. 'I don't know what you're talking about.'

'Rufus! Don't say that. We talked about this. She doesn't control you. We can leave whenever we like.'

He shakes his head, a sadness in his eyes. 'I'm sorry, Marcella.'

'Rufus—'

'I've heard enough of this,' Carmel says. 'Let's get on with it. Get her out of here.'

'But wait—'

Rufus snatches my wrist and I howl in agony. I try to pull away, but he has me firmly in his grip.

'You're hurting me,' I scream.

But he doesn't care. He tugs me roughly, snapping my head back. And then he bends over and picks me up, tossing me over his shoulder like I'm a sack of broken promises.

I struggle, but he's much stronger than me and as he starts for the stairs, bumping me on his shoulders, I give up the fight and accept my fate.

If Rufus won't help me to escape, what hope do I have?

Chapter 43

The ride, slung across Rufus's shoulders, is bony and uncomfortable. Plus, he's gripping my wrist and ankle so tightly I can feel them swelling.

There's no point fighting him because Carmel's following us, her mean eyes watching me carefully, knife in hand. Even if I managed to free myself from his grasp, I'd still have to overpower her while somehow not getting stabbed. All I can hope for is that an opportunity will present itself, a moment when they're both distracted and I can run. For now, all I can do is wait and see where they're taking me.

Rufus almost bangs my head on the ceiling as he climbs the steps up into the house. He grunts as he manhandles me along the hall towards the front door, his feet scuffing along the floor under my weight.

It's dark outside, but since I've been locked in the cellar, I've lost all sense of time and I have no idea how late it is. Or even what day it is. Rufus carries me past the cars at the bottom of the drive and into the woods along the illuminated footpath.

Finally, my tears come, bubbling up from my chest and catching in my throat. Hot, fierce tears of fear and regret that wrack my body. If they're going to kill me, I wish they'd get on and do it. Prolonging it only makes it worse. It's not cold, but I'm shivering. My mind blank. Numb.

I watch the bark kick up as Rufus lumbers onwards. Will I ever see a tree again? The sky? The moon and the stars? Feel the rain on my face? Soft sand beneath my feet? This could be my final journey. My last few minutes on this earth.

Rufus slows up. His shirt is damp with sweat and he trembles with the exertion as his breathing becomes heavier and heavier. Eventually, he jerks me off his shoulders and sets me down.

He arches his back, stretching his muscles. For an instant, I think about running. It's the slightest glimmer of a chance to get away, and I might not get another.

I glance around. Back down the path? Or should I dive into the woods and hope to lose them in the gloom?

But I'm not wearing shoes, and more to the point, Carmel has her beady eyes fixed on me.

'Don't even think about it,' she warns me, as if reading my mind.

'Listen to me, Carmel. Nobody needs to know you were involved in any of this,' I say. 'I'll tell them Rufus was acting behind your back and that you had no idea what he was doing. I'll back you up, I promise.'

'Keep your mouth shut. I don't want to hear another word.' She raises the knife to emphasise her point.

'Give me a minute,' Rufus moans, rubbing the back of his neck. 'She's heavier than she looks.'

'She can walk the rest of the way. Go on, start moving,' Carmel says, urging me on.

'Where are we going?' It's a question to which I fear I already know the answer. This is the path that leads to that door in the rock. I guess I'm finally going to find out what's behind it.

'Just walk,' Carmel hisses.

The bark is soft, but now and then a sharp edge or a stone digs into the soft skin on the soles of my feet. I wince with pain each time but don't dare to stop moving until we emerge into the clearing and Rufus pushes ahead.

He marches straight up to the door and presses a few buttons on the electronic keypad. The door clicks and he shoulders it open with a grunt.

At first, I can't see anything inside, until he steps in and automatic strip lights along the ceiling flicker and blink into life.

Carmel's hand on my shoulder encourages me to follow. I have no choice but to do what she says, shuffling reluctantly into a bare concrete hall that's about ten degrees cooler than outside. The door thuds shut behind us. A bolt snaps into place. And a shiver of fear snakes down my spine. We're sealed in and without the door code, there's no way of escaping.

Rufus hurries ahead and punches a set of numbers into another keypad on a second solid metal door. It opens with an eerie creak.

'Get in,' Carmel orders, the tip of her knife digging into my back.

I stumble into a cavernous room, my blood turning to ice.

'What the hell is this place?' My voice quivers.

It's a small, circular room with a domed roof and, in the middle, a white-tiled floor which slopes gradually down towards a drain. Directly above it, a long chain with a gruesome-looking hook hangs from the ceiling. All around the edge of the room, there are rows of metal shelves groaning with grisly looking tools. Pliers. Wrenches. Scalpels. Hooks. Handcuffs. Drills.

In between the shelving units, a number of cameras are mounted on tripods, all aimed towards the hook, swinging gently from side to side.

My legs buckle and I fall to my knees.

It's not where they bring the dead bodies. It's a torture chamber. A sadist's workshop filled with the tools of his trade. It's where Rufus brings his victims to kill them.

314

Chapter 44

'Please, no,' I sob. 'Don't do this.'

'Shut up.' Carmel slaps me hard across the face with the back of her hand.

Her knuckles catch the top of my cheek with a sharp crack and a blistering sting, which sends me sprawling across the floor and silences my cries.

She snatches my hair and pulls me up. I cry out in agony, despair flooding my soul. There's no way out of this. I'm not only going to die, but it's going to be a long, horrible, painful death.

'If you're going to kill me, just do it,' I beg.

'Get her ready,' Carmel orders. 'I'll set up the cameras.'

As she releases my hair, she punches the back of my head, sending me stumbling towards Rufus. He catches me in his arms. I lift my face and our eyes meet.

'Rufus,' I moan. 'Help me.'

He looks sad. Not like a monster at all. He looks as though he doesn't want to be here any more than I do, but it must be my imagination. He's the one who's brought me here, just as he must have brought all those women before me.

'I'm sorry,' he whispers. 'There's nothing I can do.'

From the corner of my eye, I spot Carmel disappearing into a side room. When she turns on a light inside, she's illuminated through a window which overlooks the main chamber. She moves around, checking equipment. Flicking switches and dials.

Rufus snaps a pair of handcuffs on my wrists and yanks me into the middle of the room and stands me directly over the drain. It doesn't take a genius to work out why it's there, nor what kind of bodily fluids it's intended to carry away.

A lump in my throat is so bulbous and solid, it's hard to swallow.

Ignoring my howl of terror, Rufus attaches the handcuffs to the hook hanging from the ceiling so my arms are lifted high above my head. Then he scurries across the room to a winch handle on the wall. Starts turning it. The chain rattles and clanks and my hands are pulled higher, rotating my shoulders painfully, stretching me and lifting me until I can barely touch the ground with my toes and my arms feel as though they're being pulled out of their sockets.

I scream. I can't keep my feet on the ground and as all my weight passes through my wrists and arms, an uncomfortable and persistent ache grows across my shoulders and the back of my neck.

Every time I think my feet have a toehold, steadying my body and stopping it swinging uncontrollably, I lose grip and I'm sent spinning wildly around in circles again.

I wish they'd just put me out of my misery.

Bright lights blaze on, blinding me. Warming my skin with their heat, like standing in front of a radiator. I squeeze my eyes shut, and when I blink them open again, I discover the source is a bank of lights suspended from the ceiling, all aimed at me.

Rufus grabs me by my arms, steadying me, as my momentum threatens to swing me through a complete three-hundred-and-sixty-degree pirouette.

'I can't touch the floor,' I gasp in a panic.

He shushes me quiet. 'Try to keep calm.'

'What are you going to do to me?'

The muscle fibres in my upper arm are a symphony of agony, each note a shriek of torment, while my wrists feel like they're being slowly torn away from my hands.

'Keep your voice down. Carmel can hear every word,' he whispers in my ear.

'Please, let me down. I don't want to die.'

'The more you struggle, the more painful it's going to be.' He raises his voice as he steps away, heading towards one of the shelving units.

'Is this where you brought all the women?' I gasp.

Rufus picks up a terrifying-looking hunting knife with a long blade and deep serrations. He runs his thumb along the steel, as if testing its sharpness. He glances at me and puts the knife down.

'Yes,' he says matter-of-factly.

'You sick fuck.'

He winces.

'Why?'

He shrugs. 'You wouldn't understand.'

'Well, I'm not going anywhere. I'm all ears.'

If I can keep him talking, maybe I can delay the inevitable.

He picks up a mallet with a heavy, black head that looks as if it could smash my kneecap to a thousand pieces with one blow. I shudder, but I refuse to cry again. I'm not going to give him the satisfaction of tears or begging, because I bet that's what he really gets off on. The power and the control.

He swings the mallet into his palm as if he's testing its weight. Imagining what it would be like using it on me. The damage it could do. The pain it could inflict.

I swing around again, momentarily losing sight of him. When he comes back into view, he's walking towards me with the mallet hanging menacingly by his leg.

I shake my head. 'Please, no. Don't do it.'

He puts his face up against mine, nose to nose. I recoil, turning my head away and shutting my eyes.

'I'm not a monster, you know.' He speaks quietly, as if he's afraid Carmel might hear.

My eyes flick open. 'You are the definition of a monster. You abduct innocent women. You torture them. And you kill them.' Bile rises from my stomach and scorches my throat. I spit in his face.

He steps back. Looks down at his feet as he wipes his face and I twirl around again.

'I never wanted this,' he says, sadly. 'I only ever did it to keep Carmel happy.'

'Carmel?'

'This was all her idea,' he says. 'I had no choice.'

'Are you kidding? You expect me to believe you've been abducting, torturing and killing women on Carmel's orders?'

'Yes.'

I laugh. Rufus grimaces, wounded that I find his pathetic excuse laughable. 'At least have the balls to admit what you are.'

'I don't deny I've been weak. I should have stood up to her. Told her no. But she can be persuasive. You know what she's like. And despite what you think, I do love her. At least, I did. Before I met you.'

I stare at him open-mouthed. As if this whole fucked up situation couldn't get any more fucked up.

'Bollocks.'

'Marcella, it's true.'

'If you love me, then prove it. Let me go.'

'She'd kill me. She'd kill us both,' he says. 'You don't know what she's capable of.'

'So you'd rather let me die?'

He sighs. 'No, of course not.'

He twirls the mallet around in his hands. Toying with it. In the beat of a percussionist's drum, he could kill me. He could crack my skull and crush my brain. It would be over before I even knew it. Maybe that wouldn't be such a bad idea.

'What about your baby? *Our* baby? Are you going to let her die, too? We could be a family. We could be happy. I know you're going to make a great father. A wonderful dad. Don't throw that all away.'

'Marcella...'

A pained expression falls across his face, his lip quivering, his eyes glazing.

'You targeted me, didn't you? When I turned up at the house and told you I was interested in the house and architecture, you saw an opportunity. You didn't need to go out scouring the streets for a victim, because I waltzed in here and walked right into your web.'

He shrugs. 'You were young. Attractive. No family ties. You fitted Carmel's criteria perfectly. She couldn't believe her luck.'

'So this is what you always had planned for me?'

'It's what *she* planned.'

'And now?' I ask.

'I never meant to develop feelings for you. I tried to get you to leave, but you wouldn't.'

His face tightens and his eyes narrow.

'So this is *my* fault? I've brought this on myself?' I ask incredulously.

'You should have listened to me!'

'What the hell's going on out here?' Carmel screams, marching into the chamber with a thunderous expression on her face. 'You're not even dressed yet.'

Rufus jumps away from me with the energy of a grasshopper springing off a leaf. 'I was just getting things ready.'

'And what are you doing with that, you stupid man?' She glances at the mallet in his hand. 'You weren't seriously going to start with the mallet, were you?'

'Of course not.'

He scurries away, chastened. Across the chamber to where a number of all-in-one white suits are hanging on the wall, like the police wear at a crime scene. He pulls one down and tugs it on over his clothes before tucking his curly locks under its hood.

'I'm going to enjoy this,' Carmel sneers.

'Screw you.'

'I never did like you.'

'At least I know how to keep your husband happy.'

She slaps me across the face again. Blood pours into my mouth and a red-hot poker of pain mainlines through my head.

'You should watch your mouth, you stinking whore.'

I whimper in pain.

'Truth hurts, doesn't it?' I mumble through the mess of blood and snot.

Across the room, Rufus picks up a pair of bolt cutters and scissors them open and closed, watching the jaws clamp shut with fascination. I think about what it would be like if one of my fingers or toes was trapped between the blades. The excruciating torture of it slicing through skin, muscle, ligament and bone. I shake my head to dispel the image.

'Do you know how hard it is to kill someone?' Carmel says, the smirk on her face revealing just how much she's enjoying herself. 'It can take hours and hours. A cut here. A broken bone there. The body is remarkably resilient. It can survive so much trauma, if done the right way. In a controlled way.'

My head slumps onto my chin.

'Where are they?' I gasp.

'Who?'

'The other women.'

'Somewhere they'll never be found,' she says.

'Dead?'

'What do you think?'

'But why? Why are you doing this?'

'It's my calling,' she says. 'What I was always destined to do.'

I shake my head. 'You're out of your mind.'

'Call it my hobby, if you like.' She shrugs. 'Some people enjoy playing golf. I prefer... this.' She waves a hand around the chamber. 'Oh, don't look disproving. It's in my genes. A faulty chromosome, I expect. Like how some women are predisposed to get cancer or Parkinson's. I have a taste for murder, that's all.'

'You're insane.'

She cocks her head to one side as if considering the possibility of her insanity. 'No,' she says after a moment. 'I know exactly what I'm doing. It's what the women in my family have done for generations. We can't help ourselves. Call it a blood lust, if you like.'

Rufus picks up a hammer and a handful of nails. I don't want to imagine what he's thinking.

'And Rufus? How did you get him involved?'

'He's a puppy dog. Always so desperate to win my affection. He'll do anything for me,' she says. 'Now, shall we get on?'

Rufus moves closer, his focus fixed on me. He has the hammer in one hand, while the nails in his other rattle and chink ominously.

Carmel gives an approving nod. 'The hammer and nails? Much more appropriate to start with.'

'The cameras?' he asks.

'Already rolling.'

As if their behaviour couldn't be any more perverse. 'Why the cameras? To share on the dark web with a bunch of other sickos, I suppose? So that's what this is really about? Getting your kicks and making money?'

Carmel frowns. 'We don't share the footage,' she says, as if I've offended her. 'We keep it for our own enjoyment. A memento of our work.'

'You really are deranged.'

Carmel's smile turns into an evil chuckle as she steps aside for Rufus. He holds up one of the nails. It's at least six inches long and as thick as a pencil.

So this is it.

My torment is about to begin.

A warm, damp patch spreads down my legs, soaking into my jeans as my breathing comes fast and shallow, my heart racing like a gazelle on the run from a pride of lions. Sweat stippling my brow.

'Ugh, she's wet herself,' Carmel says, turning away in disgust. 'Why do they always do that?'

'You're not really going to do this, are you, Rufus?' I croak.

He puts the tip of the nail into the fleshy part of my shoulder, holding it between his fingers.

'Here?'

Carmel nods. 'Let's start gently with this one and really take our time.'

'Stand back then,' Rufus says, lifting the hammer above his shoulder.

Carmel's face twists into an expression of pure delight, excitement dancing in her eyes. Her cheeks flushing.

'Think of our baby,' I scream. 'Think about your own child.'

Rufus pulls the hammer back. I turn my head, squeeze my eyes shut, and grit my teeth as I wait for the inevitable explosion of pain.

'Just do it,' Carmel urges him. 'Surely you can at least get this right?'

Rufus roars.

There's a stomach-churning wet smack that sounds like flesh being pulverised.

But there is no searing agony in my shoulder.

When I dare to open my eyes, Rufus is standing with his back to me, the hammer in his hand dripping with blood, and Carmel is sprawled out on the floor, face down, arms and legs twisted, with a stream of blood trailing down the tiles towards the drain.

Chapter 45

Carmel's body twitches and she lets out an obscene gurgle.

Rufus staggers backwards on weak legs and drops the bloody hammer on the floor. It makes a loud, resounding crack that echoes around the chamber like a gunshot.

'I'm sorry,' Rufus mutters, although I'm not sure whether it's directed at me, or Carmel, or us both.

I stare at Carmel's body, numb. I should feel something, shouldn't I? Relief? Disgust? Gratitude?

But all I can think about is how fortunate it is that she fell on the tiles and that the blood pumping from her head is trickling towards the drain. Easy to clean up with a hose. But I suppose that's the point.

Rufus peels off his white suit, screws it up, and tosses it angrily to one side. He runs his fingers through his tousled hair, and finally turns to me.

I stare at him, uncertain what happens next.

'Rufus?' I say, warily.

He sighs. 'I'm sorry, Marcella. I never meant for it to come to this.'

'Let me down. Please.'

He shakes his head, as if he can't believe what he's done. Then shuffles towards the winch handle on the wall and lowers me to the ground.

I catch my balance, but as my arms are lowered, it causes almost as much discomfort in my shoulders as it did when they were strung up above my head.

Rufus digs into his pocket, finds a key for the handcuffs, and unlocks them. As I rub the feeling back into my wrists, I back away. He might have saved my life, but I don't want to be anywhere near him. Just because Carmel's out of the picture, I still don't trust Rufus.

'Do you hate me?' he asks, as Carmel's arm jerks again and I have a horrific vision of her jumping up and snatching my leg, like in those old cheesy horror films.

Yes, I want to scream. I hate him for abducting all those women. For what he and Carmel did to them. For all the abuse and the suffering. The killing. And most of all, for what he's put me through. How he lied to me. How he almost let Carmel kill me.

'No, of course I don't hate you,' I lie, putting all my effort into sounding like I mean it, while maintaining my distance from him. I glance at the drills and the saws, the knives and the scalpels lined up on the shelves, and contemplate arming myself.

Rufus slumps to the floor, wrapping his arms around his knees as he pulls them up to his chest, his head bowed in defeat.

'She was telling the truth,' he says. 'There was something wrong with her. She couldn't help herself. It's like a disease that's run through her family for years.'

'Bloodlust is not a disease.' I eye up a row of knives. A machete. A meat cleaver. A carving knife. All capable of inflicting terrible pain and misery. 'A disease doesn't make you torture and kill people.'

'A condition then. I don't know.'

It's all too much to take in.

'The story we told you about the children who died in the attic with their mother wasn't the whole truth,' Rufus says as my head spins. 'They weren't killed by their father. It was their mother, Agatha. She plotted it all. First she killed the children, and then she killed her husband, Billy, before faking her own death, knowing he'd be held responsible for the murders.'

'Agatha? Carmel's great great aunt?' I remember the picture of her at the foot of the stairs. A faded image of a woman with big black eyes and waves of curly hair.

Rufus shakes his head. 'Agatha was Carmel's great grandmother.'

'That can't be right. You said she killed all her children.'

'She killed all the children she had with Billy. But after faking her own death, she moved to London and had another child, Ellen. Carmel's grandmother.'

'And she...?'

Rufus nods. 'Was a killer, too. Four husbands, apparently. She was a dab hand with poison. Every one of her murders was dismissed as an accidental death.'

I keep walking slowly, circling behind Rufus, aware I need him alive if I'm going to get out of here. There are two locked doors sealing us inside, and I don't have the codes for either of them.

But now I know the truth, I can't see how Rufus can let me live.

Unless I can convince him I'm still in love with him and that I want us to be together as a family. He's desperate to have children, which is why, I guess, he attacked Carmel and let me go. He still thinks I'm pregnant. That I'm carrying his child. All the while he believes the lie, I have a chance.

'Carmel's own mother was no better than any of them. She murdered at least half a dozen prostitutes in London,' Rufus says.

'Her mother was a serial killer too?' I gasp.

'The police were so busy looking for a male suspect, suspicion never even fell on Sandra. They never caught her.'

I frown. 'Why prostitutes?'

'Who knows? Carmel told me her mother once caught her father with a prostitute. She became Sandra's first victim, and that's how she realised how easy it was to get these women alone. They were vulnerable and happy to jump into a stranger's car for a few quid.'

The cogs in my brain whirr slowly. There's something familiar about the story. I'm sure I've seen a documentary on those unsolved prostitute killings in London in the nineteen-seventies.

'Oh, my god. The Shoreditch Strangler?'

'It was all over the papers at the time, until the killings stopped as suddenly as they'd started and the police were happy to let the case quietly fade from the public consciousness. They never even came close to catching her. Carmel only found out about it when her mother confessed on her deathbed. It's when she told her about the others. About her grandmother, Ellen, and what Agatha had done to her own children. Her mother, Sandra, convinced Carmel that it was a family trait, something that ran down the female line.'

Carmel's gone unnervingly quiet and there's no sign she's still breathing. I guess she's gone. And good riddance. The only pity is that she's not going to pay for what she's done and none of the families of those women she killed are going to see justice.

'Of course, I didn't know anything about it when I first met her,' Rufus continues. 'After we'd been married for a few years, she confessed she sometimes had some unusual, violent urges. We talked about her fantasies. And mine. They became increasingly extreme, and I was curious. I suppose there's a rotten core in me, too. I could see how it excited Carmel and I guess I fed off that.'

'And it eventually escalated to murder?' I ask, feeling sick in the pit of my stomach.

'Yes,' he whispers.

'And you were a willing participant?'

'I was in love with her. I'd have done anything for her,' he says. 'We talked a lot about abducting a woman and bringing her here. We even went out a

329

few times, found someone we thought was suitable, but didn't go through with it.'

Would Rufus notice if I palmed a scalpel and hid it under my sleeve?

'So what changed?' I ask. 'What made you cross the line?'

He shrugs. 'I don't know. It just happened. We did the first together. We spotted a woman walking home drunk. Carmel was driving and pulled over to offer her a lift. I was hiding in the back seat. At that point, we didn't plan to kill her. We were just, you know, going to play around with her a bit.'

My stomach churns in disgust.

'But she started screaming and we couldn't make her stop.' Rufus glances at me, chewing his bottom lip. 'I was appalled with myself at first, but Carm el... well, I've never seen her more alive. She was buzzing. And I suppose I kind of enjoyed it too. Holding someone's life in your hands and deciding whether they get to live or die was intoxicating. I've never known a thrill like it. And when we didn't get caught, we thought we were invincible. After all, who was going to suspect a respectable, professional couple like us?'

'Which is when you built this place?'

'It was Carmel's vision. A quiet place we could bring them to have our fun.'

I've heard enough. The walls are closing in and there's no air.

'Can we get out of here?' I ask tentatively.

Rufus is lost in thought, staring into space. 'Hmmm?'

'Can you open the doors? I want to go home.'

He breathes in slowly through his nose. 'You'll go to the police, won't you?'

'No! Of course I won't,' I lie.

'You say you won't, but you will. How could you not?'

I clutch my hand to my stomach, caressing my imaginary baby bump. 'I want us to be together,' I say. 'Just the three of us.'

A spark of hope ignites in Rufus's eyes. 'I'd like that. I've always wanted children. It was the one thing Carmel could never give me.'

'I know.'

The thought of having anything more to do with Rufus, of being pregnant with his child, sends a wave of revulsion and disgust flooding through my veins. I don't even want to be in the same room as him. He can blame Carmel all he wants, but he's as evil as she was. Twisted. Inhumane. He deserves to be behind bars for a long, long time.

'I want you to be happy,' he says, hauling himself off the ground and dusting himself down.

I edge further away, trying not to look scared. I accidentally back into one of the shelves. It wobbles, causing a cruel-looking set of truncheons and batons spiked with nails to rattle.

Rufus advances towards me, his expression grim.

He picks up a kitchen knife. It has an ebony handle, and a glistening curved steel blade, like you might find in any kitchen up and down the land.

My heart rate soars.

'Rufus...' I mumble, my gaze fixed on the weapon he's turning over in his hand.

'You deserve better than this,' he says. 'I wish you'd never come here. But if you hadn't, I'd never have met you.'

'Rufus, think about our baby.'

He glances up with a sad smile. 'Will you call her Juliet?'

'Of course. That's a lovely name.'

My feet scuff on the floor as I continue to inch away towards the heavy, locked steel door, praying for a miracle. That somehow it might miraculously spring open on its own and the police will come rushing in to end this hell.

'Juliet Van Der Proust,' Rufus muses. 'It has a lovely ring to it, doesn't it?'

'Open the door.'

'And you'll take good care of her and tell her I'm a good man?'

'I'll bring her to visit you in prison. And send you lots of pictures so you don't miss out,' I promise. 'You're going to be the most amazing, wonderful father.'

'I know I don't deserve it.' He walks towards me, still gripping the knife tightly.

I glance around, looking for somewhere to run and hide. Maybe I could lock myself in the side room where the video recording equipment is set up. But then what? Nobody knows I'm here. If he wanted, Rufus could wait and starve me to death.

'Please, Rufus, I'm tired. Let's get out of here. We can take your car and go anywhere you like.'

He shakes his head, prodding the tip of the knife with the end of his finger.

'We're not going anywhere. I'm sorry.'

Oh god, he is going to kill me. He's going to kill us both. I can see it in his eyes. He's given up. Defeated.

'Let me go,' I sob, tears rolling down my cheeks and running off my chin. 'I don't want to die.'

He's right in front of me now. I can smell the stale sweat on his clothes and the sourness on his breath. He reaches for me and touches my arm tenderly.

And then he gives me the codes to open the doors.

I shake my head. 'I don't understand.'

'Go. Be free,' he says. 'Take care of our daughter.'

'What about you?'

'There's nothing for me out there.' He turns and walks back towards Carmel's body. 'I should stay here with her.'

'Are you sure?' I can hardly believe my luck.

'Go.'

I race to the first internal door and, with trembling fingers, punch the code into the keypad. I breathe a sigh of relief as it clicks and the lock releases.

'Goodbye, Marcella,' Rufus says, his words weighted with sorrow.

I heave the door open. Lights blink on in the dark corridor outside and I hesitate momentarily to glance over my shoulder.

Rufus is kneeling at Carmel's side, staring at the knife.

Then he plunges it into his stomach, right up to its hilt.

I clamp a hand over my mouth to silence my scream as Rufus's eyes open wide with shock and horror.

Blood pumps out, soaking his hand and his shirt. He slumps back on his haunches, gurgling and spluttering, his eyes rolling back in his head.

I don't feel a scrap of regret or pity. It's a horrific way to die, but other than revulsion, I don't feel much else for him, although it's unfortunate that neither of them will face justice for the murders of all those women. It doesn't seem fair. It's a coward's way out.

I should run. Get as far away from here as I can. Call the police.

But something stops me.

This is too easy for Rufus. I can't let him die happy in the knowledge he's going to be a father.

I take a deep breath and turn on my heel. With my head held high, I march back to Rufus and crouch at his side. I study his pitiful face, his skin pale and clammy, his breath shallow.

'You make me sick,' I whisper in his ear. 'I never loved you. I didn't even have feelings for you.'

He croaks, as if he's trying to say something, but I'm not interested in hearing anything else from him.

'And I'm not pregnant, by the way. And even if I was, do you really think I'd want to keep *your* child? You *are* a monster. You and Carmel deserve each other. I just feel sorry for the families of all those poor women you killed who won't get to face you in court now.'

Rufus blinks and splutters. I can only hope I'm inflicting as much mental torment on him as he's physically feeling right now. It's the only consolation I have.

'Oh, and the real reason I came here? It wasn't because I had any interest in making a film about you, you vain bastard. I came here because of her.' I jab my thumb towards Carmel's body. 'She killed my sister. I came here for revenge.'

Rufus cocks his head to one side and frowns.

I tell him about Hannah, how Carmel was responsible for condemning her to that psychiatric hospital which ultimately led to her taking her own life.

But rather than showing any sympathy, Rufus's lips turn up into a smug smile.

The fucker.

It takes all my willpower not to pull that knife out of his stomach and use it to finish him off.

But I'm not a killer. I'm better than them.

Instead, I spit on him. Then turn my back and walk away.

'I hope your death is long, painful and drawn out,' I holler over my shoulder. 'It's no more than you deserve, you worthless piece of shit.'

I suppose at least I finally have justice for Hannah and no more women are in danger from Rufus and Carmel.

Time to get out of here. I plan to make an anonymous phone call to the police and then disappear.

I don't want to hang around being questioned by detectives for hours about what happened here, with them asking awkward questions about what I was doing here in the first place.

There's enough evidence, with the torture chamber and Rufus and Carmel's video recordings, for them to piece it all together, I'm sure. I want a clean start. A new name. A new life. It's the least I deserve.

I don't give them a backwards glance as I reach the first heavy steel door.

It creaks as I put my shoulder to it and muscle it fully open.

Almost free.

One more door and I'm out of here.

But suddenly my head is yanked back by my hair and a million needles of pain shoot through my scalp.

I'm dragged down onto the floor with unseen hands reaching around my throat.

I try to scream, but I can't breathe.

And my hopes of getting out of here alive fade.

Chapter 46

St Mary's Church, Wychwood
September 11, 1925

AGATHA

It was a pity the Reverend James Bennett had to die.
I liked him. He was always kind to me. But I couldn't
trust him. Not after hearing my confession.

We sat in the vestry with the door locked on my
insistence. I couldn't risk someone walking in and
overhearing what I had to tell him. That would have
been a disaster.

'I killed the eldest first,' I told him.

'Arthur?' he frowned.

As the words tumbled out of my mouth, his skin
became paler and paler until I thought he was going
to faint.

Technically, Arthur was Gerald's son, conceived
while Billy was fighting in France. I should have

been more careful, although when I discovered I was pregnant, I was overjoyed. Not because I was carrying Gerald's child, but because I was to become a mother.

I'd always thought that's what I wanted. The missing piece to make my life complete. Of course, I hadn't thought about the practicalities. The sleepless nights. The constant demands for feeding. The dirty nappies to clean. The disfigurement of my body which no longer felt like it was my own, but was there only to serve the needs of my young son.

'It was easy, really. A few measures of Billy's whisky in a fruit punch I made for the older children and they were all out like a light. Arthur didn't even resist when I placed the pillow over his face,' I said.

I told him exactly what I did, without embellishment or emotion. People get so hung up about death, but it comes to us all in the end. It's just that it comes to some sooner than to others.

'Are you okay, Reverend? You look a little peaky,' I said.

'And the others?'

'I killed Stanley, Frederick and Alfred the same way. They shared a room, so it was all over in a few minutes.'

After Arthur was born, Billy took to the child surprisingly easily, even though he knew he wasn't his. It was our little secret. As far as anyone else in the village was concerned, he was Billy's flesh and blood.

I didn't think he was that concerned the child wasn't his, until, after a few months, Billy suggested we should try for a baby of our own. I felt bad that I'd been unfaithful to him, and although I'd not enjoyed the experience of childbirth, I agreed we could try. I had no idea how easily I'd fall pregnant.

Four more children were born in consecutive years, and then there was Edith, born sixteen months after her older sister, Dorothy. I seemed to have found something I was good at. Falling pregnant. Billy was delighted. He'd always wanted a large family, but I began to feel increasingly trapped, my role as a mother feeling as though it was defining my entire life.

'And the girls? Dorothy and Edith?' the vicar asked, his mouth gaping open in disbelief.

'I drowned them in the bath.'

The vicar lowered his head and muttered a silent prayer.

'I warned you that you wouldn't want to know the truth,' I said. But he'd asked, and I felt I owed it to him. After all, he'd played a vital role in my plans.

'But why?' he gasped. 'How could you kill your own children?'

I shrugged. 'It wasn't the life I'd imagined I'd be leading, stuck on a farm with six children all demanding my attention, and a husband so damaged by the war, he could barely bring himself to grunt at me.'

'But to murder them all in cold blood...'

'Actually, it was a peaceful way for them to die, and now, thanks to you, they're at peace under God's watchful gaze.'

'You drowned your daughters. There's nothing peaceful about that,' the vicar pointed out. 'Those poor, poor lambs. I can only imagine the suffering they endured in their final moments.'

'And what about my suffering?' I snapped. Why did nobody ever think about what I was feeling?

'*Your* suffering?'

'I told you how Billy treated me. He made me feel worthless.'

'So you murdered him too and let everyone believe he was responsible for the children's deaths?'

'He made it too easy. He shouldn't have left his revolver in a drawer.'

'I saw his body. You made it look as though he'd taken his own life,' the vicar said.

'All I had to do was wait for him in the bedroom, put a bullet in his head, and leave the gun in his hand. It was obvious what the police would conclude.'

The vicar gulped. 'It sounds as though you had it all planned out.'

I smiled. 'I knew you'd help the police to jump to conclusions and, without my body, they'd assume Billy had killed me and blame it on the shell shock. What else could they possibly deduce, other than he must have killed the children before turning his gun on himself?' I said.

'You lied to me.'

I frowned. 'About what?'

'You used me to obscure the truth. When you came to the vicarage and told me Billy had been abusing you, that was a lie.'

340

I shook my head. 'It was all true. Billy was out of control. He was violent, to me and the children, and he had a terrible temper. All I did was open your eyes to what was going on behind closed doors.'

'But you weren't dead,' the vicar said, shaking his head as if he was trying to sift all the jumbled pieces of my story into some semblance of sense in his head.

'Apparently not.'

'So why did you come back and risk everything?'

'It's a good question. Maybe it was a mistake,' I said. 'But I wanted to say my goodbyes to the children. I guess they were as much the innocent victims as I am.'

He stared at me in disbelief, but I couldn't expect him to understand.

'And now what?'

'I'm going to start a new life somewhere no one will recognise me. I thought I'd try London. I have some money saved up that I hid from Billy. Enough, at least, that I can survive for a year or two. You won't tell anyone, will you, Reverend? I can trust you, can't I?'

He jumped up from his chair and backed away from me, clutching a cross that hung from a chain around his neck. 'You're evil,' he hissed.

That stung. How could he say that about me? It wasn't my fault I'm the way I am. It's in my nature. It was the same with my mother, and her mother before her, as she'd confessed to me just before she died.

341

She used to work for a family in Canterbury, in a big house with a couple who had a young baby. Except the baby wouldn't stop crying, day or night. It was driving all the staff insane. So my mother dealt with it. I don't know the details of how. She wouldn't go into that, but it was obvious what she meant. The baby was found dead in its cot and the doctors concluded the death had been the result of natural causes. She was never caught for what she did, and as far as I'm aware, she never killed again. She was able to curb her urges. Sadly, I have not been similarly blessed with such control.

It's not that I derive any particular pleasure from death, like lancing a boil or picking at a crusty scab. But neither do I feel any regret or sadness. In my case, I've found that murder has been more a matter of convenience.

'I think you'd better leave,' the vicar said, his voice wavering.

'But you'll keep my secret?'

'I... I don't know if I can.'

'But you have a duty.'

It didn't seem fair. I'd told him what he wanted to know and shared my darkest secret. The least he could do was hold his tongue.

'Everything I've told you has to remain confidential,' I remind him. 'That's your duty.'

'And do you think God is going to forgive your sins?'

'I've attended church regularly,' I said, 'and I've led a good life, mostly. I don't see why God wouldn't forgive my weaknesses.'

He was trembling now, his hand, still clutching the crucifix, noticeably shaking. 'You've committed a grave transgression not only in the eyes of the law, but against the divine commandments. The only way your soul can be saved after what you've done is to make your confession in a court of law. Repent your sins and let justice take its course.'

I sighed. Did he really think I was going to hand myself in after all my careful planning? I should have known it would be like this.

'All I want is another chance,' I pleaded.

'Another chance?'

'A new life. To start again. Is that so terrible?'

He was about to answer when there was a knock on the door. Someone tried the handle.

'Reverend? Are you in there?' Albert, the verger, called.

'Just a minute.'

I flashed him a warning with my eyes, trusting him not to say anything. He shuffled to the door, edging around me, and unlocked it.

'I'm just busy with something,' he said through a narrow crack. I was careful to stand out of view. Of course, it would ruin everything if Albert found out I was alive.

'Right-o. Just wanted to say I was going to head home, unless you needed me for anything else?'

'Thank you, Albert. No, that's fine. I'll lock up. See you tomorrow.'

He pushed the door closed and locked it again.

'Do the right thing,' the vicar said, turning to face me. 'It's the only route to salvation.'

I laughed. 'I don't need salvation.'

'I'm afraid you do.'

'I'm leaving now, Reverend. Please don't try to stop me, and I advise you to think seriously before revealing what was said here today, as God will be your witness.'

I wasn't sure he was going to let me go, but thankfully he stepped aside and didn't make any attempt to stop me. I turned the key in the lock and let myself out.

'I'll pray for you,' the vicar called after me.

'You do that, Reverend.'

'For all the good it will do you.'

I pulled the door closed and sighed to myself. At that moment, I really thought he might keep my secret. At least long enough for me to make my escape.

But by the time I'd made it into the churchyard, I'd convinced myself he couldn't be trusted. How could I take the risk that he wouldn't head straight for the constable's house and tell him everything?

And once the constable knew the truth, I'd always be looking over my shoulder. Not the new start I was hoping for.

He'd left me with no other choice. I had to make sure of the vicar's silence. And so I came up with a new plan. I dug around for a decent sized rock under a bush at the edge of the graveyard and found a headstone where I could hide, close to the entrance to the church. And I waited.

The Reverend Bennett must have decided he needed some considerable time praying for my soul as he remained inside for several hours. Maybe he was wrestling with his conscience, deciding whether to betray my trust, I don't know, but when he finally emerged, the light was fading and the evening drawing in.

At least that worked in my favour. As he struggled with the huge oak doors at the entrance to the church, I readied myself, creeping out of the shadows with the rock in one hand.

He didn't hear me creeping up behind him as he turned away and marched towards the vicarage.

'Reverend Bennett,' I called softly.

He whirled around, his eyes wide with surprise.

'Agatha? What are you—'

They were the last words he uttered before he died. He dropped like a rag doll, his eyes rolling back in his head, as I struck him once across the temple.

I turned him over and positioned him close to one of the gravestones, to make it look as if he'd tripped and fallen. I even used my handkerchief to dab a little of his blood on the stonework for any suspicious constables to find, in case they doubted it was an accident.

Then I tossed the rock into the undergrowth and disappeared into the night to finally begin my new life as a free woman.

Chapter 47

I can't breathe.

My vision tunnels. Everything darkens. Panic blooms.

I'm on my back, staring at the strip lights on the ceiling, lying on top of my attacker. I grab the wrists at my neck and try to pry the fingers loose. One comes away. With all my strength, I bend it back against the joint. A howl of agony threatens to puncture my eardrum, but the pressure on my throat relents at last.

With my free arm, I jab my elbow into the soft flesh beneath me. A sharp blow. Both hands leave my throat.

I roll over, scrabbling to my feet.

Carmel, her face plastered with blood, her hair sticky and wet, growls at me like a wounded animal.

'I thought you were dead,' I pant.

She stands. Sways on the spot, sizing me up.

'I should have killed you myself when I had the chance,' she hisses. 'I always knew you were going to be trouble.'

She's standing between me and the outer door. There's no way past. The only way to escape from her is back into the chamber. A prospect I hardly savour, but I have no choice.

Maybe I can grab a weapon in there. One of the knives or a club. I should have picked up that scalpel earlier.

No time to think. I snap into action, turning and running, legs pumping.

I slip back through the inner door.

Into the chamber.

Rufus is slumped in a pool of his own blood, his head on his chest, his eyes staring blankly at the ground, with the knife still embedded in his stomach.

Ignoring his body, I hurl myself at the nearest shelf. It's full of drills and bits. A car battery. A set of electrical leads. Nothing I can easily use against Carmel.

She roars with anger as she chases me. Bowls into me, rugby tackling me to the ground.

We knock over one of the cameras. It crashes to the ground with tripod legs flying. But somehow I manage to find myself on top of Carmel.

There's a hideous bloodied dent in the side of her head. It looks so unnatural, so grotesque, I know it's going to haunt my dreams for years to come.

How is she still alive?

She snarls at me as I wrap my hands around her throat. She grasps my wrists.

But I can't do it.

My life might depend on it, but I can't strangle her. Not with my bare hands. The feel of soft flesh giving way under my thumbs makes me queasy. I just don't have it in me.

I need a weapon.

There's another shelf close by, which if I stretch, I can just about reach. My hand flails around wildly, crashing through tools and equipment, desperate to find something I can use.

My finger nicks something sharp and I withdraw my hand with a gasp. There's blood all over my finger, although fortunately the cut doesn't look too deep, and frankly, it's the least of my worries.

Carmel bucks and kicks beneath me. Any second, she's going to throw me off and regain the advantage.

I just need something...

Got it!

My fingers wrap around a utility knife with a razor-sharp retractable blade.

Carmel's eyes grow wide when she sees what's in my hand. For a split second, she stops thrashing about, the first glimmer of concern in her eyes.

I don't hesitate.

I thumb out the blade and plunge it deep into the palm of her hand. After all, I don't want to kill her.

She howls in agony as I roll away, my focus totally on getting out of here.

I sprint across the room, through the inner door and skid to a halt at the keypad at the locked outer door.

Oh god, what was the number Rufus gave me?

6-7-3-2?

I punch it in, my hand trembling.

The keypad bleeps, but the door remains shut.
Shit.

Maybe it was 6-3-7-2?

Wrong again.

I glance back down the corridor as Carmel emerges from the chamber, so bloodied and battered, she looks like the Bride of Frankenstein. Not a pretty sight. Blood drips from her hand, but she's pulled out the knife.

6-7-2-3

That's it!

The bolts click and the door opens a fraction.

I throw myself at it and shove it open, spilling into the darkness of the wood.

And I run.

Arms and legs working furiously, lungs screaming, following the dim lights that illuminate the path back to the house.

Behind me, Carmel follows, unsteady on her feet. At least I'm faster than her.

But I have no plan. No means of escape. All I can do is run. I have no idea what happened to my phone. I haven't seen it since Carmel attacked me in the cellar. I assume she took it. Maybe even destroyed it. All I can hope is that there's a phone in the house I can use. Otherwise, what am I going to do? Run to the village in the dark? I'll do it if I have to, even though I'm pathetically weak with hunger, running on adrenaline alone, and my feet blistered and cut. I need to find my shoes before I go anywhere.

The silhouette of the house appears through the darkness and the trees. Thankfully, there are several lights on in the rooms downstairs, beacons guiding me on.

I crash out onto the drive, slipping on the loose gravel, wincing in pain as the stones dig into my soles.

'Marcella! Wait!' Carmel's voice is a haunting cry carrying on the still night air. 'I only want to talk.'

Yeah, talk about how to kill me.

I charge at the front door, hugely relieved to discover it flies open when I throw myself at it. I half-stumble, half-fall inside.

What now? There's no way Carmel's going to let me live.

I know too much. I know everything.

If only I had a way of calling for help. Of raising the alarm.

But it's hopeless. I don't have a phone and I don't know how to drive, so there's no point stealing Rufus's car keys from the table in the hall.

All I can do is hide. But for how long? Carmel is bound to find me eventually, and then what? I'll have to run to the village. I have no other choice.

And then from nowhere, an idea pops into my head, like a vanishing playing card appearing from a magician's top pocket.

I hurry along the hall with my heart pounding like a jackhammer in my chest.

Carmel's voice catches up with me. She's not far behind. Almost at the door. I should have locked it behind me to buy myself some time, but I'm not thinking straight.

'Don't be scared,' she says in a sing-song tone, as if she's my teacher and I'm still in Year Five.

I back up, keeping my attention fixed on the door.

It swings open ominously slowly and Carmel appears, illuminated under the light in the porch. One eye, the one under the hideous dent in her head, keeps flickering closed. When it does open, it dances left and right, up and down, as if it has a mind of its own. It's the creepiest thing I've ever seen.

'There you are,' Carmel says with a wicked grin that turns my insides to ice. 'Why were you running away, you silly girl?'

Because you were trying to kill me, you fucking insane bitch.

'Stay away from me,' I warn, holding up my hand, palm outwards.

Not that I expected that to stop her. Her grin grows broader as she steps into the house, her head and neck twitching. She shuffles towards me, one foot after the other scraping across the tiles.

'How many have there been?' I ask. 'How many women have you brought here to kill?'

A light sparks in her good eye. 'I don't know. Ten. Maybe fifteen,' she says.

'Where are they now? What did you do with their bodies?'

'In the woods.' She hesitates. Her lips curl over her teeth, stained with blood. 'Scattered around,

351

here and there.' She laughs, the sound cutting through me.

I close my eyes for a second. So much misery. Such depravity. If what Rufus said is true, that Carmel's propensity for murder is a genetic fault, something weird about the way their brains are wired, I'm just grateful she was never able to have children.

'Did you think you'd get away with it?'

'We already have,' she says, creeping closer.

I check my feet, making sure I don't trip on the rug.

'You killed my sister, Hannah.'

That throws her for a moment. She stops dead and her good eye narrows as if she's trying to recall the name.

'Hannah?' she says. She shakes her head. 'No, I don't remember her.'

'She wasn't one of the women you abducted. She died in the psychiatric hospital where you sent her.'

Carmel stares at me blankly.

'She was only arrested for starting a small fire in the stairwell of a block of flats, but you told the court she was so dangerous, she needed to be locked up indefinitely, with no hope of release. You made out she was crazy, but she wasn't. This,' I wave my hand around, 'is crazy. If anyone's crazy, it's you.'

'If you say so.'

'She killed herself because she couldn't bear it in there.'

'That's hardly my fault.' Carmel edges towards me again, placing one foot slowly in front of the other. I keep backing away.

'I came here to make you pay for what you did. I wanted you to feel the pain I felt when I lost Hannah. To make you understand what it's like to lose the thing that's most precious in your life.'

She's still smirking as we shadow dance along the hall. Thinking about Hannah again and how her life was ruined by Carmel, and how Carmel clearly doesn't care a jot about it, makes my blood steam in my veins. But I need to keep a clear head. I can't afford to let my emotions derail my plan. I'll only have one shot at this, and timing is going to be everything.

'It's true. I did sleep with Rufus.' Carmel's smirk slips a fraction. 'We screwed on the sofa in front of the big window.' I toss my head back defiantly. 'He was like an animal. Hungry and desperate. But it's hardly surprising, is it?'

'Don't,' she growls.

'I mean, you're hardly Miss World, are you, Carmel? More like a shrivelled-up, barren old hag. It's no wonder you couldn't have children.'

A dark veil of anger falls across her face. 'How dare you.'

Come on. Come on.

I'm almost at the end of the hall now, as far as I can go without ducking through the glass walkway into the new part of the house. Carmel's scowling at me with undisguised venom and hatred. I have no doubt that if she gets her hands on me, she'll kill me.

But I have no intention of letting that happen.

'I'm surprised he stuck it with you for so long. Pity, I guess.'

'Watch your mouth.'

'And fear. He told me before he died that he was killing himself because he couldn't face another minute living with you.'

With a howl, she finally launches herself at me, lunging down the hall with surprising speed and agility, dragging one limp leg behind her. The foot scuffing along the floor. Arms outstretched. Her one good eye open wide.

But her momentum is arrested the moment she steps onto the rug.

She stumbles, losing her balance as it gives way beneath her. She claws in the air, trying to catch herself, but it's too late. The ground is giving way under her feet and there's nothing she can do. Her arms flail around like windmills and for a split second, her face is a picture of shock and surprise.

And then she's gone, disappearing into the secret cellar where they kept me and who knows how many other women before me.

Her body hits the stairs with a series of dull thuds.

And then she falls silent.

I catch a breath and let it out slowly.

Is she dead?

There's a low moan and the scratch of fingernails on concrete. The rustle of clothing. The scuff of feet.

Maybe not, but there's no way I'm going down there to check.

I throw myself at the painting on the wall and shove my fingers behind it. Find the switch. Click it. And wait anxiously as the electric motors whirr and the hole in the hall floor slowly closes.

'Marcella?' Her voice drifts up from below. A pained groan of despair. 'What are you doing? Help me.'

No chance.

No chance at all.

'Marcella?'

Another voice. It sounds as if it came from directly behind.

'Hannah?'

But when I turn around, there's no one there.

Chapter 48

The room they've put me in is a soulless shell with a lingering odour of bleach masking an underlying stench of vomit. There's a desk and a few chairs, and a window which overlooks a courtyard filled with police vehicles. They've given me a cup of rank coffee, which I don't have the stomach to drink, and told me to wait while they make some calls.

They've been asking the same questions over and over until I can't think straight. But I've told them everything. Well, almost everything. I didn't think it would look too good on me if I told them the real reason I was at the Van Der Proust's house in the first place. But everything else, I've been totally honest about. How I saw Rufus dragging that woman into the house. How Carmel attacked me and tied me up in the cellar under the hall. And as much detail as I could remember about the horrifying underground chamber in the woods. To be honest, it's all a bit of a blur and not something I've wanted to dwell on.

There's a sharp knock at the door a moment before it opens.

Frazer appears behind a female uniformed officer, looking sheepish and a little uncertain.

I jump out of my seat and throw my arms around his neck. I've never been so pleased to see him in all my life.

'I wasn't sure you'd come,' I cry into his shoulder. 'But I didn't have anyone else to call.'

Eventually, he puts his arms around me. A light touch on my lower back and shoulder.

'I didn't have much choice, did I? Are you okay?'

I peel away from him and nod. 'Yeah, I'm fine,' I lie.

The truth is, I'm exhausted, mentally and physically. The police have been questioning me for hours, going over and over my story like I'm the one guilty of something. My eyes are so heavy I could sleep for days.

'How have you been?' I ask.

'Me? Yeah, okay, I guess.'

'I miss you.'

'Let's get you out of here.'

Frazer doesn't say much as we slip out of the back entrance to avoid the reporters I'm told have gathered at the front of the station. His car's parked on a back street a few minutes' walk away.

'You can stay at my flat for a few days until you get back on your feet,' he says as he blips open the doors.

'Thank you.' I'm grateful for the small mercy, but who knows, when he reflects on what I've been through, how I nearly died and how he nearly lost me forever, he'll come to his senses. I have a good feeling that there might be a chance for us to get back together and start over.

There's an empty coffee cup and a sandwich wrapper on the passenger seat, which I toss into the back before I climb into the car. I don't know what I would have done if Frazer hadn't agreed to pick me up from the police station. I have nowhere else to go.

'It sounds as though you were incredibly lucky,' he says, as he pulls away.

'Lucky?' I snort. 'It's not how I'd describe it.'

'You know what I mean.'

He takes a right, when I expect him to turn left, and I have to remind myself that he's living somewhere new now. Our past is precisely that. Ancient history. He's carving out a new life for himself, without me in it. But we'll see about that.

'They said on the news they don't know yet how many women they killed,' Frazer says, turning down the radio.

'They told me they'd found the remains of seven bodies, but were expecting to find more.'

'Where?'

'In the woods in the grounds of the house. Most of them had been dismembered and buried in shallow graves.' I stare out of the window, watching the blur of the city pass by.

I'm so, so tired.

'What the hell were you doing there, Mars?'

I shrug. 'It's a long story. Can we talk about something else?'

We drive the rest of the way in silence, Frazer brooding quietly beside me, as I lose myself in my own thoughts, glad to finally have some head space to think. Not that I think about much. I'm numb. Like someone's taken out my brain and replaced it with cotton wool.

Frazer's new place is at the opposite end of the city to our old flat. One of those faceless new-builds with a tiny square of grass for a garden and neighbours overlooking it from all sides. It's a far cry from our old flat with its quaint Victorian features and draughty windows.

It even has its own drive off the road.

Frazer holds the front door open for me and steps aside to let me in.

It smells like a stranger's house. Of stale curry, wet dogs, and cheap aftershave. Frazer's mess is everywhere. A heap of coats on the banister. Shoes abandoned across the floor. It's not bad going, considering he's only been here for a week.

I peer into the tiny kitchen. Bottles, jars and tins litter the worktops. A packet of cereal left open. A sink full of dirty dishes.

I guess some things don't change, but at least there's no evidence of another woman.

'I've made up the bed in the spare room,' he says as we stand awkwardly in the hall. Frazer makes a half-hearted effort to kick his shoes into a neat pile.

'Thanks.'

'And help yourself to anything you need. I've taken a few days off to be around. I didn't think you should be on your own.'

'That's so sweet.' I reach up to kiss him on the cheek. He's not shaved and his skin is rough with stubble. Then I kiss him on the lips.

'Marcella,' he says sternly, taking my shoulders and pushing me gently away. 'I don't think that's a good idea.'

'No, sorry,' I say, turning away to hide the flush rising from my chest up to my face.

That evening, he orders a Chinese takeaway and we eat on our laps in his living room with some candles and the TV on low in the background, showing reruns of *The Office*. The US one with Steve Carrell when it was still funny and all the actors look so young.

'What were you doing at the house, Mars?' Frazer asks again, shovelling a forkful of beef and black bean sauce into his mouth.

I top up our wine glasses, finishing the bottle and wonder where to start.

'I told them I wanted to make a film about the house for YouTube.'

Frazer contemplates this for a moment as he chews. 'Yes, but why?'

'I lost my job.'

'What?'

'The day you walked out on me, I was sacked.'

'Oh, Mars, I'm sorry. I had no idea.'

'It's okay.'

He prods at his food with his fork, pushing it around his plate.

'I'm sorry I didn't have the courage to tell you to your face. It's just that—'

'Frazer, don't.'

'I want to explain.'

I shake my head. 'Let's not talk about it.'

I've been running on adrenaline for most of the day, but the wine is finally taking its toll. I put my plate on the floor and as I tuck my legs under my body, sinking into the soft cushions of Frazer's sofa, I struggle to keep my eyes open.

'Why don't you go to bed? I'll clear up,' Frazer offers.

'Are you sure?'

'I'll see you in the morning. Or whenever you want to get up. I'll be here.'

It's odd sleeping under the same roof but in different beds and a strange house. The mattress is too soft and sags in the middle, making my lower back ache, and the pillows are so flat I might as well not bother with them. But I fall into a deep, dreamless sleep almost as soon as I switch out the light and don't wake again until it's light outside.

I roll over onto my side and peer at the clock blinking at me on the bedside cabinet. With one bleary eye, I focus on the time, confused. It's only three in the morning and yet there's so much light diffusing through the curtains. And then I remember, I'm back in the city and there's a streetlight directly outside the house. At Rufus and Carmel's house, it was always so dark. Too dark sometimes.

Typical. I'm awake now, even though my body craves more sleep.

Out of nowhere, the image of Rufus dragging that woman's unconscious body into the house pops into my head. I can see her features so clearly. Long blonde hair and huge hooped earrings. Smudged make-up. A purple bruise on her forehead.

I don't want to think about the horrors she must have endured before she died. What they did to her. How she suffered. Tortured until she couldn't take any more. I pity the poor officers assigned to view Rufus and Carmel's video footage.

Her name was Jane MacKenzie. The police told me hers was the first body they found. Or at least, bits of it. She was twenty-nine years old with a young son. It had been the first night since his birth she'd been out with the girls, I was told by one of the detectives who'd been questioning me. He probably shouldn't have said anything, but I'm glad he did. I'm glad I have a name to put to her face.

She'd had too much to drink and left the pub early to catch a taxi home. Nobody knows why she didn't make it or how she ended up with Rufus. Maybe he'd posed as a taxi driver. Or stopped to offer her a lift home. It's unlikely anyone will ever find out the truth, the detective said.

I'm sure, in time, we'll find out the stories of all the other women who were murdered too. It'll be in the news and on TV. Families talking about their anguish. Memories shared of happier times. I suppose they'll have funerals as well. It's not a story that's going away anytime soon. I only pray my part in it is kept quiet. I don't want reporters poking their noses into my business.

Who knows if Carmel will cooperate with the police? They found her clinging to life in the cellar where I'd trapped her, mumbling incoherently and badly injured. I'd managed to raise the alarm in the village, running from the house and knocking on a number of doors before a kindly, and somewhat shocked, older couple answered and let me use their phone.

Everything after that passed in a fog. The police arriving. Sirens. Blue lights. Sympathetic voices. A blanket around my shoulders. A short journey to the station. Weak tea. A medical examination. And questions. Lots and lots of questions. By the time it was over, I was reeling. My mind in total disarray, like a plague of wild locusts had torn through it and ripped it bare.

I shiver under the blankets, wide awake and suffocating under a heavy cloak of depression. If I'd acted sooner, made different choices, maybe I could have saved Jane MacKenzie. I can't shake the feeling that I let her down.

After twenty minutes, when sleep doesn't feel any closer to returning, I slide out of bed and creep across the hall in my underwear.

Frazer's door opens silently.

He's lying on his back, snoring, one leg out, hooked over the top of the duvet.

I stand in the doorway for a moment, watching him sleep with a warm fuzz in my stomach. I was a fool to let him go. We should be together. I don't want to be on my own.

I creep across the carpet and steal into his bed. He rolls over and murmurs. I wriggle closer to him and snake an arm over his warm, naked body. It feels so good. So right.

'Marcella?' he mumbles, half asleep.

'Shhh,' I whisper. 'Don't say anything.'

Our lips meet in the darkness. A soft and tender kiss. Bodies press together. Fingers run through hair. Our urgency grows together. No words spoken.

And then he's on top of me and inside me and I want to cry. Instead, I bite his shoulder and he growls.

When we're done, he rolls away and stares at the ceiling, panting.

I place my head in that special hollow in his shoulder and chase my fingers through his coarse chest hair.

'That was nice,' I murmur.

'That shouldn't have happened,' he says.

Chapter 49

It takes me a few moments to work out where I am. And then I remember. Frazer's house. Frazer's bed. A smile draws across my lips as memories of last night trickle back into my mind. There's hope for us yet.

Frazer's side of the bed is empty. He must have risen early and let me lie in. I've no idea of the time, but from the light pouring in around the curtains, I imagine it's late. Probably mid-morning already.

I gather up my bra and knickers that have somehow ended up strewn across the floor and pull on Frazer's towelling dressing gown that smells of his deodorant. All my clothes are still at Rufus and Carmel's house, but I don't suppose the police will be in a hurry to return them. I'll have to pop out later and buy some more.

Frazer's downstairs at a table pushed up against the wall in the kitchen, tapping at a laptop. He has a coffee on the go and an empty plate covered in toast crumbs.

'Morning,' I smile, combing my hair off my forehead. Until a few days ago, Frazer and I were in an intimate relationship. I don't know why this feels so awkward.

'Hi,' he says, not able to look me in the eye. 'Coffee?'

'Sure.'

He busies himself with the coffee machine, filling up the water container and heating up milk. But he makes such a meal of it, fussing over choosing a coffee pod, finding a clean mug and making sure the milk is properly warmed through, that I can't help but feel he's embarrassed that we slept together. I don't know why. It's not like it's never happened before.

'About last night—'

'It was a mistake,' he says. 'You shouldn't have come to my room. We're not getting back together, Marcella. I told you, it's over.'

'But I thought...'

'I meant what I said in my letter. It's time for us both to start over.'

My insides feel as though they've been crushed like a tinned can, ready to be tossed in the rubbish.

'I'm sorry you feel like that.' I pull his dressing gown more tightly closed, embarrassed that I'm naked beneath it. 'I'll get dressed and I'll go.'

'Where?'

I shrug, tears threatening my eyes. 'I don't know. I'll find somewhere.'

'You don't have to go, but I don't want you thinking we're getting back together just because I've let you stay for a night or two.'

He's standing with his arms crossed and a defiant look on his face. I think he actually means it.

'We were good together,' I remind him. 'And I'm sorry if I wasn't always the girlfriend you wanted me to be. I'll try harder.'

He hangs his head and sighs. 'It's not going to work.'

'Why not?'

I cross the kitchen, the tiled floor sticky beneath my feet, and try to put my hands around his waist. But he grabs my shoulders firmly and holds me at arms' length.

'I can't do this, Marcella. I'm sorry for what you went through, but it's not going to work between us.'

'I don't understand. We were so good together,' I wail.

'Because I can't trust you.'

'What? Of course you can.'

He shakes his head, his eyes screwed tightly shut. 'You lied to me.'

I don't know what he's talking about. I wrack my brains, desperately trying to recall some minor misdemeanour I've obviously made in the past and that he's clung on to for all this time. I can't think of anything. There have been a few white lies, of course. But who doesn't let those slip out from time to time?

'If I've done something wrong, I'll make it up to you,' I say. What does he want? For me to get down on my knees and beg?

367

'You know what you did,' he snaps, rage burning in his eyes. I've never seen him like this.

'No, Frazer. I don't.'

'You told me you were pregnant. You told me you were having our child.'

Oh. That.

'I thought I might have been.'

'Don't give me that.'

Well, I had to say something. He was threatening to leave me.

'Okay, I made a mistake.' I throw up my hands. I don't know what all the fuss is about. I bent the truth a little. So what? It's not as if I was sleeping behind his back with the rugby team or anything.

'How could you? It was sick and manipulative and I can never forgive you for it,' he says.

'Fine. I'll go, if that's what you really want.'

He runs a hand through his hair and sighs. 'You have nowhere else to go. I promised you could stay until you get yourself sorted out, but that's it. Nothing is happening between us.'

'I don't want to stay where I'm not welcome.'

'Don't be like that.'

No, screw him. If he doesn't want me here, I'll find somewhere else. I'm not going to stand here and argue. Although he seemed perfectly happy when I was in his bed last night. Not pushing me away then, was he?

I turn and run from the kitchen. Up the stairs and into the spare room, quickly pulling on my clothes and dumping Frazer's dressing gown on the floor.

I catch a glimpse of myself in the mirror. I look awful. My hair's a mess. My eyes are hollow and black. My skin pallid. I don't even have any make-up or a hairbrush. But it's the least of my worries when I don't know where I'll be sleeping tonight, now we've given up the old flat.

Frazer's still in the kitchen when I make it back down, scrubbing some dishes in the sink. The smell of last night's takeaway hangs heavy in the air.

'Can you at least lend me some money? I'll pay it back,' I say, fiddling with my fingers. I hate to ask for a loan, but it's the only way I'm going to get by until I can find a job.

'Sure. How much do you need?'

'A hundred?' I ask hopefully.

'That's not going to go far. I'll transfer a couple of thousand across to your account,' he says, drying his hands on a tea towel and sitting back down at his laptop.

'Thank you.'

'You don't have to leave,' he repeats.

I shoot him a tight smile. We both know that's not true. He's said his piece. It's time for me to stand on my own two feet. There's clearly no hope of us getting back together, especially if he doesn't think he can trust me. That's fine. I could do with a break from men for a while, anyway. Who needs them?

He walks me to the front door and watches me dolefully as I step outside into a bright, sunny morning.

'I still don't understand what made you go to the Van Der Prousts' house,' he says. 'And why they invited you to stay. You didn't know them. It just doesn't make any sense.'

I sigh. He might as well know. 'I went to confront Carmel.'

Frazer shakes his head, his brow furrowed. 'I don't understand. Why?'

'For revenge.'

For one reason or another, I've never told him the story about what happened to Hannah. Her mental health battles. Her run-ins with the police. Her arrest for attempted arson. Or that she took her own life inside that hospital she hated.

'Revenge? For what?'

'I should have told you before, but a few years ago, Hannah was arrested for starting a fire in a block of flats in Margate. She'd been struggling with these voices in her head for ages. She told the police it was the voice that encouraged her to do it. So when the case came to court, they brought in a psychiatrist to evaluate her.'

Frazer is staring at me blankly, almost as if he doesn't believe me. I can see he's cross I've not mentioned it before.

'The psychiatrist was Carmel Van Der Proust,' I continue. 'Not that she even remembered my sister's name. Anyway, she concluded, in her wisdom, that instead of being let off with a warning, Hannah should be sent to a psychiatric hospital for treatment. You should have seen the place, Frazer. It was like something out of a horror film. Hannah hated it. She couldn't cope. So she took her own life.' I pick at my fingers. Even the thought of that place makes me shudder.

Frazer's frown deepens. 'Marcella, what the hell are you talking about?'

'I'm sorry, I should have told you. Anyway, I went to the house because I wanted to make Carmel pay for what she'd done. I wanted to see her suffer the same way she'd made me suffer when Hannah died.'

'But that's not right,' Frazer says.

'I realise now how stupid it was. I had no idea what I was getting into.'

'Marcella, stop it. This is madness.'

Of course, if I'd known then what I know now, I'd have kept my distance. There's no way I'd have gone anywhere near Shadowbrook Farm.

'So now you know, but please, don't say anything to anyone. I may have left that bit out when I was talking to the police.'

'Because it's not true,' Frazer says.

My head snaps back. Seriously, does he think I've made this all up?

'Of course it's true,' I say, although I deliberately left out the part where I had sex with Rufus in an effort to persuade him to leave Carmel. That's a secret I'll take with me to the grave.

'Marcella, Hannah died when she was a baby,' Frazer says. 'She didn't survive the birth. At least that's what you've always told me.'

I stare at him, hardly recognising the words coming out of his mouth. What's he talking about? I've never told him that.

'Don't you remember? There was a problem with your mum's pregnancy. She had some kind of syndrome. Your sister didn't get enough blood. You took all the nutrients in the womb. She was born first, but she didn't make it.'

'No, that's not right.'

'Listen to me, Mars. You need help.'

I scoff. 'Thanks, but I'm fine.'

I don't need this right now. I turn my back on him. I need to get away.

'Please, come back in the house. Let's talk about this,' Frazer calls after me. 'Don't you remember? It's why you fell out with your mother. She blamed you for Hannah's death, even though it wasn't your fault. You said she never got over it and she never forgave you.'

'No, you're wrong,' I say. Me and mum did fall out some time ago, but I can't quite remember what it was all about now. It wasn't that though, I'm sure. I don't know why he's saying these things.

'Marcella, you need help.'

'I'm fine on my own. Thank you for picking me up from the station yesterday, and for the loan. As soon as I'm back on my feet, I'll get back in touch and pay you back.'

'Marcella...'

But I'm already walking away, humming to myself.

I thought I needed Frazer, but actually he's done me a favour. How many people get the chance to wipe the slate clean and start their lives afresh?

As I walk down the street, heading towards the city centre, my heart flutters with a rush of joy. I have enough money, thanks to Frazer, for a few weeks in a nice Airbnb while I look for a flat share and a new job.

It's a fantastic opportunity. A new beginning. I might even change my name, colour my hair and really switch things up. Wouldn't that be something? A new me with no past and my whole future ahead of me.

This is going to be the start of something amazing. I just know it is.

Chapter 50

The house is a stunning red brick Georgian town-house with a handsome frontage and tall windows, like something a child might draw. It's far more impressive than I was expecting, but I'm definitely at the right address. I double-checked my email as I stood outside, peering up the cobbled foot-path towards a huge navy blue front door with a heavy-looking brass knocker.

I straighten my skirt and dab my forehead with a tissue. It was only a couple of stops on the bus followed by a short walk up a gentle hill, but summer's come early and I'm sweating. It's important to make a good impression and I don't want to start the interview dripping all over Marc and Lucy's stripped pine floorboards or expensive deep pile carpet.

You can tell they must have money from the size of the house. It's enormous and immaculately kept. The garden at the front is only small, but it's exquisite, with perfectly manicured box hedges and pretty flowerbeds bursting with colour.

I decide on a quick spritz of perfume. A bottle of Paco Rabanne's *Lady Million* I picked up from Boots on my way over. It's a bit of an extravagance when I still owe Frazer money, but it's worth it. Appearances are everything.

With a deep breath and my head held high, I stroll confidently up to the front door and knock.

Footsteps echo inside and the door peels open. A petite woman with blonde hair and the harassed look of a parent run ragged stares out with a warm smile.

'Lara Davenport. I've come about the babysitting position,' I say, extending my hand in greeting. It's the new name I've settled on after weeks of deliberation. After all, it's me who has to live with it for the rest of my life, although I've always liked Marcella. I thought it suited me.

'Oh, gosh, yes, Lara. Do come in. I'm Lucy.' She tucks a strand of hair that's come loose from her messy plait behind her ear and waves me inside.

A little boy who can't be much more than two or three years old comes racing down the hall on a plastic tractor. He stares up at me with wide, blue eyes and a snot-encrusted nose that's bubbling from one nostril.

I swallow back my disgust and shoot him my warmest smile, bending at the waist to lower myself to his level.

'And this is Casper,' Lucy adds, as he rolls up to her legs and angles his head shyly into her thighs.

'Wow, that's a great tractor. I bet it goes really fast,' I say.

'I got it for my burf-day,' Casper tells me, before scooting around and shooting back into the bowels of the house.

'Thanks for coming over,' Lucy says as she closes the front door. 'Marc is upstairs putting the little one down for her mid-morning sleep. He'll be down in a moment.'

The house has been tastefully decorated with muted pastel colours and plenty of wood panelling, although I can't help notice there are toys everywhere. Halfway up the stairs. Cluttering the hall. And even all over the worktops in the kitchen where Lucy takes me to chat. It's one of those fancy kitchens that extends out from the back of the house, with an open plan dining space and bi-fold doors overlooking a smart patio and a bowling green flat lawn.

'What a beautiful house,' I comment.

'Thank you. There's still lots of work to do, but we're getting there. Coffee?'

She makes three mugs of coffee using a sleek, silver machine and adds a dash of milk to each without even asking me how I take it.

We sit at an enormous table by the window while Casper continues to race up and down, shouting at the top of his voice. Lucy doesn't once tell him to keep the noise down and I feel a headache coming on.

'I know it's a bit strange holding an interview for a babysitting position, but you can't be too careful, can you?' Lucy holds her mug with two hands, blowing on the coffee before taking a bird-like sip. She's painted her fingernails the colour of a rain-washed sky, but they're chipped and faded now. A woman who doesn't have much time for herself, I guess.

'No, I completely understand. And I was happy to pop over.'

'Thank you,' she says, letting out a grateful breath, as if it was a huge imposition asking me to come. 'So tell me, what experience do you have with children?'

'I've done quite a bit of babysitting over the years,' I lie. 'And obviously I love children.'

Lucy pulls a sheet of paper off a pile of paperwork heaped on the table, alongside a dirty bib and a baby's dummy.

'You were a nursing assistant until recently,' she says, scanning what I realise is a printout of my short CV. 'Is that right?'

'That's right. It was a very rewarding job, helping people when they needed it most.'

'So you're medically trained?'

'I have some knowledge, yes.'

Footsteps bound down the stairs and a booming voice announces the arrival of an attractive man wearing a thin T-shirt, cargo shorts and a wooden beaded necklace that I've only ever seen surfers at the beach wear. His face is shaded by the kind of heavy stubble which makes you wonder whether it's a deliberate attempt at a beard or if he's just not bothered to shave.

'You must be Lara,' he says, beaming. He strides towards me with an outstretched hand.

His handshake is surprisingly limp and damp. Not particularly inspiring.

He turns his attention to Lucy, holding up a baby's bottle with an inch of milk sloshing around the bottom. 'She only took four ounces,' he says. 'And she was fighting sleep. She's gone down now, though. Thank god.'

He drops the bottle by the sink and flicks on a baby monitor by the microwave. It crackles and hisses, and then I hear a low murmur and a snuffle.

'So you found us okay?' Marc asks as he takes a seat at the table next to his wife.

'Yes, no problem. I was telling Mrs Harrisbrook what a lovely house you have.'

'Please, call me Lucy,' she says.

'Lucy. Sorry.'

'You were a nurse, I hear.' Marc rocks back on his chair with his arm draped casually over his wife's shoulders.

'A nursing assistant, although they prefer to call us healthcare support workers these days.' I roll my eyes and they both smile sympathetically.

'And you've worked with children before?'

'She's had a number of babysitting jobs. We were just covering that,' Lucy snaps.

Marc doesn't seem to notice the rebuke, snatching the copy of my CV and scanning it.

'We think it's important we get out on our own, just the two of us, at least a couple of times a month,'

378

he says. 'You know, for dinner, or a movie.' He pats Lucy's hand.

She really does look knackered. The sockets around her eyes are hollow and grey and she carries an air of weariness, like she's not slept properly in weeks.

It's only a stopgap job until I can find something better paid, but it's not proving that easy, especially after getting sacked from my last post in the hospital. There are plenty of jobs around, but I can't even seem to get an interview.

I'm surviving for now on Frazer's charity, living in a cheap Airbnb on the outskirts of the city for the time being and feeding myself on handouts from the foodbank. It's all a bit demeaning, to be honest, but it won't be forever. As I keep reminding myself, it's just until I get myself back on my feet. I've managed to buy myself an inexpensive phone and a few new clothes, but the money's not going to last forever. And anyway, at some point, I need to pay it back.

'Are there any referees we could contact? Anyone who you've done babysitting for previously who would vouch for you?' Lucy asks.

'Not really, no. Sorry.'

'Oh.' Her face falls.

At almost the same moment, Casper comes chasing into the kitchen again, but loses control of his sit-on tractor as he turns the steering wheel too sharply. It tips over and sends Casper sprawling, his knee scuffing along the floor and his head catching the edge of a standalone island in the middle of the room.

He screams in pain and before I know what I'm doing, I'm up on my feet and rushing to him.

'Hey, there,' I soothe. 'Now, now.'

I pick him up gently and sit him on my knee as I crouch down, stroking his hair out of his eyes.

To my surprise, he stops crying almost immediately, looking up at me with those big, sad blue eyes.

'Rub it better,' I say, massaging his scalp. 'All better now.'

The room falls silent. I glance at Lucy and Marc, who are watching me, open-mouthed.

'Wow,' Lucy says. 'That's impressive. He's normally such a drama queen when he hurts himself.'

'He obviously likes you,' Marc adds.

A self-satisfied smile creeps across my lips as I right Casper's tractor and set him back on it.

Lucy and Marc share a look.

'I think she's just got herself the job,' Marc says. And then turning to me adds, 'That is if you want it?'

'Of course. Thank you.'

'You've not met Jemima yet,' Lucy says, frowning. 'How old is she?'

'Six months, but she's an angel. Compared to Casper at least.' She laughs, but it's more with nerves than good humour.

'I love babies.' It's what every new parent wants to hear. 'The smell of their little heads. Their chubby little hands. Their tiny little fingernails.'

'You don't have children of your own?' Lucy asks.

380

I draw a deep breath and let it out slowly. 'No.'

Let her read into that what she will.

It works. She looks suitably embarrassed and stares into her mug.

'Obviously, in addition to the fifteen pounds an hour we're paying, we'd provide a taxi to get you home. Or you'd be welcome to stay in one of our spare rooms on the nights we need you,' Marc says.

'Stay the night?' My heart skips faster.

'Only if you'd like,' he adds hurriedly. 'There's no pressure.'

'No, that would be amazing!'

I take a mouthful of coffee. It's strong. Really strong. I'll probably be jittery all afternoon.

'Do you have any questions for us?' Lucy asks.

'I guess it would be good to know a bit about you both.'

Marc looks to his wife as if seeking permission to speak. 'We're both teachers,' she says. 'He's at the posh private school, though. I'm an English teacher at the local academy.'

'Head of year,' Marc adds.

The snuffling coming from the baby monitor on the side becomes louder. The baby's obviously waking up, and sure enough, a second or two later, the snuffling turns into a full-blooded scream.

Lucy sighs, her shoulders slumping.

Marc rolls his eyes and checks his watch. 'She's only been down ten minutes. Don't worry, I'll go!'

He jumps up, marches out of the room, and bounds up the stairs.

I reach across the table for Lucy's arm.

'You look tired. Are you okay?'

She nods as she pinches the bridge of her nose. 'It's hard,' she says.

'You're not back at work yet, are you?'

'Not yet. I have to go back next term, though.'

Marc's cooing reverberates through the baby monitor he's forgotten to switch off.

'To be honest, I'm looking forward to it. To getting a break from running around after a toddler and changing nappies and constantly making up bottles of milk.'

I nod sympathetically. 'I don't know how you do it.'

'I don't have much choice, do I?'

You chose to have kids.

I think it, but I don't say it.

'Teaching though. That's a great job. You must be really good with children,' I say.

'I don't know about that, but I enjoy getting the best out of them.'

'Is it how you met Marc? Through teaching?'

'We were at the same school for a while. Waverley Manor. I don't know if you know it?'

I hesitate for a beat. 'How romantic.'

'It was,' she says. 'It seems a long time ago now. We need to remind ourselves that we have more in common than the kids. That's why Marc's keen to find a reliable babysitter. So we can start going out again. On our own.'

When Marc returns to the kitchen, he's carrying a sweet-looking baby. She has a shock of fair hair and the biggest, bluest eyes. She gives me a huge, gummy smile.

'This is Jemima,' he says, holding up her hand and making her wave at me.

'She's adorable. May I hold her?'

'Of course.'

I've never held a baby before, but I've watched enough YouTube videos over the last few days to qualify me for expert status. Marc hands her over gingerly. She pumps her arms and legs in excitement as I sit her on my lap.

'Hello, little Jemima. Didn't you want to sleep?' I sing-song, just like they do in all those videos I've watched.

'I think she likes you,' Lucy says.

I try to ignore the stomach-churning stench that's clearly emanating from her nappy. I don't want to give them an excuse to test me on my nappy-changing skills.

'It's funny you met at Waverley Manor,' I say, jiggling Jemima up and down on my leg. 'That's where my sister, Hannah, went to school. She's quite a bit younger than me though, so she might have been there at the same time as you both.'

Lucy frowns. 'Hannah Davenport. I don't remember the name.'

Marc shakes his head. 'Me neither.'

'She's my half-sister. You'd have known her as Hannah Winthrop. That's why there was an age gap between us. She was a bit younger than me. She was only fourteen when she took her own life.'

Lucy's mouth falls open in shock. 'I'm so sorry. That's awful. I don't remember that at all.'

I shrug. 'Her time at Waverley Manor wasn't the happiest of her life, I'm afraid. She was bullied quite badly and never got over it.'

'It happens to lots of kids,' Marc says. 'It's tough for them.'

'The problem is, no one took it seriously. You know, she complained about it and my parents took it up with the school. But no one did anything,' I continue.

The subtle glance Lucy shoots Marc doesn't pass me by.

'Not the head. Not the teachers. No one was interested. But maybe if someone had stopped to listen to her, she'd still be with us today.'

'I'm sure—' Lucy begins.

'Nobody cared. And now she's dead.'

Jemima coos in my lap, her pudgy hands reaching up to grab my hair.

She has such delicate fingers. Such a cute button nose. So helpless. So defenceless. I can tell by the way Marc and Lucy look at her, slightly on edge, that she means the world to them. That they'd be heartbroken if anything happened to her. Or to Casper.

'So,' I ask. 'When would you like me to start?'

A WORD FROM THE AUTHOR

I hope you enjoyed The House Guest. If you did, it would mean so much to me if you could take a few seconds to leave a rating on Amazon.

Honestly, it helps authors (particularly independently published authors with no marketing team behind them, like me) more than you probably realise to reach a wider audience.

You don't even have to leave a review these days – although any supportive words always go down well!

A star rating will suffice.

I always read all my reviews, so thank you so much for taking the time. I really do appreciate it.

If you'd like to keep up to date with all my writing news, please consider joining my weekly newsletter. I'll even send you a free e-book! You can find more details at bit.ly/hislostwife or scan the QR code below.

Or follow me on Facebook - @AuthorAJWills, find me on my website ajwillsauthor.com join me on Instagram at @ajwills_author or find me on Goodreads @ A.J.Wills

I look forward to seeing you there.

Adrian

Nothing Left To Lose
A letter arrives in a plain white envelope. Inside is a single sheet of paper with a chilling message. Someone knows the secret Abi, and her husband, Henry, are hiding. And now they want them dead.

His Wife's Sister
Mara was only eleven when she went missing from a tent in her parents' garden nineteen years ago. Now she's been found wandering alone and confused in woodland.

She Knows
After Sky finds a lost diary on the beach, she becomes caught up in something far bigger than she could ever have imagined - and accused of a murder she has no memory of committing...

The Intruder
Jez thought he'd finally found happiness when he met Alice. But when Alice goes missing with her young daughter and the police accuse him of their murders, his life is shattered.

Printed in Great Britain
by Amazon